The Presidential
or, The all-seein

Bertram Lebhar

Alpha Editions

This edition published in 2024

ISBN 9789362098979

Design and Setting By

Alpha Editions

www.alphaedis.com

Email - info@alphaedis.com

Contents

CHAPTER I.
A CABINET DISCUSSION.

The President of the United States shook his head with an emphasis which caused the other men gathered around the massive mahogany table to realize that it would be almost a waste of time to pursue the discussion. "It is my opinion, gentlemen, that if there were the slightest basis for this rumor, Mr. Throgmorton's report would not be couched in such positive terms!" he declared, pointing to a paper on the table before him. "There isn't a man in the diplomatic service more alert or level-headed than he, so far as I know. I am confident that it would be impossible for Portiforo to pull the wool over his eyes."

"Possibly Portiforo has not pulled the wool over Throgmorton's eyes," the little man who sat at the president's right suggested quietly. "He may not have found it at all necessary to do that." There was something about the speaker's tone which caused the other members of the cabinet to look at him curiously, and prompted the president to ask, quite calmly: "Will you say what you mean to imply by that remark, Mr. Attorney General?"

The little man smiled—a peculiar form of smile which seemed to be done with his eye only. "The American minister to the Republic of Baracoa has never given the impression of being exactly hostile to the Portiforo administration," he remarked dryly.

The president frowned. "Are we to understand this as an insinuation against his good faith?"

"To be quite frank, Mr. President, I have never credited Mr. Throgmorton with a superabundance of good faith," the attorney general replied. "I have known him for a long time—in fact, we were at college together, and—well, it would take more than his unsupported word to convince me that there is no truth in this startling story of Portiforo's perfidy. He and the President of Baracoa are reputed to be close friends, and it is possible that his investigation might not be unbiased."

"I protest against that remark," the secretary of state exclaimed indignantly. "I, too, have known Mr. Throgmorton for a long time, and there isn't a man living, Mr. President, in whose integrity I have greater confidence. If this hideous thing were true he would have told us so, no matter how amicably disposed he might be toward the Portiforo administration."

The president nodded an acquiescence. "I have as much confidence in Throgmorton's honesty as I have in his good judgment," he declared. "As I said before, gentlemen, he is too conservative a man to have made such a positive denial unless he had good ground for doing so. I have felt all along that this rumor was nothing more than a concoction of Portiforo's enemies; now I am sure of it."

"And nothing would cause you to change your mind, Mr. President?" the attorney general inquired.

"I would not say that. I am always open to conviction. Of course, if you could bring me a photograph of Felix in a dungeon cell, I might be ready to believe that Portiforo has him in captivity. But even at that," he added, a twinkle in his eyes, "I would have to be convinced that the snapshot was genuine."

The attorney general smiled deprecatingly. "Then I'm afraid it will never be possible to convince you, Mr. President. I don't imagine that there's a photographer in all the world who could break into a South American dungeon, snapshot a prisoner, and get out again."

"I'm not so sure of that," put in the secretary of the interior. "I know of one man who might be able to accomplish even that remarkable feat. He's a New York newspaper man named Hawley. He's on the staff of the *Sentinel*. I met him some months ago, when I was in New York, and the experience I had with him then leads me to believe that there is scarcely any feat impossible of accomplishment where he is concerned."

"Isn't that the man they call 'the Camera Chap'?" the president inquired, evincing keen interest.

"I believe they do call him that," the secretary of the interior replied. "He is truly a wonderful photographer. I believe that if Portiforo really has Felix locked up in El Torro Fortress, Hawley could get a picture of him."

The president made no comment on this, but, later that day, when the cabinet meeting was over, he said to his secretary: "I wish you would send word to Mr. Bates, of the New York *Sentinel*, that I would like to see him at his earliest convenience."

Bates, the *Sentinel's* Washington correspondent, hurried over to the White House immediately upon receipt of this information, hoping that the head of the nation contemplated favoring his paper with some exclusive information. What the latter actually said to him caused him some mystification.

"Mr. Bates," the president began, "I believe you have a photographer named Hawley employed on your paper?"

"You mean the Camera Chap, Mr. President?"

"Yes. I have heard a great deal about his exploits, and if what I have heard is true, he must be a very unusual fellow. Tell me more about him, if you don't mind."

The *Sentinel's* star correspondent launched into the subject with enthusiasm. There was not a man on his paper, from the editor in chief down to the youngest office boy, who was not proud of the fact that Frank Hawley was connected with it. The Camera Chap occupied a position unique in the newspaper world. He commanded a large salary, and his extraordinary achievements had made him famous in every newspaper office in the country, and caused other managing editors to envy the *Sentinel* for having him under contract.

It took Bates more than half an hour to tell of some of Hawley's most notable performances, and the president's face lighted up as he listened. "Why," he exclaimed enthusiastically, "the Camera Chap must be a remarkable character! Does he ever come to Washington? I should very much like to meet him. You might make it a point to mention that to your managing editor the next time you communicate with your office, Mr. Bates."

"I will be sure to do so, Mr. President," said the *Sentinel* representative, who, being far from dull-witted, and well acquainted with the chief executive's methods, surmised that there was behind this request some special motive.

As a result of the message which Bates sent over the wire which connected the *Sentinel's* Washington bureau with the home office, a tall, slender young man, with a prepossessing countenance and a twinkle in his keen eyes, arrived at the capital the following afternoon.

Bates greeted him effusively. "Welcome to our city, Hawley, old man!" he exclaimed. "I don't know whether the president contemplates offering you a position in his cabinet or whether he merely wants his picture taken, but, whatever the reason, he's very keen to meet you. His secretary called me up this morning to make sure you were coming; and when I told him that you were on your way to Washington he sent over this note for you."

Bates handed Hawley a square envelope, on which the address of the executive mansion was embossed. The Camera Chap opened it, and read its contents over twice, the expression of surprise on his face intensifying as he did so.

"Are you sure this isn't a practical joke?" he inquired half incredulously, handing Bates the note.

An envious look came to the other's face as he glanced at it. "That's going some!" he exclaimed. "You certainly are lucky, old man. Some of us Washington correspondents pride ourselves on being pals with the president, but he's never invited any of *us* to lunch at the White House."

CHAPTER II.
A MATTER IN CONFIDENCE.

When the Camera Chap went to keep his luncheon appointment the following morning, Bates, who had some business to attend to at the treasury department, accompanied him as far as the White House grounds. As they were walking along Pennsylvania Avenue, a splendid touring car, with a silver crest on the door panels and a liveried footman on the box, passed them by. It contained two women, one of them a blonde, the other very dark. The former, recognizing Bates on the sidewalk, bowed graciously.

"That is Mrs. Fred V. Cooper, wife of the attorney general," the correspondent explained to his companion, noting that the latter was staring at the automobile, as though fascinated. "She's one of the beauties of Washington."

"And the other woman—the dark one—who is she?" the Camera Chap demanded eagerly.

Bates smiled. "There's a woman with a history," he said. "She is Señora Francisco Felix, wife of the former president of the Republic of Baracoa. You remember reading about him, of course?"

"Oh, yes. He's the chap who disappeared a couple of years ago."

"Disappeared is a gentle way of putting it," returned the other, grinning. "He sneaked away in his private yacht, one memorable night, and the good people of Baracoa awoke next morning to find that they were minus a president, and incidentally the greater part of the national treasury. The scamp took away with him every bolivar he could lay hands on. The little republic would have gone bankrupt if General Portiforo hadn't stepped in and saved the situation."

Hawley nodded. "Yes, I remember. What is his wife doing in Washington?"

"She's been living here ever since her husband absconded. I guess she didn't find it exactly comfortable in Baracoa after the scandal. She and Mrs. Cooper are great friends; they've known each other since they were girls. The señora was educated in the United States; I believe she and the attorney general's wife were in the same class at Vassar. She—why, what's the matter, old man?"

Hawley had given vent to a sharp exclamation, at the same time gripping his companion's arm excitedly. "Did you notice that swarthy chap in the taxicab which just passed?" he asked.

"The fellow with a beard? Yes. What about him?"

"Don't happen to know who he is, do you?"

Bates shook his head. "I suppose he's connected with one of the Spanish-American embassies. There are so many of those fellows running around Washington that it isn't possible for us to know them all. Why the interest in him?"

"This isn't the first time I have seen him. I saw him in New York a couple of weeks ago. He was shadowing Señora Felix."

"Señora Felix!"

"Yes; this is not the first time I've seen her, either, although I did not know who she was until now. The other day, Bates, I witnessed a queer incident outside the Hotel Mammoth. I was passing there just as that woman came out of the Thirty-fourth Street entrance and entered a taxicab. My attention was attracted to her not only because of her striking beauty, but because of the nervousness she displayed. As she stepped into the cab she kept glancing about her in all directions, as though aware that she was being watched. As she drove off I noticed a man skulking in the doorway of a store on the opposite side of the street. It was that same dark-skinned, bearded chap who just passed us. I saw him hurry across the street and rush up to another taxi that was waiting at the cab stand. I heard him instruct the driver to follow the woman's cab, no matter where it went. He spoke in English, but with a decidedly foreign accent. My curiosity was aroused, and I decided to see the thing out. I, too, jumped into a taxi and joined in the procession.

"Straight down Fifth Avenue we went, as far as Washington Square. Then the three of us turned into a side street, and came to a stop. The woman's cab had halted outside the door of a dingy-looking house in a neighborhood which had seen better days, but which now consists mostly of cheap rooming houses. The bearded man's cab had drawn up about fifty yards away. He jumped out quickly, and I alighted, too, as inconspicuously as possible. A surprise awaited us both. The first cab was empty. The woman had disappeared."

Bates laughed knowingly. "She must have been wise to the fact that she was being shadowed, and took advantage of a chance to drop out somewhere along the trail."

"Of course. It's an old trick. You ought to have seen our bearded friend's face when he found that he had been fooled. He said a lot of things to himself in Spanish. I have enough knowledge of that language to know that his utterances weren't fit for publication. Wonder if he's shadowing her again now."

"Most likely," said Bates. "I suppose he's one of Portiforo's spies. Naturally, the present government of Baracoa would be interested in the movements of Señora Felix. I presume they hope, by watching her, to get a line on where her husband is."

"You think she knows that?"

"It is more than a bare possibility. Felix hasn't been heard of since he landed from his yacht on the south coast of France two years ago, but it is exceedingly likely that he has been in communication with his wife. I understand they were a very devoted couple. In fact, it was a surprise to everybody that when he skipped he didn't take her along. Well, here we are at the White House grounds. See you later, old man. I am burning up with curiosity to know what the president wants of you."

Bates' curiosity in that respect was not destined to be gratified that day, nor for many days after. When the Camera Chap returned from his interview with the president, and dropped in at the *Sentinel* bureau, he was provokingly uncommunicative.

"It was a fine lunch," he said. "The White House chef certainly knows his business; and the president is a genial host. He is one of the most democratic men I have ever met."

"But what did you talk about?" Bates asked impatiently. "I know very well that he didn't send for you merely to make your acquaintance. What did he want, old man? You can trust me, you know."

"Of course I can," the Camera Chap agreed cheerfully. "We discussed many things—ranging all the way from Park Row to South America."

"South America!" the correspondent exclaimed eagerly. "What did he have to say about that?"

Hawley's eyes twinkled. "He asked me whether I'd ever been out there, and when I told him no he expressed great surprise, saying that I certainly ought to make it a point to go; that he felt sure I would find many interesting things to photograph in that part of the world."

Hearing which Bates had a shrewd suspicion that the president had suggested some particularly interesting thing to photograph in some part of South America; but, although he was a past master in the art of extracting information from unwilling lips, his efforts failed to draw out the Camera Chap further along this line.

It was the president's closing remark to Hawley which had compelled the latter to adopt this sphinx-like attitude.

"I will not pledge you to secrecy," the chief executive had said. "I will merely urge you to be discreet, Mr. Hawley. I think I am able to estimate a man at first sight, and if I did not feel that you could be relied upon I would not have asked you to undertake this mission. You realize, of course, that in addition to the risk you will be running, a human life may depend upon your discretion."

CHAPTER III.
PAXTON'S WARNING.

Inasmuch as the president had not pledged him to secrecy, the Camera Chap decided to take one person into his confidence regarding his visit to the White House. He knew that Tom Paxton, managing editor of the *Sentinel*, could be trusted, and there were reasons why Hawley felt that it was necessary to have him know the purpose of the undertaking on which he was about to embark. So he returned to New York that night, and arrived at the *Sentinel* office just as Paxton was closing down his desk with the intention of going home.

"Back so soon!" The boyish-looking managing editor greeted him, grinning. "I supposed it would take you at least a couple of weeks to tell the president all you know about how to run the ship of state. Seriously speaking, though, old man, I'm glad you've returned. I've got a little job for you up in Canada that needs your immediate attention. It——"

"I'm sorry, Tom," the Camera Chap interrupted, "but I'm afraid I'll have to ask you to hand that assignment to somebody else. I can't touch it. I've got to have a couple of months' leave of absence—to begin at once."

Paxton looked his astonishment. "What are you going to do with it?"

"I am going to South America," Hawley announced. "To Baracoa, to be precise. I suppose you recall, Tom, the sensational disappearance of President Felix, a couple of years ago?"

"Of course," Paxton replied. He had a phenomenal memory for contemporaneous history. It was the boast of the *Sentinel* staff that he could give, offhand, facts and figures of any event of importance in any part of the world within the past ten years.

"Francisco Felix," he went on, as though reading from a book, "the poor Baracoa laborer who became president. They called him 'the South American Abraham Lincoln.' He was the idol of the people—the most beloved and respected executive Baracoa has ever had—until he proved himself to be a crook by absconding with the contents of the national treasury."

The Camera Chap smiled. "That is the story which is generally accepted," he said quietly. "But there is a possibility that the world may have done President Felix a great injustice."

"What do you mean?" Paxton asked, looking searchingly in the other's face.

"It now appears," said the Camera Chap, "that instead of being a fugitive and an absconder, Felix may really have been the victim of a daring conspiracy; that instead of being free in some part of Europe at this moment, living in luxury on his loot, the unhappy man is in reality eating out his heart in a South American dungeon—where he has been ever since that fatal night that he is supposed to have skipped from Baracoa in his private yacht. In other words, Tom, it was all a frame-up. According to this story, Felix was kidnaped by the Portiforo party, who, realizing that he was too strong with the people to be deposed by an ordinary revolution, took this means of discrediting him and seizing the reins of government."

Editor Paxton smiled incredulously. "Sounds pretty far-fetched. Yet I don't know," he added musingly. "Almost anything is possible down in that part of the continent; and I recall that there were some circumstances about Felix's disappearance which struck me at the time as queer. There is the fact, for instance, that he has never been seen since the day his yacht reached the south coast of France."

"He wasn't seen even then," Hawley reminded him. "At least, there is no proof that the man who came ashore was really Felix. The only persons who saw him were some French peasants, and, of course, they wouldn't know Felix by sight."

"There was the crew of the yacht," Paxton suggested. "You are forgetting, perhaps, that later on they were caught and they admitted the whole business."

"It is possible that they were in the conspiracy," Hawley argued. "Every member of the crew could have been a Portiforo agent, carefully instructed as to the story he was to tell."

The managing editor nodded. "Yes; that's possible. By George!" he added, a glint in his eyes, "what a wonderful story—if it should be true. Where on earth did you get hold of it?"

"At the White House," the Camera Chap replied, sinking his voice almost to a whisper.

"What! You don't mean to say the president believes it?"

"Not exactly. In fact, he is strongly inclined to think that it is a preposterous theory concocted by Portiforo's enemies. Still, there is a doubt in his mind. That is why I am going to Baracoa."

"He is sending you there to investigate this yarn?"

"To find Felix, if he is really in Baracoa, and to bring back a snapshot of him," Hawley said simply.

"Good stuff!" Paxton approved. "If we had photographic evidence the United States would be in a position to intervene, and demand Felix's immediate release. That, of course, would mean the finish of Portiforo, and I happen to know that there are reasons why Washington wouldn't be exactly sorry to see a change in the government of Baracoa. But I say, old man," he added anxiously, "do you appreciate the magnitude of the job you're tackling? Do you realize the danger?"

"Surely I do," Hawley answered. "The president warned me that I would have to be very careful—that if the story happened to be true, and Portiforo should find out the object of my trip to Baracoa, the consequences would be serious. They would probably seek to remove the evidence—by murdering poor Felix before I had a chance to get to him."

Paxton frowned. "Yes, I have no doubt they would do that. They would make short work of Felix. But I wasn't referring to him; I was thinking of what might happen to you if they were to nab you in the act of trying to get that snapshot." His tone was very grave. "I am afraid, old man, that they would stand you up against a stone wall, with a handkerchief around your eyes and spray you with lead from their guns."

The Camera Chap laughed. "Not as bad as that, I guess. A dungeon cell and a ball and chain would be about the limit."

"I'm not so sure," Paxton muttered. "What protection does the president promise you in case you are caught?"

"He didn't promise me any protection," the Camera Chap replied cheerfully. "On the contrary, he gave me clearly to understand that I am going into this thing at my own risk. He explained that if I am apprehended in the act of violating any of the laws of a friendly nation, the United States government wouldn't have any right to intervene."

"I thought so," growled Paxton. "Why the deuce couldn't he have given this job to a secret-service man instead of you?"

"I didn't ask him that," Hawley answered, smiling. "But don't worry, Tom. I'm going to get along all right. They're not going to catch me, you know."

The managing editor shook his head forebodingly. "I've a good mind to refuse you that leave of absence," he said. "I'd do it, too, if I didn't know that you'd go, anyway—and if you were working for anybody else but the President of the United States. When do you expect to start?"

"To-morrow. The *Colombia*, of the Andean line, sails for South American waters at two p. m. I've engaged passage on her."

"You're certainly not losing any time," Paxton chuckled. "Would you like me to send somebody along to help you, old man? You can have the pick of our staff."

The Camera Chap declined this offer. "I'm ever so much obliged," he said, "but I have decided that I had better work alone. It seems to me that this is one of those cases where one head will be better than two." He extended his hand. "Good-by, Tom. I'll trot along. I've got to go home and pack my trunk."

"Good-by, old man," said the managing editor, gripping the outstretched hand with a fervor he rarely displayed. "Good-by, and good-luck to you! You'll need all the luck you can command; for this is by far the most dangerous job you've ever tackled. By the way, let me give you a little tip that may prove valuable. If you should happen to get into trouble, and have to appeal to the American minister to save you, you'd better not let him know, if you can help it, that you are a member of the *Sentinel* staff."

"Why not? I should think——"

"Minister Throgmorton doesn't like the *Sentinel*," Paxton interrupted dryly. "He has good reason for his prejudice. We have been roasting him editorially ever since he was appointed. So, under the circumstances, I scarcely think he would move heaven and earth to help a *Sentinel* man."

CHAPTER IV.
SEÑORA FELIX.

The Andean line steamship *Colombia* was about to weigh anchor when the Camera Chap came aboard. He was not the only passenger who narrowly missed being left behind. As his taxicab drew up at the wharf two women were just alighting from an electric brougham. One of them was a blonde, and the other a pronounced brunette. Hawley gave a start of surprise at sight of them.

"Bon voyage, dear," the blond woman was saying. "I trust that everything will come out all right, and that you will soon be back in Washington. After all, your father's condition may not be as serious as the telegram makes out. You know how doctors sometimes exaggerate."

The dark woman smiled faintly. "I pray that it may be so," she said; "but I am greatly worried. They would not have sent for me unless it was very serious. Au revoir, and thank you a thousand times for all your kindnesses."

"All aboard, ladies!" the officer at the gangplank cried. "Please hurry."

The women embraced, and the blonde, whom Hawley had recognized as the wife of the United States attorney general, reëntered the brougham. The other hurried up the gangplank, the Camera Chap following close behind her.

"Señora Felix!" he said to himself. "I didn't expect to have her for a fellow passenger. Lucky, I guess, that I decided to take this boat."

On board the señora was greeted by a younger woman, whom she addressed as Celeste, and who, Hawley learned later, was her maid. They went immediately to her stateroom.

Hawley soon learned that Señora Felix's departure from the United States was no secret. He had brought an evening newspaper on board, and on an inside page he came across the following heading, so inconspicuously displayed that it had first escaped his notice:

"Fugitive President's Wife Goes Back.—Victoria Felix, 'Grass Widow' of Baracoa's Missing Chief Executive, Sails To-day for Her Native Land After Two Years' Exile in Washington.—Serious Illness of Her Father Given as Cause of Trip."

From the quarter of a column of smaller type which appeared beneath this heading he learned that Señora Felix's father was Doctor Emilio Hernandez, a prominent physician of San Cristobal, the capital of Baracoa.

He had been seized with a paralytic stroke, and his daughter had been hurriedly summoned.

It was not until the vessel was well out at sea that the Camera Chap saw the señora again. She did not appear in the dining saloon for the evening meal, nor did she show herself on deck during the first day of the voyage. He inquired of one of the stewards, and learned that she was indisposed. But on the second day he saw her reclining in a steamer chair on the promenade deck, apparently absorbed in the pages of a French novel. He stood with his back against the starboard rail at a sufficient distance from her chair to avoid making his attention too marked, and covertly studied her.

She was slender, dark-eyed, about forty, and of aristocratic bearing. She was still beautiful, although suffering had imprinted deep lines on her olive skin. The set of her chin and the shape of her delicate mouth denoted character; in that respect the young man who was so intently watching her felt that he had never seen a face which impressed him more favorably. He recalled what Bates had said about the probability of her knowing the whereabouts of her fugitive husband, and he decided that the Washington correspondent must be wrong about that.

"If Felix isn't the martyr I believe him to be—if his disappearance was voluntary, that woman was not a party to it, either before or afterward," he told himself confidently. "A woman with a face like hers wouldn't shield a crook, even if he was her husband. I take her to be the kind that would go through fire for a man worthy of her love, but a woman who wouldn't have a particle of use for a moral weakling."

As he was thus soliloquizing, the subject of his thoughts looked up from her book, and their eyes met. A faint tinge of pink made itself visible beneath her dark skin, as though she were embarrassed by his scrutiny. She frowned slightly; then resumed her reading.

Feeling that he owed her an apology for his seeming rudeness, Hawley was debating in his mind whether it would be discreet to take her into his confidence as to his mission to Baracoa, when an incident occurred which diverted his attention. Two men strolling along the promenade deck suddenly halted a short distance from where the señora was sitting, and stood leaning with their elbows resting on the rail. Hawley recognized both of these men. One of them, in fact, occupied the stateroom opposite his own. He was a clean-shaven, swarthy man of middle age, who was down on the passenger list as Señor José Lopez. The first time he had seen him on the boat it had struck Hawley that there was something familiar about the fellow's face, but so far he had cudgeled his brain in an effort to recall when and where he had seen him before.

The other man was of striking appearance. He was tall, and of soldierly carriage. His dark, curly hair was gray at the temples, but, apart from this evidence of years, his handsome face was so youthful looking that he could easily have passed for a man in the early thirties. His complexion was ruddy, his dark eyes were sparkling. His well-waxed mustache, the ends of which were as sharp as stiletto points, gave his countenance a decidedly foreign aspect, otherwise he might have been taken for an American. The Camera Chap had learned that his name was Juan Cipriani, that he was a native of Argentine, and on his way back to that country.

The pair had been engaged in conversation as they approached, and now, as they leaned against the rail, they continued talking. They spoke in Spanish, and it seemed to Hawley that their voices were pitched above their normal register.

"In my opinion, it is a piece of impertinence for her to return to Baracoa," the one known as Cipriani said emphatically. "If she has any delicacy she must realize how unwelcome she will be to the people whom her rascally husband robbed and betrayed."

"But if her father is dying," the other argued tolerantly.

"Bah!" retorted Cipriani, with a contemptuous gesture. "Who would believe that story? You can depend upon it, my friend, her sole purpose in going back there is to make trouble. If your President Portiforo were wise he would instruct his port officers to refuse to permit her to leave the ship. That is the only way to deal with a woman of her stripe."

"But, after all, it is scarcely fair to blame her for her husband's sins," Lopez suggested mildly. "We must admit that the abominable Felix treated her as shabbily as he did my unfortunate country. I understand that she has not once heard from him since he fled."

The other laughed ironically. "Are you so ingenuous, my friend, as to believe that? You can be sure that he has been in constant communication with her, and that she is only waiting for a chance to join him and help him spend his stolen fortune. No doubt, she would have done so before now if she had not feared that she was too closely watched to—— I beg your pardon, sir—what did you say?"

This last remark was addressed to the Camera Chap, who, unable to contain himself any longer, had stepped up, frowning angrily, a menacing glint in his eyes. He knew Spanish well enough to make out most of their conversation, and although he had stood some distance away, every word that they had uttered had reached his ears. He knew, too, that the señora had heard. She was making a brave pretense of being absorbed in her novel, but the book trembled perceptibly in her hand. Up to this point

Hawley had hesitated to interfere, feeling that such a course might only add to her embarrassment; but now he decided that this cruelty must be stopped. If these men were permitted to go on there was no telling what they might say next.

"I say that your conversation is offensive," he repeated quietly, but with emphasis. "I ask you to stop it immediately."

He spoke in English, and Cipriani answered him in that language, which he spoke fluently, although with a marked accent. "It seems to me that you are impertinent, sir," the latter said, his dark eyes flashing. "Might I inquire in what way our conversation could possibly be offensive to you?"

The Camera Chap lowered his voice. "Don't you realize that every word you are saying is being heard by Señora Felix? What kind of men are you, any way, to insult a woman like this? I thought you South Americans boasted of your chivalry."

Señor Cipriani glanced toward the woman in the steamer chair. Suddenly she rose and walked away with dignity. A look of astonishment came in Cipriani's face. "Señora Felix!" he repeated. "My dear sir, you don't mean to tell me that is she?"

"Of course. Didn't you know it?"

Cipriani shook his head. "How unfortunate!" he murmured, and if the regret in his tone was feigned, it was skillfully done. "I assure you, sir, that I would rather have had my tongue cut out than intentionally make such remarks in the presence of the lady. I would apologize to her most abjectly, but I fear that would only be making matters worse. You see, I've never met the señora—this is the first time I have seen her since she came aboard." Then, seized with a sudden thought, he turned upon Lopez, his face flaming with rage. "But you must have known her!" he declared hotly. "It is not possible that you did not recognize the wife of your former president. Why did you let me go ahead? Why did you not warn me of what I was doing?"

The clean-shaven, swarthy man shrugged his shoulders. "I did not notice that the señora was sitting there," he said deprecatingly. "I was so engrossed in your interesting remarks that I did not observe our surroundings." As he spoke he smiled—an expansive grin which bared his large, exceedingly white teeth, which somehow reminded the Camera Chap of the fangs of a wolf.

"Now, where the deuce have I seen that man?" Hawley asked himself. "The more I see of him, the more I feel that we met before we came aboard, but to save my life I can't place him."

CHAPTER V.
BOLD CURIOSITY.

Muttering an apology, Lopez walked away, and as he strode rapidly across the deck toward the companionway, the Camera Chap noted curiously that his footsteps were uncannily noiseless. Cipriani, too, seemed to observe that fact, for he remarked, with a smile: "Our friend certainly is most appropriately named. Does not his walk suggest to you the lope of a wolf?"

"Exactly what I was thinking," said the Camera Chap. "Who is he?"

"His name is José Lopez, and he hails from Baracoa. That is all I can tell you about him. I have just made his acquaintance. We got to talking about his country, and that is how we came to discuss Señora Felix. I wish I could express to you how deeply I regret that I so cruelly hurt her feelings. If you are acquainted with the lady and——"

"I am not," Hawley hastily interrupted. "I merely know her by sight. She was pointed out to me the other day in Washington."

"Ah! You are from Washington?" It seemed to the Camera Chap that the other looked at him very keenly.

"Not guilty," he said, with a laugh. "New York is my stamping ground. I merely happened to be in Washington for a couple of days."

"I see. And you are now bound for——" Cipriani paused interrogatively.

"I am going as far as Puerto Cabero."

Once more the other looked at him searchingly. "Might I inquire the object of your visit to Baracoa, if the question is not too personal?"

Hawley smiled. "I haven't any great objection to answering it," he said. "I am an artist, and I am going to make some pictures. I understand that the landscapes there are very fine."

"An artist," the other exclaimed. "That is interesting. I should very much like to see some of your work."

"Perhaps some day I will show you," said the Camera Chap, his eyes twinkling. "And now, having answered your question, may I ask you one in return?"

"I am at your service, señor."

"I would like to know why you are so bitterly prejudiced against Señora Felix. She doesn't strike me as being the sort of woman who deserves the unkind things you said about her."

Cipriani shrugged his shoulders. "You are young, my friend. When you have lived as long as I you will not judge by appearances," he said gravely.

"But that isn't answering my question," Hawley insisted. "Have you any special reason for believing that the señora knows where her husband is?"

"Only my knowledge of human nature," Cipriani replied. "As I said before, it is only logical to suppose that Felix has communicated with his wife since he ran away. I understand that they were a most devoted couple. I presume that when he fled they had an understanding that she was to join him later on; probably she has found it impossible to do so because of the close watch that Portiforo has kept on her."

"How do you know that Portiforo has been keeping a close watch on her?" Hawley asked quickly.

Cipriani seemed discomfited by the question. He winced, and his ruddy face changed color; but his confusion quickly passed. "Of course, I do not know it," he said suavely. "I only assume it. Is it not logical to suppose that the government of Baracoa would keep the wife of an absconding president under close surveillance? If you had ever lived in South America you would not have asked that question. There are more spies down there than there are people to spy on."

He threw the stub of his cigarette into the sea, and took a gold case from his pocket to supply himself with another. "May I offer you one of these?" he said. "They are of my own manufacture. I am in the cigarette business in Buenos Aires."

"No, thank you," said Hawley. "I prefer a pipe." He felt in his pocket. "That reminds me; I left my brier in my stateroom. I'll go and get it. See you again, sir."

The South American smiled and bowed, but as the Camera Chap walked away the smile abruptly left his face, and was replaced by an anxious expression. "We must find out more about that interesting young man," he mused. "I don't think he is going to Baracoa to paint landscapes."

When Hawley reached his stateroom he made a disconcerting discovery. The room had been entered since he was there last, and somebody had been through his baggage. He knew that such was the case because certain articles were not as he had left them. Nothing was missing—a close inventory of his effects satisfied him as to that; but the contents of his trunk and his suit case were slightly disarranged.

With a frown he stepped out into the corridor, and went in search of the steward. "Didn't happen to see anybody go in or out of my room during the last two hours, did you?" he inquired.

The man looked worried. "No, sir; I—I didn't actually see anybody—go in or out," he stammered. "But, now that you speak of it, I saw something that was rather queer."

"What was that?"

"As I was passing your door, ten minutes ago, I saw a man fumbling with the lock. It looked to me as if he was just locking the door; but when I stepped up to him he explained that he had made a mistake, and was trying to get in, thinking it was his own room."

"Ah!" Hawley exclaimed. "Do you know who he was?"

"Yes, sir; it was the gentleman who occupies the room across the hall from yours—Señor José Lopez."

"The deuce!" muttered Hawley. "No wonder he has such a catlike tread. Evidently he needs it in his business. Begins to look as if he might be one of Portiforo's spies sent—— By Jove! I've got the answer, now, as to where I've seen his face. What a chump I am not to have remembered before. It was the absence of his whiskers that fooled me. His appearance is considerably changed without them, but I'm quite sure, now, that he's the same busybody who was trailing Señora Felix in a taxicab."

CHAPTER VI.
A MEETING AFTER DARK.

If the Camera Chap had witnessed a meeting which took place that night between Señora Felix and a certain tall, soldierly-looking male passenger, and if he could have overheard their conversation, he would have been greatly amazed and perplexed.

It was well on toward midnight. The musicians had long ago ceased playing, and most of the passengers had turned in. The promenade deck was as deserted as Broadway after four a. m. The señora, as she stood at the rail, pensively watching the moonbeams playing upon the waves, was as motionless as a wax figure. She was wrapped in a long, black silk shawl so arranged about her head that most of her face was hidden, but the tall, soldierly-looking man who stepped up to her had no difficulty in recognizing her.

She turned swiftly at the sound of his footfall behind her, and an exclamation of pleasure escaped her lips. "So you managed it all right!" she whispered in Spanish.

"Yes, señora; but it is very unwise. I got your message, and I felt that I had to obey this time—but it must not occur again. The risk is too great."

"I know," she acquiesced. "As you say, it must not occur again. From now on we must be as strangers; but I felt that I must have this one talk with you. I am so very anxious."

A frown darkened his handsome features. "It is exceedingly unfortunate, señora, that you should have sailed on this boat," he said ungraciously. "Your presence here is likely to prove disastrous. If only you had waited for another week."

"I couldn't," she answered deprecatingly. "They sent me word that my father's condition was most serious, and I felt it my duty to go to him at once. But I had no idea that you would be here. I understood that you were to sail next Tuesday on the *Panama*."

"Such was my original intention," he answered; "but there were good reasons why I had to alter my plans. I certainly would have delayed my sailing, however, if I had suspected that there was the slightest chance of your being here. I greatly fear the fact that we are traveling on the same boat is regarded as more than a mere coincidence by our friend who calls himself José Lopez."

A worried expression came to the señora's face. "How much does he know?" she inquired.

"I would give much to be able to answer that question," her companion replied, with a grim smile. "Of this much I am sure, however: He already has a strong suspicion that my name is not Juan Cipriani, and that my destination is not Buenos Aires. He forced his acquaintanceship upon me in the smoking room to-day, and began straightway to cross-examine me in a manner which, no doubt, he considered adroit, but which I saw through immediately. In an attempt to lull his suspicion I went through that painful little scene in front of you. I need scarcely assure you, señora, of my profound regret at being obliged to hurt your feelings so cruelly."

"That is all right," she answered. "I realized the necessity. You managed it very skillfully. I feel sure that he must have been convinced that you were unacquainted with me, and that we have no interest in common."

"I am not so certain of that," the man answered, shaking his head. "The best that we can hope is that I succeeded in establishing a doubt in his mind; but I fear that he guessed it was all a trick contrived to deceive him. For the rest of this voyage, I am afraid, he will be watching us closely—on the alert for the slightest glance that passes between us. You must be very careful, señora."

"I will," she promised. "Where is he now?"

"Asleep in his stateroom. I made sure of that before I came here to keep this appointment." The man paused. "But it is not him alone we have cause to fear," he exclaimed suddenly. "There is somebody else on board whose presence is a grave menace to us. That good-looking young American who so impulsively came to your rescue this afternoon—do you know who he is?"

The señora shook her head. "That was one of the reasons I felt it necessary to have this talk with you. I, too, am uneasy about that young man. In spite of his interference in my behalf this afternoon, I have reason to suspect that he belongs to our enemies."

Her companion frowned. "Would you mind telling me your reasons for thinking that, señora?" he asked.

"The first time I noticed him was in New York, several days ago," the woman explained. "It was that day I visited your headquarters. You remember my telling you that I had been followed?"

The man nodded. "That was the time you worked that clever trick with the taxicab," he said, with a smile. "But I understood you to say that it was Lopez who was shadowing you?"

"There were two of them. Lopez was in one cab, but there was another taxi behind his. It contained that young American. I had previously noticed him watching me as I came out of the Mammoth."

Her companion uttered a sharp exclamation.

"And that wasn't the only time," the señora went on. "I saw him in Washington, the day before he sailed. I was driving in Pennsylvania Avenue, and I noticed him on the sidewalk. That may have been a coincidence, of course, but I am afraid not. I noticed that he was observing me very closely. And then, again, he came on board this ship at exactly the same time I did. He was close behind me as I walked up the gangplank. All of which leads me to believe that he is on this vessel for the purpose of spying upon us. I have had Celeste make inquiries about him, and she has learned that he is a New Yorker named Hawley. He claims to be an artist on his way to Baracoa to paint some landscapes, but I am sure that that is only a bluff. The man is one of Portiforo's spies."

Her companion smiled. "You are mistaken about that, señora. I, too, have been making inquiries about this young man. I was fortunate enough to get hold of a fellow passenger, an American, who could tell me all about him. He is not connected with Portiforo—but he is just as dangerous to us as if such were the case."

"Who is he?" the señora asked quickly.

"Hawley is his right name, and, as he has said, he is an artist. But he does not wield a brush. He makes his pictures with a camera. He is a newspaper photographer—on the staff of the New York *Sentinel.*"

The señora gave vent to a faint cry. "Hawley, of the New York *Sentinel!*" she exclaimed agitatedly. "I have heard of him. He is that wonderful photographer they call the Camera Chap."

Her companion nodded. "I see that you realize, señora, how careful we must be of him. The press is as much to be feared by us as our enemies in Baracoa. If a Yankee newspaper were to get hold of our secret we should be lost. I don't know what he is after, but I shall——"

"I do," the señora interrupted tensely. "Now that I know who that young man is, I understand fully why he is going to Baracoa. And he must be stopped," she added, her voice vibrant with emotion. "He must not be permitted to go ahead. We must find some way of preventing it."

CHAPTER VII.
DISCOURAGING NEWS.

It was not until the *Colombia* was approaching Puerto Guerra, the first port of call in Baracoa, that the Camera Chap exchanged a single word with Señora Felix. Possibly he could have conversed with her before that had he desired to do so, for she spent much time on deck, and on several occasions, as he passed her steamer chair, he caught her dark eyes regarding him with keen interest. Several incidents arose, too, which seemed to offer him an opportunity to make her acquaintance, and, modest young man though he was, he could not help suspecting that these incidents were arranged by her in an effort to bring about that result.

Once, for instance, as he walked past where she sat, she dropped the magazine she was reading, and it seemed to Hawley that it was done somewhat ostentatiously, as though she fully expected him to pick it up. On another occasion her shawl fell from her shoulders to the deck as she was promenading, when Hawley was standing near by, and once more it seemed to him that the act was done deliberately.

But even at the sacrifice of having to appear boorish, he ignored these and other advances—if they were advances—for although, under other circumstances, he would have been delighted to make the fair señora's acquaintance, he had decided that it would be most indiscreet to do so now. He had made up his mind to keep away from her throughout the entire trip.

It was the mysterious, soft-treading passenger known as Señor José Lopez who was responsible for this decision on his part. There was no doubt now in Hawley's mind that the fellow was a spy, a secret agent of the Portiforo government, and such being the case he deemed it highly necessary to keep Lopez from guessing that there was aught in common between himself and the wife of the missing president of Baracoa. The slightest evidence of friendship between himself and the woman, he surmised, might give the spy cause to suspect the real object of his mission to South America.

But one evening, as the vessel was approaching the hilly coast line of Baracoa, a steward handed him a note. The missive was in a woman's handwriting, and although it bore no signature he guessed at once from whom it had come. It was short—merely a couple of lines stating that the writer would appreciate it very much if Mr. Hawley would make it a point to be on the promenade deck after eleven o'clock that night.

Guessing whom he would meet there if he kept this appointment, the Camera Chap's first thought was to ignore the summons. But upon reflection, he changed his mind. "It would be a pretty shabby way to act," he told himself. "Besides, I'm too curious to know what she wants of me to be able to resist the temptation. I'll take a chance—provided I can dodge that infernal busybody with the gumshoes. I'm afraid I can't afford to keep the appointment if he's going to be there. However, I think I'll be able to get rid of him."

That evening most of the passengers retired unusually early. The *Colombia* was to dock at sunrise the following morning, and everybody, even those who were not going ashore, desired to be awake early to get the first sight of land. At nine-thirty, as the orchestra finished its final selections, Hawley exchanged "Good night" with several of his acquaintances, and went to his stateroom. A few minutes later, Señor José Lopez came down the corridor with his noiseless, catlike tread, and stood listening intently outside the Camera Chap's door.

The latter grinned as he heard the eavesdropper's soft breathing. He was aware of the fact that his neighbor across the hall paid him this attention each night, never going to bed until he had made sure that Hawley had retired. That cautious young man now went through the formality of disrobing. Señor Lopez heard the thud of his shoes as he allowed them to drop noisily to the floor. Shortly afterward there was the click of the electric light being switched off, and soon after that a sound like a buzz saw in action satisfied the eavesdropper that the occupant of the room was well settled in the land of dreams. Then Lopez stole across the corridor to his own stateroom, and turned in with an easy mind.

A little more than an hour later the Camera Chap arose, dressed himself in the dark, and, with his feet incased in a pair of tennis shoes, emerged from his stateroom, and moved along the corridor with a secrecy which would have done credit to Lopez himself.

When he reached the promenade deck and strode past the long row of empty chairs, there was not a person to be seen. He was beginning to wonder if he were not the victim of a practical joke, when suddenly he espied a shrouded figure, which looked almost ghostly in the moonlight, coming toward him. With a cautious glance behind him, he stepped forward to meet her.

"It was very good of you to come," the woman said softly. "But I knew that you would—just as I feel confident that you will grant me the favor that I am going to ask of you." As she spoke she drew aside the silken, fringed mantilla which concealed all of her face except her eyes, but even before she did this the Camera Chap knew with whom he was talking.

"If there is any service I can render you, señora, you have only to name it," he avowed impulsively. And he meant it, for as he gazed into her dark, sad eyes all the chivalry in him was stirred, and he thrilled with pity for this frail, unhappy woman. At that moment he would have been prepared to go to the rescue of her husband with a sword instead of a camera if more could have been gained that way.

"I am glad to hear you say that," Señora Felix said gratefully. "I trust that you will not change your mind, Mr. Hawley, when I tell you that the favor I am going to ask of you concerns the errand which has brought you to Baracoa."

The Camera Chap gave a start of surprise. "Then you know——" he began excitedly, but suddenly on his guard, abruptly checked himself. "The errand which has brought me to Baracoa!" he exclaimed, with well-feigned bewilderment. "I beg your pardon, señora; I'm afraid I don't quite understand."

The woman laughed softly. "You can be quite frank with me," she said. "I know who has sent you to Baracoa, and what you expect to find—in the fortress of El Torro." She paused, and an anxious expression flitted across her face. "And the favor I'm going to ask of you, Mr. Hawley, is—to give up this undertaking."

The Camera Chap stared at her in astonishment. "To give it up!" he exclaimed incredulously. "Surely you can't mean that, señora! If you really know who sent me and what I hope to accomplish, it seems to me you are the last person in the world who should make such a request of me."

The woman sighed. "There is a good reason for what I ask. You would be running a great risk, and——"

"Don't worry about the risk, señora," the Camera Chap interrupted cheerfully. "If that's your only reason for asking me to quit, I'm afraid I'll have to refuse to listen to you."

"It isn't the only reason," she rejoined. "If there was anything to be gained by it, I'm afraid I would be selfish enough to let you go ahead in spite of the danger you would incur; but when I know that you have come on a wild-goose chase, I feel it my duty to prevent you from sacrificing yourself."

"A wild-goose chase!" the Camera Chap repeated.

"Yes; for your president is misinformed," the señora declared tensely. "My husband is not confined in El Torro. He is not in Baracoa. There is no truth in the rumor which has brought you here."

It was almost as if she had struck Hawley a physical blow. Although, of course, he had realized all along that there was a possibility of the story turning out to be baseless, and although the president had intimated that he himself placed no stock in the sensational rumor, and was merely sending Hawley to Baracoa in order to remove the last possible doubt from his mind, somehow the Camera Chap had been confident until that moment that he was embarked on no fruitless mission. Instinctively he had felt that Felix was a martyr instead of the rogue which the world believed him. But now this statement, coming from the missing man's wife, seemed to dispel all hope that such was the case.

"Do you know where he is, señora?" he inquired, his disappointment evident in his voice.

The woman hesitated, and he caught the shade which flitted across her face. "I do," she said at length, almost in a whisper. "He is—in Europe."

"You are quite sure, señora? Is it not possible that you, too, have been deceived?"

She shook her head. "No; that is not possible—for I have been in constant communication with him. I received a letter from him only last week." She smiled sadly. "So you see, Mr. Hawley, there is nothing for you to do."

CHAPTER VIII.
THE LOST CAUSE.

The Camera Chap was noted on Park Row, among other things, for the buoyancy of his nature and his refusal to permit disappointments and setbacks to ruffle him. But he was scarcely in a cheerful frame of mind as he took his leave of Señora Felix and went back to his stateroom. To have traveled several thousand miles only to discover that he had come on a fool's errand, and, what was worse, to have had all his dreams shattered, was a severe strain even for his abundant stock of philosophy.

For a long time he sat on the edge of his berth, meditating on his conversation with the wife of the missing president. One thing puzzled him exceedingly: Why had the woman taken him into her confidence to the extent of telling him that she knew the whereabouts of her husband? Why was she so keen to dissuade him from persisting in his undertaking? He took no stock in her assertion that solicitude for his welfare had caused her to take this step. Surely, he told himself, she would not have jeopardized her husband's safety and confessed herself an accessory to a crime merely to save a stranger from getting into trouble. There must be some more weighty reason which had prompted her to intrust him with her secret.

Suddenly his face lighted up, and he gave vent to a joyous ejaculation. "Of course, that must be it," he muttered. "The poor little señora! I hate to doubt the word of a lady, but I'm afraid I'll have to take your statements with a grain of salt."

His mind more at ease now, he climbed into his berth, and was soon in a sound sleep. He was awakened early in the morning by the voice of the steward in the corridor notifying those passengers whose destination was Puerto Guerra that their port had been sighted.

Hawley hurried into his clothes and went on deck. He was not going to disembark at that point; he had decided to land at Puerto Cabero, farther on along the coast of Baracoa, and only a few miles from the capital. Yet he was anxious to get his first sight of the land which was to be the scene of his activities.

The ship was picking her way through the coral reefs as he walked to the bow, and stood gazing with interest at the palm-fringed harbor. There he was soon joined by other passengers, among them Señora Felix. She was not going ashore at this port; like Hawley, she was booked to land at Puerto Cabero, but she had left instructions to be awakened as soon as land was sighted, and she now stood against the rail, a pathetically wistful expression on her sad countenance as she stared at the blue-black mountains which formed a background to the quiet little village of thatched houses.

There was only one pier in the harbor. It projected from a low stone structure which, the Camera Chap overheard somebody say, was the custom house. A handful of swarthy-faced men in blue uniforms stood on the pier, languidly watching the approach of the steamship. When the *Colombia* had docked and began to unload freight, these men gathered around six huge packing cases which were carried ashore, and studied them with great interest.

A fat official whose blue uniform was decorated with much gold lace gave some orders to two of the men, who grinned and began to pry off the lid of one of these packing cases. As she watched this act from the deck of the ship an involuntary exclamation escaped Señora Felix. It was only a slight murmur, but it reached the ears of the Camera Chap, who was standing near by. He glanced at her, and observed that her hands were gripping the top of the rail so hard that the knuckles showed white through the nut-brown skin. Evidently she was under a great nervous strain.

Abruptly his attention was drawn from the woman at his side to what was taking place on shore. A force of men on horseback, fifty strong, had galloped up to the group of soldiers gathered around the packing cases. The newcomers were wild-looking fellows, raggedly dressed, and all of them armed. They uttered loud cries as they surrounded the handful of soldiers, who promptly threw up their hands in surrender.

Astonished as the Camera Chap was by this spectacle, he presently witnessed something which amazed him still more. A man rushed from the ship to the pier, and as he went down the gangplank he was greeted by cheers from the wild-looking horsemen. The man was the tall, handsome passenger whom Hawley had known at Señor Juan Cipriani, of Buenos Aires. He was clad now in a gorgeous uniform of blue and gold, and he brandished a sword which flashed in the sunlight. As he joined the group on the pier they gathered around him, and welcomed him with shouts of "Viva Rodriguez! Viva el general!" He acknowledged this ovation with a graceful sweep of his sombrero, and as he happened to turn toward the ship, Hawley saw that his face was aglow with enthusiasm.

Something caused the Camera Chap to glance, just then, at Señora Felix. A great change had come over her. Her face, too, was radiant with happiness, and she was sobbing softly.

But suddenly she uttered a cry of mingled horror and dismay; she clutched the rail in front of her, as though to save herself from falling. The Camera

Chap had only to glance toward the dock to realize the cause of her agitation. With the swiftness of a moving-picture drama, the scene there had changed. A regiment of infantry, springing up apparently from nowhere, had surrounded the group of horsemen. The latter were now surrendering as meekly as the handful of soldiers had previously surrendered to them. The only man making the slightest attempt to fight was Cipriani. He was struggling frantically in the grasp of two burly infantrymen.

These two successive bloodless victories struck Hawley as so ludicrous that he would have laughed but for the evident grief of the woman beside him. There was not the slightest doubt that this latest development meant tragedy to her, however amusing it might appear to a disinterested spectator. Making a valiant effort to regain her calm, she hurried below to her stateroom.

The Camera Chap did not see her again until the *Colombia* arrived at Puerto Cabero. But before they arrived at the latter port a steward stealthily handed him at note. The missive was unsigned, but he recognized the handwriting, and although to anybody else its wording might have been vague, he had no difficulty in grasping its meaning. The note ran:

"Pay no attention to what was said to you last night. What you have witnessed has changed the situation. Now, our only hope lies in your discretion and your ability to carry out the mission intrusted to you."

CHAPTER IX.
THE GIRL IN PINK.

As the *Colombia* steamed into the harbor of Puerto Cabero the following day, the Camera Chap caught sight of a turreted, forbidding-looking gray edifice on the east shore, and he did not have to make inquiries in order to know what this building was. Although he had never seen it before, he knew that he was gazing on the fortress of El Torro, which, in addition to being the main defense of Baracoa's chief seaport, was also internationally famous as the living tomb of several ill-starred wretches whose political activities had earned for them the grim decoration of the ball and chain.

According to the rumor which had brought Hawley to South America, it was within this building that Portiforo had the unhappy Felix locked up; therefore the Camera Chap viewed it with more than idle interest. As he noted the sentries marching to and fro in front of the gray walls it impressed him as being "a pretty formidable sort of a joint," and he didn't imagine that it was going to be exactly a picnic to get inside of it.

"I observe that the señor is interested in El Torro," exclaimed a voice close behind him. "It is a place much easier to enter than it is to leave."

Coming as though in response to his unspoken thought, the words startled Hawley. He wheeled swiftly, and found himself gazing into the swarthy countenance of Señor José Lopez.

"What do you mean by that remark?" he demanded sharply. Then, suddenly on his guard, he added more mildly: "What makes you think that I am particularly interested in El Torro?"

The other bared his large teeth in a wolflike grin. "I judged that such was the case from the manner in which the señor was staring at it," he replied quietly.

The Camera Chap laughed. "It is a picturesque pile," he declared. "From an artistic standpoint it appeals to me greatly. I certainly will have to make a picture of it before I return to the United States. That is, of course, if it isn't against the rules."

Lopez shrugged his shoulders. "I dare say there will be no objection to Señor Hawley making as many pictures as he desires—of the outside of El Torro," he remarked.

"Now, I wonder what the deuce he meant by that!" Hawley reflected, as the other walked away. "I'd give a lot to know whether that confounded spy suspects anything."

Until that moment he had felt confident that he had his inquisitive fellow passenger guessing as to the object of his visit to Baracoa, but the significant remark which the latter had just let drop made him exceedingly uneasy. There being no doubt in his mind that Lopez was a secret agent of the Portiforo government, he feared that he was going to have a hard time losing him when they got ashore; in fact, he was now even prepared to be challenged by the immigration authorities, and told that his presence in Baracoa was not desired. But, greatly to his relief, both these fears proved unfounded. When the vessel docked, the pier authorities manifested no more interest in him than in any of the other passengers; on the contrary, the customs officers were so careless in their examination of his baggage that they did not even discover the big camera in his trunk. And when he went ashore, Lopez made no attempt to shadow him; in fact, he saw the latter board a train without even a glance in his direction.

Another circumstance which surprised him somewhat was that Señora Felix was also permitted to land without undue attention from the authorities. In view of what had happened at Puerto Guerra, and her obvious interest therein, he had been wondering ever since whether she would not be placed under arrest as soon as she attempted to land, on a charge of being in some way connected with the affair, and he was very glad to find that such was not the case.

Hawley watched the landing of the señora with great interest. He observed that as she and her maid stepped from the pier, many people stared at her, recognizing her as the wife of their missing president; but nobody spoke to her, with the exception of a blond-haired, blue-eyed girl in a pink dress, who stepped up and greeted her effusively.

This young woman aroused the Camera Chap's curiosity. It was quite evident that she was not a native of Baracoa; at first sight he would have been willing to bet all the money he had in his pocket that she was of his own people. She appeared to be still in her "teens," and was of such an attractive personality that almost any one would have bestowed more than one glance upon her, even if his interest had not been intensified by the fact that she was there to welcome Señora Felix.

For a few minutes the two women stood chatting together in the plaza in front of the steamship pier, Celeste, the señora's maid, hanging respectfully in the background. Then, followed by the latter, they made their way toward a touring car standing near by, which they entered. The girl in pink gave some instructions to the liveried negro at the wheel, and the car dashed up one of the steep roads which led to the capital.

Not once since she had come ashore had the señora appeared to notice the Camera Chap—he suspected that she studiously refrained from doing so for reasons which he fully appreciated—but just before the automobile started she whispered something to her fair companion, and the latter turned in her seat and looked deliberately toward where he was standing. There were several other persons in his vicinity, and it might have been any of these at whom her glance was directed, but Hawley, modest man though he was, felt positive that he was the object of her scrutiny, and somehow the thought afforded him much satisfaction.

He was not left long in ignorance as to the identity of this prepossessing young woman, for, as the car started off, the conversation of two natives standing near him supplied him with that information.

"Is it not somewhat surprising that the daughter of the American minister should be on such friendly terms with the wife of the abominable Felix?" Hawley overheard one of them remark in Spanish. To which the other responded, with a shrug: "Nothing is surprising about those Yankees."

The Camera Chap was too much absorbed in the information he had gleaned even to feel like resenting the slur upon his countrymen. So the girl in pink was Miss Throgmorton, the daughter of the American minister to Baracoa! And she was on such intimate terms with Señora Felix that she alone had come to welcome the latter back to her native land! Here was an interesting discovery, indeed.

At that moment there flashed through his mind what his friend and managing editor, Tom Paxton, had said about the sentiments of the United States minister to Baracoa toward the *Sentinel,* and all men connected with it. He devoutly hoped that the daughter did not share her father's prejudices in that respect, for he had already fully decided that if it were possible he was going to make Miss Throgmorton's acquaintance before he had been many days in Baracoa.

CHAPTER X.
AN UNPLEASANT SURPRISE.

The Camera Chap did not linger long at Puerto Cabero. He had decided to make Santa Barbara, the capital, his headquarters, that city being only ten miles away from the seaport. It is situated on a highland three thousand feet above the sea level, and, as Hawley traveled on the antiquated railroad, he marveled at the manner in which the line twisted and turned like a huge corkscrew.

When he arrived at his journey's end he found the city in gala attire. The streets and shops were decorated with flags and bunting, and a band was playing in the plaza. At the Hotel Nacional, where he registered, he inquired whether he had struck town on a national holiday, and was informed that the festivities were the result of the extraordinary scene he had witnessed at Puerto Guerra the previous day.

"You see, señor," explained the hotel clerk, who spoke very good English, "President Portiforo has ordered a day of public rejoicing because of the defeat of General Rodriguez."

"Rodriguez!" exclaimed Hawley, who recalled that he had heard the man whom he had known as Juan Cipriani hailed by that name by the group of wild-looking horsemen on the pier. "What was he trying to do? Was he starting a revolution?"

The clerk nodded, and proceeded to tell Hawley a story which fully enlightened him as to the significance of the drama he had seen enacted at the customhouse at Puerto Guerra. The Camera Chap learned that the big packing cases which the steamship *Colombia* had brought, and which were invoiced as containing farming implements, had in reality contained machine guns intended for the use of the new revolutionary party which General Emilio Rodriguez, alias Juan Cipriani, had come to Baracoa to lead.

Rodriguez, Hawley was informed, was a native of Baracoa, but had been in Europe for the past ten years. He had held a commission in the French army, which he had resigned in order to come back and attempt to overthrow the Portiforo government; which attempt, however, had been rendered futile by the alertness of President Portiforo.

"But you don't mean to tell me that that chap was going to have the nerve to buck against the government forces with that handful of men I saw at the pier?" the Camera Chap exclaimed in astonishment. "Why, there couldn't have been more than fifty of them in all."

The clerk smiled deprecatingly. "That was only the beginning, señor. If Rodriguez's plans had not miscarried, he was to have taken to the hills with that escort, and there proclaimed the revolution. He had been assured that the people would flock by thousands to his banner, and that as soon as he gave the word the army was prepared to revolt and go over to him. But things didn't go just as he expected. President Portiforo learned of the plot in time to nip the revolution in the bud. A few days ago he raised the pay of everybody in the federal army, from the commander in chief down to the newest recruit, and thereby kept the troops loyal to him. He set a trap for Rodriguez, and when that unhappy man stepped off the boat at Puerto Guerra yesterday, expecting the whole country to be ready to respond to his call to arms, he was seized and thrown into jail." The clerk grinned. "One has to get up very early in the morning in order to catch our President Portiforo napping, señor," he said.

"So I have heard," the Camera Chap responded dryly. "What do you suppose will happen to Cipriani—I mean Rodriguez?"

The clerk shrugged his shoulders. "There is only one fate for those who conspire against the government of Baracoa," he said quietly. "I understand that the president has already signed his death warrant."

Hawley was silent for a while after that. "Do you happen to know," he inquired suddenly, "whether your former president, Francisco Felix, was mixed up in any way with this revolutionary plot?"

The clerk stared at him in astonishment. "If such is the case, it is the first time I have heard of it!" he declared. "Might I inquire what put such a thought in your head, señor? Have you any information to that effect?"

"I?" exclaimed Hawley, with a deprecating smile. "I arrived at Baracoa only a few hours ago. What should I know about the affairs of your interesting country?"

Later that day, Hawley got his first sight of Miguel Portiforo, President of Baracoa. There was a big military parade in honor of "the overthrow of the revolution," and the president rode at the head of his troops in an open carriage, flanked on each side by an escort of cavalry.

Standing in front of the Hotel Nacional, the Camera Chap gazed with great interest upon the man with whom he realized he must expect to match wits in order to carry out the delicate and difficult errand which had been intrusted to him. At first sight the president did not impress him as being a man of formidable personality. Although he wore a glittering uniform of scarlet and gold, he was far from presenting a military appearance. He was undersized and exceedingly fat, and his bloated face was as round as a pumpkin. As he smiled in acknowledgment of the plaudits of the crowds, he looked like an easy-going, jovial old boy, who would have been more at home at a banquet table proposing a toast to "the ladies—God bless 'em," than ruling with an iron hand over the political destinies of a turbulent South American republic.

That was the first impression which the Camera Chap formed of Miguel Portiforo, but just then an incident happened which quickly caused him to change his estimate of that dignitary. As the president's carriage was passing, a man in the front rank of the crowd on the sidewalk outside the Hotel Nacional stepped forward, and, gesticulating wildly, began to abuse Portiforo in a tone loud enough to reach the latter's ears. The man was staggering as though intoxicated. Hawley learned later that he was a humble shoemaker of Santa Barbara, who, when in a normal condition, was as meek and law-abiding a citizen as was to be found in all Baracoa, but who now had been celebrating the overthrow of the revolution to such an extent that he was not responsible for what he said or did. Although the fellow's condition was obvious, Portiforo made no allowance for it. Glancing at the latter, the Camera Chap was appalled by the change which had come over him as the drunken man's abuse fell upon his ears. The jovial smile had disappeared. In its stead had come an expression terrible to behold. The beady eyes were snapping with rage. The thin lips were parted in a snarl. Curiously the president's plump face seemed suddenly to have lost all its roundness, and to have been remolded into lines sinister and cruel. It was not until he had seen several soldiers rush forward, seize the offender, and drag him off, struggling and screaming, that his features relaxed, and the jovial smile returned.

"I wonder what will happen to the poor beggar," said a dapper, good-looking young man who was standing close behind Hawley. "I suppose they'll give him the limit, eh?"

"I am afraid so," replied his companion, a blond-haired, blue-eyed young woman. "Inasmuch as the city has been put under martial law, Portiforo can do as he pleases with him, and that brute isn't likely to show much clemency to a man who has publicly insulted him."

"Be careful," entreated the young man nervously. "Aren't you taking an awful chance, Virginia, talking like that in public? There may be people around us who understand English, and even though you are the daughter of the United States minister, you can't—well for the love of Methusaleh! If it isn't old Frank Hawley, of the *Sentinel*!"

Regretting the impulse which had caused him to turn his head at this hint of the girl's identity, Hawley stared at the speaker in some consternation, for the recognition was mutual. The Camera Chap was well acquainted with Miss Throgmorton's dapper companion. The latter's name was Gale, and he was a reporter on the New York *Daily News*, the *Sentinel's* most bitter rival. Incidentally he was the last man in the world whom Hawley would have desired to meet in Baracoa.

CHAPTER XI.
A DIPLOMAT'S DAUGHTER.

Between the Camera Chap and Gale there existed a feud of long standing, the intensity of which was based upon more than mere loyalty for their respective newspapers. Hawley knew the *News* man, from past experience, as the trickiest, most unscrupulous member of the journalistic profession he had ever matched wits with on an assignment, and for that reason disliked him exceedingly. But dislike would hardly be a strong enough word to characterize the sentiments of Gale toward Hawley. Jealousy and resentment for many past defeats at the latter's hands had engendered in him a feeling of downright hatred for the clever, good-humored chap who generally managed to turn the tables on him in spite of his underhand methods.

There was nothing of this feeling evident in Gale's manner now, however, as he greeted the Camera Chap. On the contrary, if he had loved the latter like a twin brother his demeanor could scarcely have been more cordial. "Well, this is, indeed, a big surprise, Hawley, old scout," he exclaimed exuberantly. "I didn't have any idea that you were in Baracoa."

"I scarcely expected to find you here, either," the Camera Chap replied quietly. "Might I inquire what you are doing so far away from Park Row?"

"I'm not down here on business," the other replied. "I was so busy covering the street cleaners' strike last summer that I didn't have time to take a vacation then, so the boss is giving me a few weeks now. I thought I might as well run down here and visit my old friend, the American minister."

"Oh, an old friend," Hawley repeated, glancing at the girl.

"Yes, I have had the honor of knowing Minister Throgmorton for a long time, and when he was appointed to this position he was kind enough to extend me a standing invitation to come to Baracoa and be his guest. As you say, it's a long way from Park Row, but I am having a great time."

Hawley looked at him searchingly, but said nothing.

"And now, how about yourself, old top?" the *News* man demanded. "Tit for tat, you know. What particular bunch of trouble has brought you down this way? Haven't come to lead a revolution, have you?"

"Scarcely," the Camera Chap replied, smiling. "It is a curious coincidence, but I, too, happen to be here on a leave of absence. I haven't had a vacation in three years, so I figured that the paper owed me a holiday."

"What made you select Baracoa?" Gale demanded suspiciously.

"Why not?" the Camera Chap rejoined. "I've always had a hankering to visit South America. Some people prefer going to Europe, but I've always believed in seeing our own hemisphere first."

Gale was not satisfied by this answer. "Brought your camera along with you?" he inquired abruptly.

"Of course. I wouldn't travel without it—even on a pleasure trip. I hope to land some good snapshots before I go back."

"Snapshots of what?" Gale demanded quickly.

Hawley shrugged his shoulders in a manner which would have done credit to a native of Baracoa. "That is hard to say, at present," he answered. "I have no doubt that in a land as interesting as this, there must be many attractive things to photograph."

As he spoke he looked into the eyes of Gale's fair companion, and saw lurking in their blue depths an appreciative twinkle which warned him that she knew his secret. Evidently her friend, the señora, had taken the girl into her confidence. The situation disturbed him greatly. He wondered uneasily whether the American minister's daughter could be relied upon to keep what she knew to herself, or whether she would pass it along to Gale, with whom, evidently, she was on friendly terms.

"Miss Throgmorton," said Gale suddenly, "may I present my friend, Mr. Hawley? You remember my telling you the other day about Hawley, of the *Sentinel*?"

"Oh, yes," the girl replied mischievously, as she extended her hand; "I recall your telling me how often you scooped him on pictures. I really felt quite sorry for you, Mr. Hawley, when I heard Mr. Gale's stories. Newspaper work must be a cruel game."

The Camera Chap smiled, and Gale looked somewhat sheepish. In boasting of his exploits to his host's daughter, he had departed from the truth to an extent which covered him with glory, but did not do justice to the *Sentinel* man.

"Suppose we change the subject," Gale said quickly. "Possibly Mr. Hawley might find it painful, you know. By the way, Frank, old man, I wonder if you'd mind taking care of Miss Throgmorton for a few minutes, while I go and make some inquiries about the attempt that was just made on President

Portiforo's life? Even though I'm on my vacation, I can't afford to pass up a story like that."

"The attempt on Portiforo's life?" the Camera Chap repeated, in astonishment. "What do you mean?"

"Didn't you see that fellow try to throw a bomb at him just now?"

"Why, Mr. Gale!" Miss Throgmorton cried indignantly. "You know very well he didn't do anything of the sort. The man was intoxicated, and he didn't do anything except call Portiforo names. Surely you are not going to send your paper such an exaggerated account!"

"I am positive I saw something in his hand that looked like a bomb. He was just about to throw it when they grabbed him," insisted Gale, according to whose code of journalistic ethics it was always justifiable to "color" a story, provided one could get away with it. "So long, folks. I'll be back in a little while," he said, as he walked off.

The Camera Chap was grateful for this unlooked-for opportunity to speak to the girl alone. "I must have a talk with you, Miss Throgmorton," he began, in an eager whisper; "but not here. There is too much danger of our being overheard. I hope you will not consider me presumptuous, but it is really very important. Isn't there some place near here where we can talk in safety?"

The girl nodded. "The Botanical Gardens are only a short distance from here," she suggested. "They will be deserted now; every one is on the street watching the parade. I, too, am anxious to have a talk with you; in fact, even if we hadn't met now, I was going to make it a point to communicate with you and arrange a meeting. I have a message for you—from a mutual friend."

Hawley smiled. He thought he could come pretty near guessing the identity of the sender of the message. "Don't say any more about it now," he warned her hastily. "Wait until we reach the gardens."

They forced their way to the rear of the throng on the sidewalk, and a few minutes later were strolling along the graceful walks of the Botanical Gardens, which, although usually crowded at that hour of the day, were now, as the girl had surmised, as desolate as a desert island.

"Did I understand Gale to say that he is stopping at your house?" Hawley began abruptly.

"Yes; he is spending his vacation with us. My father has taken a great fancy to him. When dad was a deputy police commissioner in New York, Mr. Gale wrote some very flattering things about him in the *News*, and he has never forgotten it. Dad just hates to have the newspapers publish nice things about him," she added, with a laugh.

"I don't care very much for Mr. Gale myself," she added frankly. "In fact, I do not like him at all. When he first came to us I did. I was so favorably impressed with him that I was on the point of taking him into my confidence about—poor President Felix."

Although her words greatly interested the Camera Chap, his face was as a mask. "President Felix?" he repeated, with an interrogative inflection.

"Yes. You see, I felt that I must share my secret with some one, and I believed at first that Mr. Gale would be just the person to help get that poor man out of El Torro," the girl said. "But after I had studied him for a few days," she added, "I decided that he wouldn't do at all; he isn't trustworthy. I feel sure that if he got even a hint of the story he would publish it in his paper, regardless of the consequences."

Hawley felt pretty sure of that, too. Inwardly he rejoiced that Miss Throgmorton had changed her mind about taking the perfidious Gale into her confidence. Aloud he said, after a cautious glance all around him: "So you suspect that President Felix is confined in El Torro?"

Her reply almost took his breath away. "Suspect!" she exclaimed tensely. "I know it. I have seen him!"

CHAPTER XII.
ON THE RIGHT TRACK.

The Camera Chap stared at the girl with as much incredulity written on his face as if she had just told him that she had been present when Columbus landed in the New World. "You have seen him!" he exclaimed. "Surely you can't mean that you have been inside El Torro?"

"Yes, I do!" the girl declared, smiling slightly at the effect her announcement had upon him. "I mean just that. I have been inside El Torro, and I have seen President Felix."

"When was this?" Hawley demanded.

"Several months ago. I saw him only once—and then only for one brief second. Since then I have been trying my hardest to get in there again, but I haven't been able to manage it."

"How did you manage it that time?" the Camera Chap inquired, his manner still slightly incredulous, although he did not intend it to be so. "I shouldn't imagine that it was an easy thing, even once."

Virginia hesitated. She was debating with herself as to whether this prepossessing, frank-looking young man from her own country could safely be taken into her confidence. "I feel that I can trust you, Mr. Hawley," she said suddenly. "If I didn't I shouldn't tell you what I am going to tell you now. For if it were to become known to others the consequences might be serious."

She glanced around her in all directions, and even when she had ascertained that there was nobody within earshot, lowered her voice almost to a whisper. "There is a certain young man of my acquaintance," she began, "who is an officer in the Baracoan army. His name is Reyes—Captain Ernesto Reyes. You must promise me to forget that name as soon as you have heard the story, Mr. Hawley."

"I have forgotten it already," the Camera Chap assured her.

The girl smiled. "I met him at an embassy ball, about a year ago, and we became very good friends. He was attached to El Torro and had charge of the prison guard. It was through him that I was able to visit the prison."

"He permitted you to enter the prison?"

"Yes; he smuggled me in there. He was running a great risk, of course."

"So I should imagine," said the Camera Chap. "He must be very fond of—President Felix," he added dryly.

Virginia blushed. "No; I'm sorry to say that isn't the case. If it were so it would make things so much easier for us. It wasn't out of any consideration for President Felix that Captain Reyes allowed me to visit his prison. It—there were other reasons. Captain Reyes is far from being a Felix sympathizer. On the contrary, he has a deadly grudge against him. I guess that is why Portiforo has put him in charge of El Torro prison; he knows that there is no chance of Felix being allowed to escape while he is in charge."

Hawley frowned. "Why is he so bitter toward Felix?" he inquired.

"He has cause, I must admit," the girl explained, her face clouding. "Captain Reyes' father was a colonel in the Baracoan army when Mr. Felix first became president. He was caught conspiring against the government, and Felix ordered him to be shot. I don't know anything about the merits of the case, but, right or wrong, I suppose it is only natural that the son should hate the man who signed his father's death warrant."

Hawley nodded. "But if he feels that way about it, whatever could have possessed him to consent to your communicating with the prisoner?" he exclaimed.

Virginia's blue eyes twinkled. "He didn't consent to any such thing," she said demurely. "He didn't have any idea that I desired to see President Felix, or that I had the slightest interest in him. He supposed that my anxiety to inspect the dungeons was prompted solely by morbid curiosity."

"Still, I can't understand his being so rash as to let you in there," said Hawley.

The girl's face dimpled. "He couldn't help himself; I called his bluff," she announced, laughing apologetically at her own frank use of American slang.

"His bluff?"

"Like most of his countrymen, Captain Reyes has the habit of indulging in very extravagant language when he is talking to women," Miss Throgmorton explained naïvely. "One evening when he was at our house he was assuring me, with his hand on his heart, of his readiness to lay down his life for me, and I laughed at his protestations and told him that in my native land that brand of talk was known as 'hot air.' He urged me to put him to the test, and, after pretending to consider for a while, I told him that I wouldn't ask him to risk his life, but that if he really wanted to show that he was willing to take chances for my sake, he could do so by taking me on a tour of inspection through El Torro prison."

Hawley chuckled. "Clever work! You knew, then, that President Felix was there?"

"I had heard the rumor, and I thought it was a good chance to find out whether it was true. I could see that poor Captain Reyes was startled by my request. He protested that it was against the rules to admit visitors to El Torro. He begged me to put him to some other test. But I insisted that it must be that or nothing. I taunted him with being afraid to take a chance, and at last I got the poor man so worked up that he gritted his teeth and said that he would do it, no matter what the consequences might be."

"Good for him!" said Hawley. "He must be a pretty plucky chap."

"He is no coward," said the girl soberly. "I hated to demand such a sacrifice of him; for although I didn't let him know it, I realized that I was making him do something which, if he had been caught, would have meant the ruin of his career—and, perhaps, worse. But it was for a good cause, and I considered myself justified. Anyway," she added brightly, "thank goodness, nothing like that happened."

"He got away with it, all right?"

"Evidently; for that was several months ago, and he is still in command of the prison guard; which wouldn't be the case, of course, if even a hint of my visit to El Torro had reached the ears of Portiforo."

"So he is still in charge of the prison guard!" murmured the Camera Chap, inwardly resolving to make the acquaintance of Captain Ernesto Reyes at the earliest possible opportunity. "Do you mean to say that he took you all over the prison—even to the cell in which they've got Felix locked up?" he continued wonderingly. "Surely it would have been an easy matter for him to avoid showing you that particular cell."

The girl laughed. "He didn't find it so easy. He did attempt to hurry me past that cell, but, to borrow your own expression, he couldn't get away with it. I peeped through the hole in the panel before he had a chance to stop me."

"The hole in the panel?"

"They have put sheets of tin over the bars of President Felix's dungeon to prevent anybody in the corridor from getting a glimpse of him," the girl explained. "But the tin had rusted, and there was a tiny hole in one corner which evidently had escaped the attention of the prison officials. It was through this hole that I got my peep at the unfortunate man."

"How did you know he was in there?" the Camera Chap queried.

"I didn't know, of course. I merely guessed it. As soon as I saw that covered door it flashed through my mind that it would most likely be the place where they would have him. And Captain Reyes' manner confirmed my suspicions. When I inquired of him why the door of this cell was covered with sheets of tin instead of being grilled like all the other doors on that gloomy corridor, he became perceptibly nervous. He explained that the cell was unoccupied, and was used as a storage room; but while he was talking I heard the sound of somebody coughing behind that screened door, and I knew that he had lied to me. Captain Reyes heard it, too, but evidently he was in hopes that it had escaped my ears, for he tried to hurry me away by telling me that he had something exceedingly interesting to show me in another part of the prison. But I broke away from him and stepped close up to the door. It was then that I discovered the tiny peephole which the rust had eaten in one part of the tin, and before he could stop me I had put my eye to it."

"And you saw?" The Camera Chap's voice was tense with eagerness.

Virginia shuddered slightly. "I saw a man seated at a rough wooden table reading a book. Just at that moment he happened to look up, and I got a good view of his face. He had changed terribly since I had last seen him. His hair was snowy white, his face was pitifully thin, and looked as if it didn't have a drop of blood in it. His eyes were sunken. But it was President Felix; I am absolutely positive of that."

The Camera Chap's face was grim. "You say that he was reading. Was his cell light enough for that?"

"Oh, yes; there was plenty of light, and air, too. I must say in justice to Portiforo that he has made his prisoner as comfortable as possible under the circumstances. The dungeon is much bigger than the other cells, and there is a large window, barred, of course, which commands a view of the sea."

Hawley's face lighted up with excitement. "I rather like the idea of that window!" he murmured, as if to himself. "Our friend Portiforo is much more accommodating than I dared hope."

Guessing what was in his mind, Virginia shook her head. "I'm afraid you won't be so optimistic when I tell you that there is a sentinel on guard every hour of the night and day outside of that window," she said. "You couldn't possibly get to him in that way."

Hawley received the announcement cheerfully. "I expected that," he informed her. "I didn't suppose for a minute, you know, that Portiforo would be so careless as to leave the window unguarded. Still, it's easier to tackle the problem of a flesh-and-blood sentry than an inanimate stone wall. But go on with your story, please. What happened after you took that peep at Felix? Captain Reyes saw what you were up to, of course?"

The girl smiled. "Of course; and the change that came over him was truly startling. His face went white with rage, and his voice trembled as he accused me of being a spy, and of having tricked him. I was actually afraid at first that he was going to order poor little me arrested and put in irons. It was a great relief to me when he apologized."

Hawley smiled. "You made him apologize?"

Virginia nodded, and her blue eyes twinkled. "When he was through with his violent outburst," she said demurely, "I decided that it was my turn to become indignant. I told him haughtily that I didn't see why he should make such a fuss just because my curiosity had got the best of me. I complained tearfully that I was sorry now that I had consented to come to his horrid old prison, and that I had been through jails in my own country, which I found much more interesting. I guess my words and my manner must have satisfied him at length that I had not recognized the prisoner, for, after he had asked me a few questions, he suddenly became very remorseful for his rough treatment, and begged me to forgive him. Later on, when we were good friends again, I inquired of him carelessly as to the identity of the man I had seen in that cell, and he informed me glibly that he was a political agitator named Pedro Velasquez, who had been in captivity for the past fifteen years. He was even ingenious enough to tell me that the poor fellow had gone out of his mind, and had hallucinations that he was President Felix. I smiled at this and replied that there certainly wasn't much resemblance between the prisoner and President Felix as I remembered him, which was literally true."

The Camera Chap bestowed upon her a look of frank admiration. "You're a wonder, Miss Throgmorton!" he declared impulsively. "I don't know any girl who could have handled the situation more cleverly. I suppose," he added anxiously, "you told your father of your discovery?"

Miss Throgmorton shook her head. "No; I decided that it wouldn't do to tell dad a word about it. He thinks so highly of Portiforo that I felt sure that he would only laugh at my story, and tell me that my imagination had got the best of me. Besides, I had to consider Captain Reyes. I was afraid that if I told my father of my visit to the prison he might mention the matter to President Portiforo, and thus get Captain Reyes into trouble. I haven't confided my secret to anybody except yourself and Señora Felix. By the way!" she exclaimed. "Speaking of the señora reminds me that I have a message for you from her. She told me to assure you that she has the greatest confidence in your ability and discretion, but she wishes to urge upon you the necessity of being most careful. On no account must you attempt to see her at her father's house. The place is watched by spies all the time. If for any reason you should wish to communicate with her, she suggests that it be done through me."

The Camera Chap bowed. "A very sensible arrangement," he said, "and one that is eminently satisfactory to me."

The girl laughed, and her color deepened. "I think we'd better be getting back," she suggested. "The parade must be over, for people are beginning to come into the park."

As they stepped outside the Botanical Gardens they encountered Gale. That young man frowned at the sight of them. "Why, here you are!" he exclaimed reproachfully. "I've been looking all over for you. I thought you promised to wait for me outside the Hotel Nacional."

"We got tired of watching the parade, so we thought we'd walk around a bit," Hawley replied. "Did you get the information you wanted about the attempted assassination of Portiforo?" he inquired quizzically.

Gale nodded. "I found out the fellow's name and business," he replied. "That's all I needed. It's a peach of a story. I'm going to put it on the wire in a little while. Would you like to send it to your paper, too, old man?"

Hawley smiled. He knew from past experiences that when Gale offered to share a story with a rival newspaper, it was never out of motives of altruism, but because the story was so much the product of his imagination that it gave him a greater sense of security to have his statements backed up by another sheet. "No, thanks," he said dryly. "I guess I won't touch it. I'm a snapshotter, and sending stories is somewhat out of my line. Besides, I'm on my vacation, so why should I work?"

Gale looked at him searchingly. "Of course, you wouldn't think of working on your vacation, would you?" he rejoined, with an ironical smile.

When, a few minutes later, the Camera Chap took his leave, the *News* man turned eagerly to Virginia. "Did he happen to drop you any hint of what he's doing in Baracoa, Miss Throgmorton?" he inquired.

The girl's blue eyes opened wide in childlike wonder. "A hint?" she said innocently. "Why didn't he tell us outright that he's spending his vacation here?"

Gale smiled sapiently. "Vacation or no vacation, that fellow didn't come here to study the scenery!" he declared. "He is here for a purpose, and before I'm many days older I'm going to find out what it is."

CHAPTER XIII.
TRUTH WILL OUT.

It was not often that the Washington correspondent of the New York *Daily News* visited the home office of that newspaper, particularly when Congress was in session. Therefore Ben Stephens, the managing editor, looked up from his desk in astonishment one afternoon when that young man stepped into his office.

"I've got a line on something so important," the latter explained, "that I was afraid to trust it to the wires. I might have sent it in by mail, of course, but I thought it would be more satisfactory to run into town and talk it over with you. I think you'll agree that it's one of the hottest tips that ever came out of Washington."

"A scandal?" eagerly exclaimed Stephens. "Haven't caught a United States senator with the goods, have you?"

The correspondent smiled. "Not exactly. It's a scandal, all right, and a whopping big one, but a little farther from home than that. You remember that chap Felix, President of Baracoa, who skipped with the national treasury a couple of years ago?"

The managing editor nodded. "What about him? Have they caught the rascal?"

The Washington correspondent lowered his voice. "According to the tip I've got, he never went away," he announced. "It was all a frame-up on the part of his political enemies, headed by Portiforo. They've got him locked up in a dungeon of El Torro fortress, where he's been ever since the night he's supposed to have beaten it."

Stephens smiled skeptically. "What kind of tobacco do you smoke?" he sneered.

"It isn't a pipe dream," the other said earnestly. "At least, I'm pretty well satisfied that the tip is straight goods. It comes from a most authoritative source." He dropped his voice even lower. "I got it from Attorney General Cooper."

The managing editor's face lighted up. "From Cooper himself?"

The correspondent hesitated. "Well, I didn't exactly hear it from his own lips, but it came from him, all right. The fact is I got the tip from one of the servants of the attorney general's household—his butler. But the fellow is absolutely to be relied on. I have had him on my pay roll for the last six months, and he's never given me a wrong steer yet. You remember that scoop last winter about the wife of that European ambassador losing twenty-five thousand at bridge? Well, that tip came from him. That chap is a regular bear for news. There is mighty little going on at the capital that he doesn't hear about."

Stephens grinned appreciatively. "Where did he get this fairy story about Felix?" he demanded.

"From Mrs. Cooper's maid. You know that until recently Señora Felix has been stopping at the attorney general's house. She and Mrs. Cooper are very chummy. Naturally they talked together frequently about the matter, and the maid managed to overhear most of what they said, and passed it along to my trusty informant. It seems that the women have been getting at the attorney general to put the proposition before the president, and have him order an investigation, and a few weeks ago Cooper brought it up at a cabinet meeting."

Stephens became more interested. "Have you asked the president about it?" he inquired.

"No, indeed! I was afraid that instead of telling me anything, he'd make me promise not to print a line about what I already knew, and then I'd have to take my choice between passing up the story or being in bad at the White House. Either that, or else, seeing that the *News* has the tip, he'd hand out the story to the whole Washington bunch; for the president makes it a rule not to play any favorites."

Stephens nodded. "Under those circumstances, you were quite right not to take any chances. Still," he added pensively, "I don't see what we can do with the tip in its present form. It would hardly pay us to send a man down to Baracoa."

"Why not?" the correspondent protested. "It's a big story if it's true and——"

"Yes, if it's true!" the managing editor interrupted doubtfully. "If I thought there was a ten-per-cent chance of there being anything in this wild rumor, I wouldn't mind the expense of sending five men down there to dig up the story, even if we had to charter a private yacht, but with all due respect to your friend, the attorney general's butler, this sounds to me like the effects of a combination of Welsh rabbit and strawberry shortcake, with a couple of slabs of custard pie thrown in. I don't feel like spending even ten cents on such an impossible yarn."

Then, suddenly, his face lighted up. "By Jove! I was forgetting!" he exclaimed. "We don't have to send a man down there. We've got a man in Baracoa now—and a good one, too."

"Who is it?"

"Gale, of our city staff. He's taking a month's vacation, and that's where he went to spend it. He sent us a good story from there a couple of days ago about an attempt on the life of Portiforo. I couldn't have picked a better man than Gale for an assignment of this sort. He's got more gall than any other reporter on our staff. If Felix is locked up in El Torro fortress, I'll bank on Gale being able to locate him. I'll wire him to-day to get busy."

Thus it came about that a week after the Camera Chap's arrival in San Cristobal, Gale received a dispatch, the laconic but comprehensive contents of which caused him to seek an immediate interview with his host, the United States minister to Baracoa.

Minister Throgmorton was in his library in conversation with a tall, bearded man, when Gale knocked on the door. "I beg your pardon, I didn't know you were busy," the *News* man said. "Perhaps I'd better come back later. It isn't anything important."

"Come right in," the United States representative responded genially. "I want you to meet General Replife, minister of war in President Portiforo's cabinet. General, permit me to present my friend, Mr. Gale, a New York journalist of distinction. Now, Gale, what can I do for you?"

"It is nothing important," Gale repeated. "I merely wanted to ask you whether it would be possible for you to get me a pass to go through the fortress of El Torro."

"El Torro!" exclaimed Minister Throgmorton sharply. "For what reason do you want to go there?"

Gale shrugged his shoulders. "Merely on a sightseeing tour, sir," he replied, conscious, as he spoke, that the dark eyes of General Replife were fixed scrutinizingly on his face. "I've heard that it is an interesting sort of place, and I shouldn't like to return to New York without being able to say that I had included it among the places I visited."

Minister Throgmorton frowned. He was a stout, pompous little man, with an odd little gray beard, which sprouted from his chin like a miniature whisk broom. "I am afraid that is out of the question," he said. "I believe visitors are not welcome at El Torro, eh, general?"

The minister of war bowed. "There is a strictly enforced rule to that effect, señor," he replied.

"I know there is," said Gale, smiling. "That is why I have come to you, Mr. Throgmorton, to ask you to use your pull to get me in." He hesitated; then, with a sudden show of candor: "I might as well be quite frank with you, sir. It isn't merely idle curiosity which makes me desirous of visiting the fortress. I don't know whether I have mentioned it to you before, but the study of prisons has always been my hobby. I have visited nearly all the big jails in the United States, and some in foreign countries. Some day I hope to get up a magazine article on the subject."

"Ah!" exclaimed General Replife, addressing the minister. "Then it is the dungeons of El Torro, not the fortifications, in which your friend is interested? I think that might be arranged, Señor Throgmorton. If you will vouch for this gentleman, there will be no objection to his being shown through the prison part of the fortress. I will make out a permit now."

Gale expressed his gratitude and delight; but, as a matter of fact, he was secretly disappointed. When entering the room, he had been fully aware of the identity of his host's distinguished visitor, and he had made his request, not with the idea of having it granted, but with the expectation that when he heard it, Portiforo's minister of war would be filled with consternation. In that case Gale would have had cause to believe that there was something in the tip which his paper had instructed him to investigate. But now, General Replife's willingness to let him go through the prison caused him to doubt that Felix was confined there.

"Present this order to the commandant of El Torro, and he will show you all that you wish to see," said the minister of war graciously, handing him the paper which he had just made out. "I trust you will find there, señor, some interesting material for the magazine article you wish to write."

CHAPTER XIV.
A MYSTERIOUS SUMMONS.

The end of the Camera Chap's first week in Baracoa found him not much nearer to the fulfillment of his mission than on the day of his arrival. He had made several trips on the crooked little railway which connected the capital with Porto Cabero, and as unobtrusively as possible had hung around the cafés and public places of the seaport. As the soldiers from the fortress, when off duty, patronized these places, he was in hopes that by mingling with them, and keeping his eyes and ears wide open, he might pick up something which would aid him in the performance of his task.

In addition to this he had chartered a motor boat and made many excursions into the harbor, hovering around El Torro fortress, and making a careful, though futile, study of the exterior of that grim edifice. Although none of these efforts had as yet been productive of results, he was not discouraged. With characteristic patience and optimism he felt confident that sooner or later he would hit upon a solution of the big problem which confronted him.

During this time he had held several consultations with his fair confederate, Virginia Throgmorton. The latter, who was fond of horseback riding, was in the habit of taking long rides daily out into the country. At her suggestion, the Camera Chap hired a mount, and went for frequent canters in the same direction. Thus they were able to meet and compare notes, safe from prying eyes and ears—or, at least, so they believed. But one afternoon, when Hawley galloped off into the outskirts of San Cristobal, to keep one of these trysts, Virginia met him with a troubled expression on her usually serene countenance.

"This is the last time that we must meet here—or anywhere else, for that matter!" she declared firmly. "I'm afraid we've been inexcusably careless."

"Careless?" the Camera Chap repeated wonderingly. "My dear Miss Throgmorton, what's the matter?"

The girl turned in her saddle, and shot nervous glances about her in all directions. "We ought to have foreseen the folly of this," she said severely. "We might have known that we couldn't meet like this without being found out."

"You don't mean to say that such a thing has happened?" exclaimed the Camera Chap.

Virginia nodded gloomily. "My father was asking me about you this morning," she announced. "He wanted to know how many times I had met you. He also evinced painful curiosity as to where I go, and whom I meet, when I take my daily canter. I could tell from his mode of questioning that he knows about these meetings."

"Who could have told him?" said the Camera Chap. "I have always been careful when coming out here to make sure that I was not shadowed."

"So have I," returned the girl, with a rueful smile. "Nevertheless, we have evidently been spied upon. I have a shrewd suspicion that it was Mr. Gale who told my father. He and dad were talking very confidentially together as I came into the room this morning, and I'm almost positive that I heard your name mentioned."

Hawley frowned. "I guess that is very probable," he said. "I've run into Gale quite often during the past few days, and I've had reason to believe that the encounters weren't accidental—that he's been paying me the compliment of watching me very closely. I hope he doesn't suspect the reasons for our meeting, Miss Throgmorton. He's the last man on earth that I would want to have know what I am doing here."

Virginia sighed. "My great fear is that Portiforo, too, has learned about these meetings of ours," she said anxiously. "If so, I am afraid that he'll put two and two together. They know that I visit Señora Felix, and they might easily assume from the fact that you and I meet so often that your presence in Baracoa is in relation to her cause. That, of course, would be fatal to your chances of success—and," she added, with a shudder, "perhaps fatal to President Felix, too. We ought to have thought of that before; but at least we must take the precaution of avoiding each other from now on. You must hold no communication with me whatever—not even through a third person. We cannot be too careful."

The Camera Chap was forced to admit the wisdom of this decision. From that day he seemed suddenly to have lost all interest in horseback riding, for he took no more canters into the outskirts of San Cristobal. And when, on one or two occasions, he encountered Miss Throgmorton, riding or walking on the streets of the capital, he merely saluted her formally, and passed her by without a word.

One evening, about a week later, as he was entering his hotel, a man stepped up close to him and covertly slipped a small envelope into his hand. "Don't open this, señor, until you are alone in your room," he cautioned in a hurried whisper.

The contents of the envelope puzzled the Camera Chap exceedingly. In the seclusion of his room he read and reread the mysterious message in English, and evidently in a man's handwriting:

"It is of urgent importance that you call upon Doctor Gaspard Bonsal, at nine o'clock, this evening. The address is Avenida Juarez, opposite the cathedral. Please come alone, and make sure that you are not followed before entering the house."

Hawley's first impulse was to go downstairs and ask the hotel clerk whether he knew of any such person as Doctor Gaspard Bonsal, and, if so, what he knew about him. But, on second thought, he decided that in the event of the mysterious message being genuine, and not the hoax he was inclined to suspect that it might be, such a step might prove unwise. The clerk was a talkative chap, and might repeat to others any questions that were put to him.

So Hawley decided to take a chance and call upon the mysterious Doctor Gaspard Bonsal without taking the precaution of making any inquiries about him. There was one fact which he considered slightly reassuring. Although there was nothing about the note to indicate whether the person referred to was a physician, a horse doctor, or a doctor of philosophy, Hawley recognized the address as being in the most exclusive residence section of the capital. He had walked several times along the Avenida Juarez, and had noted the pretentious residences which lined that well-lighted thoroughfare, particularly in the vicinity of the cathedral; so he felt satisfied, at least, that this was no ruse to lure him into some dark alleyway in the slums of San Cristobal.

The address was only a short distance from the hotel, and Hawley proceeded there on foot, carefully observing the warning which the message had contained to make sure that he was not followed. He had no difficulty in picking out Doctor Gaspard Bonsal's house, for there was a brass plate on the door bearing that name. This discovery added greatly to his confidence; nevertheless, as he climbed the low stoop and pressed the bell button, he took the precaution of keeping one hand in his coat pocket, with a businesslike grip on the automatic pistol it contained.

The door was opened by an aged negro servant, who, without asking any questions, ushered him into a handsomely furnished reception room, and quietly disappeared.

A few minutes later, as Hawley was appreciatively studying one of the oil paintings which lined the walls, a gray-bearded, fine-looking old man entered the room.

"You are Mr. Hawley?" he inquired. He spoke excellent English, although his appearance was decidedly Latin.

"Yes; and I presume I have the honor of addressing Doctor Bonsal?" As Hawley spoke, his hand came out of his pocket; for the sight of this fine, courtly old man removed his last apprehension.

Doctor Bonsal bowed. "I must apologize most profoundly for having summoned you here in such a mysterious way," he said, with a smile, "but I assure you, sir, it was most necessary. The circumstances are such that we cannot be too careful. Had I sent my carriage for you, as I would have liked to do, it might have aroused suspicion."

"That's all right," Hawley assured him. "It was only a short walk."

"You are quite sure that you were not followed here?" There was great anxiety in the other's tone.

"Positive. At least, if there were any spies trailing me, I'm satisfied that I'm a good case for an oculist," said the Camera Chap, with a laugh. "I kept a sharp lookout for them."

"I trust you were not deceived," remarked Doctor Bonsal gravely. "If you will be good enough, Mr. Hawley, to accompany me into the next room, I think you will immediately realize the wisdom and necessity of these extreme precautions."

He drew aside some sliding doors, and the Camera Chap followed him into the room adjoining. A woman was seated there. She rose as they entered, and, as he gazed into her dark, sad eyes, Hawley gave a start of astonishment. Although he had suspected ever since entering the house that Señora Felix was connected in some way with this mysterious summons, he had not expected to find her there.

CHAPTER XV.
THE PLEA.

Although only a few days had elapsed since the Camera Chap had last seen Señora Felix, he was shocked at the change which had come over her in that time. There were dark circles under her eyes, and her face was drawn and haggard. She seemed to be on the verge of a nervous collapse.

"I suppose it is a surprise to you to find me here, Mr. Hawley?" she began, with a pathetic smile.

"Somewhat, I must confess, señora, in view of the warning you sent me not to attempt to communicate with you," he replied.

"I felt that I must see you, in spite of the great risk," she said. "I feared that there was slight chance of persuading you to grant the great favor I am compelled to ask of you, unless I made the appeal in person. I am confident that no matter what it will mean to you, you will not refuse to be moved by the pleadings of a most unhappy woman. So I induced our good friend, Doctor Bonsal, to arrange this meeting."

The venerable physician acknowledged this reference to himself by a bow. "It was the only safe way, sir," he explained simply to Hawley. "The señora's home is watched so closely that it would have been out of the question for her to receive you there. As I am in attendance, professionally, upon her father, and it is known that she calls here frequently to consult me about his condition, it looked to me like a feasible plan to have you meet here."

"An excellent idea," the Camera Chap returned. "You spoke of a favor you wished to ask of me, señora. Without waiting to hear what it is, I assure you that if it lies within my power to grant it——"

"It does," she interrupted eagerly. Then, with startling abruptness: "I want you to leave Baracoa immediately, Mr. Hawley. I want you to give up this mad attempt to help my unfortunate husband. No good can come of it— nothing but a great deal of harm. The steamship *Panama*, bound for New York, is due to arrive at Puerto Cabero to-morrow. If you are sincere in your desire to be of service to us, you will prove it by engaging passage on her."

The Camera Chap smiled regretfully. "I am afraid I cannot promise to do that, señora—not unless there is a very good reason. May I inquire why you have so suddenly lost faith in me? The other day, on the *Colombia*, you sent me a message that your only hope was in my ability to carry out the mission intrusted to me; and later you sent me another message that you had the greatest confidence in me. What can have happened to cause you to change your mind?"

The señora sighed. "I have not lost confidence in you," she said. "From what I have heard of your great skill and courage, I think it quite likely that you would succeed in doing what you have been sent to do."

The Camera Chap stared at her in astonishment. "Then why——" he began.

"Because whether you succeed or fail," she broke in passionately, "the result must be the same. When I urged you, the other day, to persevere in your desperate undertaking, I had not stopped to consider that. I believed, then, that your success would bring about my poor husband's freedom. But now"—she paused, and a look of great fear came into her dark eyes—"now I know that inevitably it would mean his death. Whatever the outcome of your adventure, its price would be my husband's life—and that is too great a price to pay, even for his vindication."

"But it won't be that way if I get the snapshot," Hawley protested confidently. "I can understand your fears, señora; but, believe me, they are groundless. If we can get photographic evidence that President Felix is locked up in El Torro they won't dare touch him. Portiforo is too smart a man to try anything of that sort. Once he knows that we've got the evidence, he'll realize that the game is up, and that he'd only be making matters worse for himself if he were to attempt to assassinate your husband. So you see," he concluded cheerfully, "if I can get the picture everything will be all right."

The señora shook her head. "You don't know Portiforo," she said bitterly. "He'd assassinate my husband first, and argue about the genuineness of the photograph afterward. If for no other reason, he'd do it out of revenge. No, Mr. Hawley, you cannot save my husband that way. The only way you can help us is by doing nothing."

"But maybe your fears are exaggerated," the Camera Chap suggested, as a new argument presented itself to his mind. "If Portiforo is capable of committing such a cold-blooded murder, why hasn't he done it before now? Surely it would have been much safer for him to have put President Felix to death in the first place, instead of throwing him into prison. Doesn't the fact that he didn't take that course indicate that he draws the line at assassination?"

"It wasn't mercy, sir, which made Portiforo spare his victim's life," said Doctor Bonsal quietly. "It was necessity. At least, so we have cause to believe."

"Necessity?" Hawley repeated curiously.

"Yes; our theory is that he was compelled to do so. General Replife, although one of Portiforo's intimates and fellow conspirators, was under great obligations to President Felix," the physician explained. "It is our belief that it was he who saved him from assassination. Replife had a little more conscience than the others, and although he was willing to take part in the dastardly plot, his past friendship for Felix caused him to insist that the victim's life be spared. He persuaded Portiforo that their ends could be served just as well by locking up the president in El Torro as by murdering him. And Portiforo, afraid to antagonize Replife, was forced to consent to this plan. That is our theory, and we feel sure that it is the correct one."

"Well, if it is," argued Hawley, "isn't that good reason to assume that President Felix's life isn't in danger? If Replife wouldn't stand for assassination before, the chances are that he won't stand for it now. So you see, señora, there is nothing to fear."

Señora Felix looked at him in astonishment. "Can it be possible that you have not heard the news?" she exclaimed. "General Replife was shot down by an assassin as he was leaving the war office this afternoon. There is now nobody to prevent Portiforo from doing as he pleases with my unfortunate husband."

CHAPTER XVI.
THE SEÑORA OR THE PRESIDENT.

"To-day's tragedy has made the situation a hundred times worse than it was before," moaned Señora Felix despairingly, looking appealingly at Hawley and the old physician. "Replife was a bad man, but, at least, there was a spark of humanity in him which made him unwilling to countenance the murder of his former benefactor. He was our only hope. Now that he is gone, it will take only the slightest provocation to make Portiforo do away with my poor Francisco." She paused, and a shudder shook her frail frame. "Who knows that he has not already been butchered! I cannot help fearing that the assassin's act was inspired by Portiforo, who realized the necessity of getting out of the way the only man who stood between him and his helpless victim."

She covered her face with her hands, and burst into a violent paroxysm of weeping. The Camera Chap and Doctor Bonsal looked at each other helplessly. The latter shook his head commiseratingly. Presently he walked over to the grief-stricken woman and placed his hand gently on her shoulder. "Courage, my dear señora," he murmured, his voice as tender as a woman's. "Be brave, I entreat you, my dear friend. After all, we have not yet heard from the hospital. Until we get word from Doctor Picard we will not give up hope."

He turned and explained to Hawley: "We have hope that Replife's injury may turn out to be not so serious as was at first reported. He has been taken to the Red Cross Hospital, and an operation, I understand, is to be performed. My good friend, Doctor Picard, the house surgeon, has promised to apprise me as soon as there is news."

Hawley nodded. "Let's hope that when it comes it will be good news!" he exclaimed briskly. "Señora, I know from my newspaper experience that such reports are usually exaggerated. There may still be lots of fight left in General Replife. And even if there isn't," he added confidently, "even if the worst comes to the worst, so far as he is concerned, you are wrong in saying that there will be nobody to prevent Portiforo from doing as he pleases with President Felix."

"What do you mean?" cried the woman and Doctor Bonsal, in an eager chorus.

"I am referring to a powerful old gentleman named Uncle Sam," Hawley said smilingly. "Portiforo no doubt is wise enough to realize that he would have the United States to reckon with if he tries any treachery of that sort."

The señora breathed a murmur of disappointment. "Your government can do nothing—absolutely nothing," she said hopelessly.

"I beg your pardon, señora, but you are mistaken about that," the Camera Chap protested. "Once the photographic evidence is placed in the hands of the President of the United States, nothing——"

The woman interrupted him with a cry. "I tell you that must not be," she exclaimed, almost fiercely. "Surely, Mr. Hawley, after what you have heard, you will not persist in going on with your impossible adventure? You must realize that our only hope of saving my husband's life, now, lies in our ability to prevent anything from being done which would provoke that tyrant to take desperate measures."

"Señora Felix is right, sir," Doctor Bonsal chimed in earnestly. "I sincerely trust that you will not refuse to be guided by her wishes in the matter. You must appreciate the logic of our contention. If Portiforo and his villainous associates have cause to suspect that their infamous secret is known, they will doubtless make short work of their victim. As the señora says, our only hope lies in our ability to continue to make them believe that nobody—not even she—is aware of the truth regarding our martyr president."

Hawley looked at him in surprise. "Do you mean to say that Portiforo doesn't know, now, that the señora suspects the truth?" he demanded incredulously.

"We have strong hopes that such is the case," the venerable physician answered. "Señora Felix has been very clever. I believe, sir, that there are few women who could have conducted themselves with such rare tact and courage as she has displayed." He bowed reverently to her. "When it becomes possible to let the truth be known, the story of what this brave little woman has done will thrill the whole world."

"For two years," he continued, his fine old face glowing with enthusiasm, "she has submitted patiently to the badgerings of Portiforo's spies, who have tried by every means their ingenuity could devise to ascertain whether she had any inkling of the monstrous conspiracy. For two years she has played her difficult part with consummate skill, listening with a silence that was truly sublime to the sneers and abuse that were heaped upon her husband, stifling the impulses of her tortured soul, which yearned to cry out to the whole world that Felix was a martyr, instead of a rascal. For two years she has hung her head in shame, pretending, for the edification of Portiforo's spies, that she believed herself to be the deserted wife of an absconder—that the letters she received from him after his disappearance were genuine."

"The letters?" the Camera Chap exclaimed wonderingly.

"I beg your pardon," said Doctor Bonsal, somewhat confused; "perhaps I should not have spoken of them." He turned inquiringly to the señora.

"It is all right," the latter reassured him. "Since Mr. Hawley has been told so much, he might as well know everything. I know that we can trust him absolutely. The letters which Doctor Bonsal refers to," she herself explained, addressing the Camera Chap, "are the ones which I have received from my husband since that fatal night. You remember, perhaps, my telling you, on board the *Colombia*, that I had been in receipt of letters from him?"

The Camera Chap nodded. "Forgeries, I suppose?" he suggested. "Of course, President Felix never wrote them?"

Her reply astonished him greatly. "I believe he did write them," she said. "They might be forgeries very skillfully done, but I think not. I am almost positive that they are in his own handwriting."

Hawley stared at her in bewilderment. "But I don't quite understand, señora. You can't mean that they've actually permitted him to communicate with you?"

"Not permitted—forced him to do so!" rejoined the woman, her dark eyes flashing. "If those notes are genuine, they must have been written under compulsion."

"Might I inquire what they said?" the Camera Chap said eagerly.

The señora sighed. "The first one said merely that he was alive and well, and that I must not worry. The others—there have been at least a dozen of them, so far—were to the same effect, but some of them contained the additional assurance that he was very comfortable, and would send for me as soon as he considered it safe to do so."

The Camera Chap frowned. "How did these notes come to you, señora?"

"Through the mails."

"To your Washington address?"

"Yes. They were postmarked Paris, France. That was the whole object of the diabolical subterfuge—to make me believe that my husband was over there, at liberty, living on the proceeds of his crime."

Doctor Bonsal nodded gravely. "Of course, that was the motive of those notes," he said, "and the señora was clever enough to pretend to be completely deceived by them."

"Splendid!" the Camera Chap exclaimed. Then, as a thought came to him: "But there is one other question that I would like to ask. It concerns that chap, Cipriani, or Rodriguez, whichever his name is. He, of course, señora, knew the truth about your husband?"

The woman hesitated, and her questioner caught a swift glance which passed between her and Doctor Bonsal.

"Why do you ask that?" the physician demanded sharply. "What do you know about Rodriguez, sir?"

"Not very much," Hawley replied. "I saw, of course, what happened on the customhouse dock at Puerto Guerra, the other day, and later, when I arrived here, I learned from the clerk at the hotel the significance of what I had witnessed. I was informed that General Rodriguez had come to Baracoa to start a revolution."

Once more a swift glance passed between the old man and the señora. It was evident to the Camera Chap that the pair were exceedingly disconcerted by this turn in the conversation.

"Did—did this hotel clerk say anything which gave you cause to believe that Rodriguez knew President Felix's fate?" Doctor Bonsal stammered. Happening to glance at the señora, the Camera Chap observed that her lips were parted, and that her whole attitude indicated that she awaited his answer with great suspense.

"Oh, no," he assured them; "the clerk didn't know anything about that. You need have no apprehensions on that score. It was your own actions that day, señora, which caused me to believe that you were in sympathy with Cipriani's venture. I was standing close beside you at the ship's rail, and I couldn't help observing how greatly you were agitated by what occurred on shore. And then, there was the note you sent me later. From these things I got the impression that Cipriani was working for you—that his revolution was started with the object of getting President Felix out of El Torro."

Doctor Bonsal glanced nervously toward the window, the shades of which were drawn. "Not so loud, señor, I beg of you," he whispered. "If a mere hint of what you have just said should reach our enemies, we are done for. Tell me, have you expressed this theory of yours to anybody else?"

"Certainly not," the Camera Chap replied indignantly. "Pardon me, doctor, but your question is almost a reflection on my intelligence."

The señora uttered an audible sigh of relief. "We might have known that we could rely upon Mr. Hawley's discretion," she said. Then, addressing the Camera Chap: "No doubt you can surmise the reason for our great apprehension?"

Hawley smiled. "I think I can. The government believes that Rodriguez's revolution had nothing whatever to do with your cause. Isn't that the idea?"

The señora nodded. "We took every care to convey that impression," she said sadly. "As Doctor Bonsal has said, if Portiforo had any suspicion of our noble friend's real motive, the consequences would be fatal—as fatal as if you were to persist in your efforts to get into El Torro to photograph my husband."

"And that reminds me," said Doctor Bonsal, with a smile, "we have wandered away from the subject we were discussing. I trust, Mr. Hawley, that you will find it convenient to sail on the *Panama* to-morrow?"

A look of distress came to the Camera Chap's face. "I am sorry, but I'm afraid I cannot do that," he said regretfully. "I would like to oblige you, señora, but you must appreciate my position. Even if I were willing to quit, I would not be free to consult my own wishes in the matter, or even yours. I am here under orders—orders that must be carried out before I can think of leaving Baracoa."

Señora Felix's face became very stern. "Surely you and your president would not sacrifice a human life in order to gratify your selfish ambitions!" she exclaimed indignantly.

"Selfish ambitions!" Hawley protested. "Oh, come now, señora; that's scarcely a fair way of putting it."

"It is fair!" she rejoined passionately. "For you this adventure, if successful, simply means one more feather in your cap—one more triumph to be added to your roll of journalistic achievements. For your president it means a diplomatic victory scored—a chance to replace the present administration of Baracoa with one more favorable to the policies of the United States government. And for these reasons you are determined to go ahead now, regardless of the inevitable consequences which have been so clearly pointed out to you. What other term can I use to characterize your motive than selfish ambition?"

"But, my dear señora," argued the Camera Chap, with an uneasy feeling that there might be some justice in her viewpoint, "we can't let President Felix remain in El Torro. Wouldn't that be almost as bad as death itself? There may be a certain amount of risk to my plan, but I feel confident that if the matter could be put up to your husband he would be willing to run the chance of having me go ahead. You see, there isn't any other way of getting him out. If there were, I might be willing to give up my attempt. If a better plan——"

He was interrupted by an exclamation from the woman, and again he detected an interchange of swift glances between her and Doctor Bonsal.

"Do you mean that, sir?" the latter demanded eagerly. "Have we your word for it that if you knew that another plan was under way, you would abandon this undertaking and sail for New York on the *Panama* to-morrow?"

"If it was a better way than mine," Hawley stipulated guardedly. "I'd have to be convinced of that, of course."

The physician flashed a glance of interrogation at the señora, who answered him with a nod. "We have put ourselves so much in your confidence already, Mr. Hawley," he said quietly, "that we might as well go a little further. I know that we can trust you." He glanced nervously toward the shaded window, and lowered his voice to a whisper. "We have important tidings," he announced. "General Rodriguez made his escape to-day from the arsenal, and is now at liberty. You realize what that means?"

The Camera Chap smiled faintly. "Another revolution, I suppose?"

"Yes," said the old man fervently. "And this time one that will not fail. So you see, sir, there is a much more practical plan than the one you are now abandoning."

CHAPTER XVII.
A SERIOUS CHARGE.

A knock on the door of the room interrupted the conversation at this point, and startled Doctor Bonsal and his guests. It was only the old black servant who had admitted Hawley to the house. He handed his employer an envelope. "Your pardon for interrupting, master," he whispered, "but it is from the hospital and you said it should be brought to you at once."

"Quite right, Pedro," the physician responded eagerly tearing open the envelope. As he read its contents he uttered a joyous exclamation.

"Here is good news," he said, turning to the señora. "This is from my good friend Doctor Picard. He tells me that an operation has just been performed on General Replife, and the bullet removed. It had lodged in the chest, narrowly missing the heart. Doctor Picard says that the minister of war's condition is still very grave, but there is no immediate cause for alarm. It will be several weeks before he will be out of danger, but he has a fighting chance of pulling through."

"Thank God," the woman murmured fervently. "There is hope now— unless that which we dread has already happened," she added, with a shudder.

"Of course it hasn't!" declared Doctor Bonsal reassuringly. "You can depend upon it that Portiforo wouldn't dare take extreme measures until he was quite sure that Replife wasn't going to get well and call him to account. He will await the result of the minister of war's injuries. And, in the meantime, our dearest hopes may be realized. Doctor Picard tells us that even though Replife's injuries prove fatal, he may linger for several weeks—and within that time much may happen," he added significantly.

He turned eagerly to the Camera Chap. "I trust, sir, that if anything was lacking before to convince you of the necessity of giving up your venture, this will remove your last doubt. We have, now, new reason to hope that the life of our beloved president will be spared for some days. Portiforo will not take any desperate step unless he is spurred on to do so by the fear that his secret has leaked out. We can truly say that our fate lies in your hands, and we throw ourselves upon your generosity."

"And upon your sense of honor as well," the señora supplemented quickly. "You gave us your promise, Mr. Hawley, that if we could assure you that we had a plan more promising than yours, you would leave Baracoa immediately."

"But I am not sure that your plan is more promising than mine," Hawley replied, with a smile. "Don't think that I'm trying to evade you, but I must remind you that your friend Rodriguez has tried his revolution once and failed. What guarantee have we that he will succeed this time? And even if he does make good with his revolution, how is he going to get President Felix out of El Torro? I don't see why there wouldn't be just the same objection to his plan as to mine. The revolutionists may capture the fortress, but——" He paused significantly.

The señora was about to make a reply when there came a startling interruption. Pedro, the aged servitor, who had departed from the room after delivering Doctor Picard's note, now came rushing in, without going through the formality of knocking. He was in a state of great excitement. His eyes were rolling, and his face was almost white.

"Master," he gasped, "the house is surrounded by soldiers. There are two of them knocking at the front door now."

A faint cry of alarm escaped from the señora. She seemed to be on the verge of collapse. Doctor Bonsal's face had turned very pale, and the Camera Chap saw that he was shaking as though suddenly seized with a chill. His lips moved as though he were about to speak, but no words came from them.

Hawley, the only cool member of the group, was the first to break the silence. "Pardon me for suggesting it, doctor," he said, as a sound of a violent pounding came to his ears, "but wouldn't it be a good idea to find out what those fellows want? From the way they are going at it, if you don't answer them pretty soon, they'll have the door in splinters."

The physician made a heroic attempt to pull himself together. "I think I know what they want, without asking them," he said, with a grim smile. "But you are right; nothing is to be gained by keeping them waiting. I will go and attend to them."

He made a step toward the door, but the señora intercepted him. "Not you!" she protested frantically. "You must not go to them. It is for you that they have come. You must find some way of escaping from the house."

The old man shrugged his shoulders. "I'm afraid that won't be possible, my dear friend," he replied, now quite calm. "Did you not say, Pedro, that the house was surrounded by soldiers?"

"Yes, master," the panic-stricken servant replied. "The garden is full of them. There are more than twenty of them, and they have every means of escape covered."

Doctor Bonsal turned with a sad smile to Señora Felix: "You see! To attempt flight would be useless. Besides, even if it were possible for me to get away, it would be most unwise. It is necessary that I go to those men at the door before they come in here. It is our only chance of preventing them from discovering the presence here of you and Mr. Hawley—and that, of course, must be prevented."

"But I cannot let you go," the señora cried, still clinging to him. "It means your doom. That tyrant will show you no mercy. You——"

"Hush, my child," he said gently. "After all, I am an old man, and my days upon this earth are numbered. It does not matter much what becomes of me—we must think only of the cause that is so dear to us. If only we can get those men to depart without learning that you are here, I shall be satisfied."

He gently disengaged himself from her grasp, and turned to the Camera Chap. "Whatever happens, Mr. Hawley, I am going to ask you to remain in this room with Señora Felix, and not attempt to leave the house until you have made sure that the soldiers have gone. I would try to conceal you both, but there is no time for that. Besides, it would be useless; if they insist upon searching the house they would find you anyway, and——"

A crash and a shout of triumph interrupted him. "They've broken down the door. I must go at once," he whispered, and hurried out into the hall.

"What do you wish, gentlemen? What is the meaning of this violence?" the Camera Chap heard him demand, with great dignity.

"You are Doctor Gaspard Bonsal?"

"At your service, señor."

"We have an order for your arrest," came the startling announcement. "I regret to say, señor, that you must go with us at once."

The Camera Chap made an impulsive move toward the door, but Señora Felix stopped him with an imploring gesture. "You can do nothing," she whispered, the tears streaming down her face. "I beg of you not to make matters worse by interfering."

"But what does it mean?" Hawley demanded. "Why are they arresting that——"

"Listen!" the woman interrupted tensely.

"I am at your service, gentlemen," they heard the venerable physician say again. "But might I inquire the nature of the charge against me?"

"You are accused of aiding and abetting General Rodriguez to escape from the arsenal prison," came the grim reply. "If you are innocent, doctor, you have no cause to fear. You will have a fair trial."

"Very good, señor," exclaimed the aged man, his voice trembling. "I am ready to go with you."

The Camera Chap, an expression of astonishment on his face, turned to the señora. "Is it true?" he whispered.

She nodded, and, sinking into a chair, covered her face with her hands. Then, suddenly, she jumped to her feet, and stood quivering like a hunted animal as another voice reached them: "How about searching the premises before we go, captain?"

The Camera Chap glanced almost instinctively toward the heavy portières which draped the window. They did not offer a very promising chance of concealment for himself and the señora, but they appeared to be the best that the room offered. Fortunately, however, it did not come to that. He and the woman exchanged a glance of congratulation as they heard the man addressed as captain reply carelessly: "No; we need not bother to search the house. We had no orders to do so. All we want is our prisoner."

"I am ready to accompany you, gentlemen," said Doctor Bonsal.

CHAPTER XVIII.
A NEW MENACE.

Mindful of the warning which Doctor Bonsal had given him, Hawley made sure that none of the soldiers had remained behind to watch the house before he ventured to leave the ill-starred physician's residence. When he was satisfied that the coast was clear, he and Señora Felix went through the garden at the rear of the house, and out of a small gate, thus making their departure as unobtrusively as possible.

As soon as they were outside, Hawley and the señora parted company, the woman entering an automobile with a closed top which had been standing in readiness for her on a quiet road a short distance from the garden gate.

"Remember your promise! I shall expect to hear to-morrow that you have sailed on the *Panama*," were her parting words to him, and before he could make any reply she was gone.

Hawley felt that this was taking an unfair advantage of him, inasmuch as the promise which he had given had been a tentative one. He was not sure, though, that he was not going to return to New York the following day as she desired; for the arguments which he had heard, and the stirring events of that evening, had made such an impression on him that he was seriously thinking of giving up the undertaking.

The thought of returning to the White House with a report of failure was not a pleasant one, but he wished to do what was right in the matter. The bitter remark of Señora Felix that selfish ambition was the sole motive of his mission to Baracoa had got under his skin. Being an exceedingly fair-minded man, he could not help asking himself whether there was not some justice in her accusation.

The President of the United States had not taken him into his confidence as to what he purposed to do in the event of the Camera Chap's being successful in getting the photographic evidence of Portiforo's rascality. He had instructed Hawley merely to get the picture and bring it to the White House, giving no hint of what measures he intended to employ to prevent Portiforo from wreaking summary vengeance on his victim. Hawley knew that the present incumbent of the White House was a man of but scant sentiment, and he could not help wondering whether the great man, satisfying his conscience with the argument that individuals could not be considered when public policy was concerned, was not ruthlessly willing to sacrifice poor President Felix in order to bring about the exposure of Portiforo and a welcome change in the administration of Baracoa.

But, on the other hand, the Camera Chap was reluctant to believe that this could be his distinguished employer's attitude. However lacking the President of the United States might be in sentiment, he had the reputation of being an eminently just man. Besides, was not Señora Felix the intimate friend of the wife of a member of his cabinet? Which made it very unlikely that the president would have taken this step unless he had up his sleeve some plan for protecting President Felix from the murderous impulses of the conspirators.

These conflicting thoughts left the Camera Chap in a very unsettled frame of mind. He conscientiously sought to put aside his own wishes in the matter. As the señora had bitterly stated, it would be a great feather in his cap to get that picture—the most notable achievement of his whole career; but he was prepared to give it up, provided he was satisfied that such a course would be for the best, so far as Felix was concerned. For the martyr of El Torro was the only man to be considered. The Camera Chap was fully resolved as to that. If the photographic evidence of the monstrous conspiracy could not be obtained without fatal results to the victim, it would be better, he decided, to leave things as they were.

Deep in thought as he wrestled with this problem, Hawley was walking along the Avenida Juarez on his way back to the hotel, when he encountered two men coming arm in arm up the street toward him. One of this pair, who wore the uniform of an army officer, staggered as he walked as though under the influence of liquor. The other, a good-looking, dapper young American, was in civilian clothes, and displayed no outward evidence of being in the same condition as his companion.

The sight of these two together was a startling surprise to the Camera Chap; for the dapper young American was Gale, of the *News*, and the man who staggered was Captain Ernesto Reyes, of the engineers' corps, in command of the prison guard of El Torro.

Hawley had not as yet met Reyes. Although, when Virginia Throgmorton had first mentioned the army captain, he had registered a resolve to make the latter's acquaintance as soon as possible, he had since changed his mind as to the wisdom of such a step. It had suggested itself to his imagination that situations might subsequently arise wherein it would be an advantage not to be recognized by the custodian of El Torro prison; so, instead of seeking his acquaintance, Hawley had cautiously avoided him. But he knew Reyes by sight, and was quite sure, now, of the identity of Gale's companion.

Until this moment he had been unaware that Captain Reyes and the *News* man were acquainted. The discovery that they not only knew each other, but, apparently, were boon companions, came as a shock to him. He wondered uneasily whether it was a mere coincidence, or whether Gale had reasons of his own for getting into the good graces of the man who had charge of President Felix.

He was not left long in doubt on this point. Before he had a chance to dodge, Gale recognized him, and, tugging at the arm of his staggering companion, came quickly toward him.

"Well, if this isn't an odd thing, I'd like to know what is," he began exuberantly. "I mean our meeting you right here and now, Hawley, old scout. Strangest thing that's happened to me in a dog's age."

"I don't see anything so very remarkable about it," replied Hawley, noting that although Gale was steady on his feet, there was a thickness in his voice that was not normal. "San Cristobal is not a very large city, and the Avenida Juarez is one of its principal thoroughfares; so what is so strange about our meeting here?"

"Because we were just this minute talking about you, old pal," Gale explained, "and my old college chum, here, was saying how much he would like to meet you. Isn't that right, Ernesto?"

Captain Reyes blinked his eyes rapidly and murmured something which was so unintelligible that the Camera Chap couldn't even tell whether it was English or Spanish.

"You were talking about me?" exclaimed Hawley, his eyes fixed searchingly on the *News* man's flushed face. "That's very flattering. May I inquire in what way I figured in your conversation?"

Gale chuckled. "I was explaining to my friend here what you are doing in Baracoa," he said. "And why you spend so much of your time hanging around Puerto Cabero."

Splendid as was his usual self-possession, Hawley was unable to refrain from giving a start of surprise at this announcement. But he was quickly on his guard. "That was very kind of you," he said pleasantly. "What did you tell him?"

Gale grinned. "I told him about the work you hope to do with your little camera."

The Camera Chap raised his eyebrows interrogatively. "I'm afraid I don't quite understand," he said quietly.

"Oh, yes, you do," the *News* man rejoined, with an ironical laugh. "See here, Hawley, what's the sense of our playing hide and seek with each other any longer? Wouldn't it be a much more sensible idea for us to get together on this assignment? I need you and you need me, so what's the matter with forming a partnership?"

"A partnership to do what?"

Gale's reply made him wince. "To find old boy Felix, of course," the *News* man exclaimed boisterously.

"To find Felix!" the Camera Chap repeated, with well-simulated bewilderment.

Gale laughed raucously. "Still keeping up the bluff, eh? Don't you suppose that I know what you're here for? I must admit that you had me guessing at first, but as soon as I got that query from my office, I was wise right away. I knew then that we were both following up the same tip." He chuckled. "Thought you were going to have it exclusive, eh? Well, as I've often told you before, the *Sentinel* will have to get up mighty early in the morning to get ahead of the good old *News*."

"I'm afraid you're telling me more than you ought to," said the Camera Chap, making a valiant attempt to conceal his uneasiness. "You'll be sorry to-morrow for slipping me these hints about this mysterious tip of yours."

The other grinned. "You think I'm feeling so good that I don't realize what I'm doing, eh? Well, you're mistaken about that. I wouldn't be mentioning anything about Felix, now, if I wasn't quite sure that I'm not slipping you anything that you don't know." He put his hand in his coat pocket. "Just to prove to you how sure I am that you and I are shinning up the same tree, I'll show you the telegram I got from the office."

"Not now," the Camera Chap protested hastily, with an involuntary glance toward the swaying figure of Captain Reyes.

But the *News* man went on fumbling in his pocket. "Can't seem to find it," he muttered thickly. "Wonder what the deuce I've done with it." Then his face lighted up. "By Jove! I remember now. Can't show you the query the office sent me about Felix being locked up in El Torro, Hawley, old scout, because I haven't got it. I left it with old boy Portiforo."

The Camera Chap stared at him incredulously. "You did what?"

"I left it with his nibs, the President of Baracoa. Ernesto and I have been dining with him at the palace this evening. That's why we're feeling so good now. His bubble water was the best I've ever sampled. Some class to your little friend Gale—dining with presidents and cabinet ministers."

"Do you realize what you're saying?" Hawley demanded sharply. "You can't really mean that you showed Portiforo the tip you got from your office. You're too level-headed, I'm sure, to do a fool thing like that. It must be the wine that makes you tell me such nonsense. Come, pull yourself together, Gale, and talk sense."

"I am talking sense," Gale replied, with a show of indignation. "Sure I showed Portiforo the telegram. What was the harm in that? He knew all about the tip already."

"He knew about it?" Hawley exclaimed, with an anxious frown.

"Sure! That's why he invited me to come and eat with him. He wanted to pump me as to how much I knew about this Felix business. You can't keep anything from that wise old guy. He's the slickest article I've ever been up against."

———

CHAPTER XIX.
A FORCED PLAY.

The next morning, Hawley received a note at his hotel. It was from Virginia Throgmorton, and it said:

"I must see you at once. Something very alarming has happened. I am going out riding this afternoon, as usual. Will you meet me at the same place? If you can't be there tell bearer."

Hawley sent word by the bearer, one of the men-servants of Minister Throgmorton's household, that he would surely be there. The steamship *Panama* was due to arrive and leave that afternoon, and if he kept this appointment he would be unable to sail on her; but he had already fully decided that he was not going back to the United States just yet. He hated to disappoint Señora Felix, but the latest developments had removed from his mind all doubts as to what course he should follow.

Virginia Throgmorton's pretty face wore a very grave and perturbed expression when Hawley galloped up to the old trysting place on the steed he had hired for the occasion. "I don't think I was followed," she began, "but if I was it can't be helped. I have some news so important and serious that I had to run the risk of meeting you once more."

"Is it about our friend Gale?" the Camera Chap inquired, having a shrewd suspicion of the cause of the girl's anxiety.

"Yes; how did you guess—or do you know about that dinner last night?"

"I know a little about it, I think," Hawley answered. "I met Gale last evening on Avenida Juarez, as he was returning from the palace, and he told me that he had been President Portiforo's guest at dinner."

A shade flitted across the girl's face. "Did he tell you what took place at that dinner?"

The Camera Chap nodded grimly.

"What is to be done?" exclaimed Virginia, in a tone of deep concern. "Poor Señora Felix! I fear that all her brave efforts to save her husband have been in vain. Now that Portiforo knows that the press of the United States is aware of his secret, he will take no chances. In order to avert discovery he will resort to desperate measures."

"The situation is pretty bad," Hawley admitted. "Still, it might be worse, I think. I've been doing a lot of thinking since I met Gale last night, and I believe I've hit upon a way of lulling Portiforo into a sense of false security."

"What is it?" the girl demanded eagerly.

"I understand, from what Gale told me last evening," the Camera Chap explained, "that Portiforo invited him to dinner for the double purpose of finding out how much he knew, and denying vehemently that there was any truth in the rumor. Now, my idea is that if Gale can be made to believe that Portiforo spoke the truth—that there is absolutely nothing in the rumor of President Felix's confinement in El Torro, he will wire his paper to that effect, the *News* will publish the story, knocking the supposed lie on the head; the story will be cabled back to San Cristobal, and Portiforo will be satisfied that he has nothing to fear from the press of the United States."

"But how are we going to make Mr. Gale believe Portiforo's denial?" Virginia queried. "He doesn't believe it now. He was arguing with father about it at the breakfast table this morning. He said that Portiforo was very crafty—that he couldn't fool him, but that he intended to keep right on until he got the proof."

"And what did Mr. Throgmorton say to that?" Hawley inquired, greatly interested.

"Dad got angry and said that he had given Mr. Gale credit for having more sense. He asserted that Portiforo was a most estimable gentleman, and the best president that had ever ruled over Baracoa, and that this preposterous rumor about Felix was a base slander concocted by the enemies of the present administration. Dad asked Mr. Gale about his visit to El Torro fortress. It seems that Mr. Gale went all through the prison the other day, on a pass from the minister of war. Dad wanted to know how he had been treated there. Mr. Gale said that he had been received very cordially, that Captain Reyes had taken him all over the prison, and that he had discovered nothing to confirm his suspicions."

"Then he didn't see the cell with the covered door?" Hawley remarked.

"Evidently not; at least, he didn't mention it. Still, he is far from satisfied. He argued with father that the prison officials knew he was coming, and could easily have removed President Felix before he got there. So you see, Mr. Hawley," Virginia pointed out, "we would have a hard time trying to make him believe that there is nothing in the story."

The Camera Chap smiled. "I think I have found a way of convincing him," he said quietly. "In order to carry out my plan, Miss Throgmorton, I shall need your assistance."

He proceeded to outline his plan, and Virginia's face lighted up as she listened. "Excellent!" she exclaimed. "You can certainly count on me to do my part."

"And Señora Felix? Do you think you will be able to persuade her to let us have those letters?"

"I feel sure that she will consent," the girl replied. "She doesn't know yet of Mr. Gale's interview with Portiforo. When she hears of it, she will be willing to do anything in her power to avert this new menace. And she is bound to be impressed with your ingenious plan. It was really very clever of you to think of it, Mr. Hawley, and I want to thank you for making my heart much lighter than it was when I came out here. I felt, then, that all was lost."

Then, suddenly, her face clouded. "But, after all," she said sadly, "even though we succeed in reassuring Portiforo, that isn't getting poor President Felix out of prison." She looked at the Camera Chap wistfully. "Don't you think that you'll soon be able to find a way of getting that picture, Mr. Hawley?"

The Camera Chap smiled. "I am going to whisper a little secret," he said; "I believe I have found a way already. I was out in the harbor in the motor boat this morning, taking another peep at El Torro, and, suddenly, an inspiration came to me as to how the thing might be done. It is a good plan, and I feel confident that it would succeed; but in order to carry it out, I shall have to find a partner—preferably a woman."

"Preferably a woman!" Virginia caught him up eagerly. "Well, you won't have to look very far, Mr. Hawley. What's the matter with me?"

"You!" he exclaimed, as though the thought had never even remotely suggested itself to him. "Do you mean to say that you're ready to volunteer, Miss Throgmorton, without even knowing what the job calls for?"

"I don't care what it calls for," she responded, her eyes flashing. "If there's anything that I can do to help get poor President Felix free, I'm eager to do it. Won't you let me help you, Mr. Hawley?"

"I'll consider your application," he replied gravely. "That's the best I can promise now. But, first, we must attend to the business of getting rid of Gale. We can't do anything until we've made him believe that President Felix isn't in El Torro."

CHAPTER XX.
WHAT GALE OVERHEARD.

The morning after his dinner with President Portiforo found Gale in a very unsettled frame of mind. Save for a severe headache, he had fully recovered from the effects of the elaborate banquet which the President of Baracoa had given in his honor, and he retained a clear recollection of the conversation which had passed between him and his host. It was that conversation which now puzzled him.

Portiforo had discussed the startling rumor about Felix with, apparently, the utmost frankness. In fact, it was he himself who had broached the subject. Over the cigars and coffee he had surprised Gale by abruptly inquiring, with a quizzical smile, how that young man was getting along in his quest for the missing President Baracoa. Quickly recovering his self-possession, the reporter had attempted to deny that he was interested in any such quest. Then Portiforo had laughed, and told him that he might as well own up, as he was fully aware of the real cause of Gale's recent tour of inspection through El Torro fortress.

Later on, it occurred to the *News* man how the president had probably come into possession of this information. Stephens, his managing editor, had sent him the assignment by wire, and it was more than likely that, in this land, where spying was a fine art, the government maintained a close surveillance over all messages that were received and sent from the cable office. But this simple solution of the mystery did not suggest itself to him immediately, and his perplexity greatly amused his host.

"But do not fear, my dear Señor Gale, that I am in the least bit offended by your activities," the latter had reassured him. "I realize that you are merely doing your duty. I must express my amazement, though, at the credulity of your editor. Surely he must be a person of scant intelligence, to be deceived by such a preposterous story."

"He hasn't been deceived by it," Gale answered. "I have no doubt, Mr. President, that my editor suspects there is nothing in the rumor; but, just the same, we have to investigate it. You would be astonished to know how many ridiculous tips come into a big newspaper office—rumors that have not a vestige of fact behind them. But we investigate them all. We can't afford to take any chances. And that is why I have been instructed to look into this matter."

The reply had seemed to afford Portiforo much satisfaction. "It is well," he said. "Nothing could please us more than to have this absurd story thoroughly sifted to the very bottom by a fair-minded, highly intelligent journalist such as I know you to be—for I have heard of your worthiness and great skill from my good friend Señor Throgmorton. We court investigation. For, while I feel confident that no intelligent person will give serious consideration to this heinous fabrication of our enemies, at the same time it is exceedingly distressing to me and the patriotic and high-minded gentlemen connected with my administration to have such a rumor circulating in the United States. Therefore, I am hopeful, my dear Señor Gale, that before you leave Baracoa you will be in a position to dispose once and for all of these base calumnies. You have my assurance that nothing will be done to impede your efforts."

Was Portiforo on the level? That was the question which was perplexing Gale now. He was too astute and sophisticated a man to be entirely deceived by the Baracoan president's air of sincerity, for in his newspaper work he had been thrown with New York politicians who had been equally perfervid in declaring that they "courted investigation," and experience had taught him that this wasn't always to be taken as a sign of innocence. But the result of his investigations to date seemed to favor Portiforo. His tour of inspection through El Torro prison and his skillfully disguised questioning of the soldiers of the garrison and many residents of Puerto Cabero and San Cristobal had failed to unearth a single clew. His conversations with Captain Reyes, whose friendship he had managed to cultivate without difficulty, and who impressed him as being a frank and rather simple-minded chap, had proved equally unproductive.

Then, too, there was the attitude of Minister Throgmorton. As Virginia had told the Camera Chap, Gale had discussed the matter with the United States representative at the breakfast table that morning, and the latter had waxed highly indignant at such insinuations being made against his good friend Portiforo, who, he declared, was the very soul of honor.

Being a pretty good judge of men, the *News* reporter was not disposed to regard Minister Throgmorton as one of the most brilliant and keen-witted diplomats he had ever met; still, he considered it scarcely likely that Portiforo and his friends could have got away with such an audacious kidnaping plot without the American minister knowing something about it. Therefore, the latter's faith in the President of Baracoa went a long way toward influencing Gale's judgment.

That afternoon Gale received a second dispatch from Ben Stephens, his managing editor. It was terse and to the point. It read:

"Have you dropped dead? If not, why don't we hear from you regarding assignment?"

Gale was strongly inclined to wire back that he had made a thorough and laborious investigation of the tip and begged to report that somebody had handed the *News* a large and juicy citron. There was only one reason why he did not take this step. That reason was—the Camera Chap. He was afraid that Hawley might have been more successful than he in picking up a clew corroborative of President Felix's incarceration in El Torro.

Much as he disliked the Camera Chap, he had a wholesome respect for that wide-awake man's shrewdness and ability, and he didn't deem it safe to throw down the story until he was sure that his rival was ready to quit.

So he wired back to Stephens that he was still alive, and had been working hard on the assignment, but was not yet ready to report. That evening, however, something occurred which caused him to send another dispatch.

Shortly after dinner, Gale was writing some letters in the library of the legation when he heard voices in the garden below.

"You have no right to come here!" he heard a girl exclaim petulantly. "It was very indiscreet. I must ask you to go away immediately. If you were discovered here it might cause a lot of trouble. My father——"

"I am sorry, but I had to see you at once," a man's voice broke in. "I have made an important discovery—one that necessitated an immediate interview with you, Miss Throgmorton."

Gale pricked up his ears. Even before he had heard her name mentioned he had recognized the girl's voice. He believed, too, that he knew the identity of her companion. In order to make sure he switched off the lights of the room, and, going to the French window which commanded a view of the garden, stepped softly onto the balcony.

By the light of the moon he was able to discern the familiar outline of a tall, slim man who was standing with his profile turned toward the balcony.

"Be careful!" he heard the girl say fearfully. "Suppose there should be somebody listening. Every word you say can be heard in the house. Can you not wait until some other time to discuss this matter, Mr. Hawley? Or, if it must be now, let us go to the other end of the garden. We shall have more privacy there."

Gale waited until they had disappeared, then hurried down the short flight of steps which led from the balcony to the grounds, and went in swift but stealthy pursuit of them. He did not have much difficulty in locating the pair. They were seated on a rustic bench beneath a bamboo tree, and the Camera Chap was talking excitedly in a voice raised above its normal pitch.

"Why did you do it?" Gale heard him ask. "That's what I can't understand. What could have been your object in trying to make a fool of me."

"But I haven't tried to make a fool of you, Mr. Hawley," Virginia protested meekly.

Hawley received this with an ironical laugh. Gale was astonished by his demeanor. On Park Row the Camera Chap enjoyed the enviable reputation of never having been known to lose his temper. It was said to be one of the reasons for his success. But now it was evident that he was far from being in an amiable mood.

"For three weeks I've been hanging around Puerto Cabero, tying knots in my brain, trying to find a way of getting inside the fortress, in order to corroborate that story you told me the first day I met you," Hawley said bitterly. "If you don't call that making a fool of me, Miss Throgmorton, I'd like to know why. Perhaps you'd still like me to believe that Felix is locked up in El Torro?"

"Well, isn't he!" Virginia inquired, a tinge of mockery in her voice.

"Isn't he!" echoed Hawley. "As though you didn't know! I suppose your subtle friend, the señora, hasn't taken you into her confidence regarding the letters she has been receiving from her husband, eh?"

"The letters!" the girl repeated, her voice trembling. "Why, what do you mean?"

Hawley laughed triumphantly. "I guess you know what I mean, Miss Throgmorton. I am referring to the letters which our missing friend, Felix, has been writing his wife from Paris."

Gale heard Virginia utter a little cry of dismay. "Who told you?" she began. Then, as though suddenly on her guard: "If there are any such letters, why should you expect me to know about them?"

The Camera Chap's answer caused the eavesdropper to give a start of astonishment. "Because," he charged sternly, "you happen to have those letters in your possession now. It is no use attempting to deny it, Miss Throgmorton. If you knew the source of my information you would realize that. Your friend Señora Felix handed you the package of correspondence to-day. She asked you to take care of them for her; possibly because she was afraid to keep them herself, for fear that Portiforo's spies might ransack her house and find them. At the present moment they are concealed in a drawer of your desk, tied up with pink ribbon. You see that I know what I'm talking about."

"This is most extraordinary!" Virginia exclaimed. "How could you possibly know—unless—do you combine burglary with your newspaper work?"

"Not guilty," Hawley replied. "If you suspect that I have been near your desk, you are mistaken. Don't ask me how I got the information, because that's a secret I am not at liberty to disclose. We newspaper men have our own little methods of finding out things. I give you my word of honor, though, that I haven't seen the letters. If I had, perhaps I shouldn't be here now." He suddenly dropped his aggressive manner. "I haven't come to reproach you, my dear Miss Throgmorton, for the way you and your wily friend, the señora, have deluded me. I have come to talk business with you."

"Business!" Gale heard the girl exclaim, with an inflection of astonishment.

"Yes. I have come to return good for evil by offering you a chance to make a nice little sum of pin money. I might as well be frank with you: The scoop would be worth a lot to the paper I represent. The *Sentinel* would pay handsomely for the privilege of reproducing that correspondence. If you will give me an opportunity to photograph those letters, and will promise that no other newspaper man shall see them, I will——"

What the great newspaper was prepared to offer in return for such an accommodation Gale did not learn, for before the sentence was finished he was on his way back to the house. It had suddenly occurred to him that there was a delicate little job which required his immediate attention.

CHAPTER XXI.
HOW IT WORKED.

Half an hour later, Virginia Throgmorton entered the legation library and, stepping up to a dainty little mahogany desk in a corner of the room, opened one of the drawers and uttered an exclamation of dismay.

Gale, who was seated at a table in the center of the room, looked up from the letter he was writing, and regarded her solicitously. "Anything wrong?" he inquired.

"It was horribly careless of me to leave the key in the lock," the girl murmured, as though speaking more to herself than to the reporter. "Still, I cannot imagine who could have taken them. It is most mysterious."

"Lost anything?" Gale asked curiously.

Virginia hesitated. Then, with sudden decision: "Yes; some letters are missing from my desk—very important letters."

"Love letters?" Gale inquired, with a grin.

"Not exactly," the girl replied coldly. "How long have you been in this room, Mr. Gale?"

"Not very long. Not more than five minutes, I should say. Why do you ask?"

"I was wondering if you had noticed anybody tampering with my desk."

The reporter smiled deprecatingly. "My dear Virginia! If I had, don't you suppose I would have called them to account?" Suddenly a glint came to his eyes, as an idea occurred to him. "One minute, though! I think, perhaps, I can solve this mystery for you. Tell me, were these letters of such a character that they would be of value to a newspaper?"

Virginia sighed. "They would be of great value to a newspaper," she answered, "but——"

"Then I guess I've got the answer," Gale interrupted. "This morning, as I was coming downstairs, I encountered a man coming out of this room. He seemed to be in a great hurry, and it struck me, also, that he appeared very nervous. I would have stopped him and demanded what he was doing here, only I supposed at the time that he had been calling on your father. After he had gone, though, I discovered that your father wasn't in the house. I have no doubt, now, that it was the chap who stole the letters from your desk."

"And you haven't any idea who he was?" Virginia asked, an odd break in her voice.

"Yes, I have," Gale answered. "It was the Camera Chap—Hawley."

"Good heavens!" Virginia gasped. "Are you sure, Mr. Gale?"

"Absolutely so," he answered. "Even if I hadn't seen him," he added maliciously, "I might have guessed that the robbery was his work. I know his methods. That fellow Hawley is so unprincipled, Virginia, that he'd steal the crutch from a cripple."

Feeling very well satisfied with himself and his evening's work, Gale went out and repaired to a certain café which he knew was the haunt of a man whom he greatly desired to see.

"I believe you were telling me, the other day," he said, when he had found his man, "that you used to be employed by former President Felix?"

"I was his private secretary," the other answered.

"Then you ought to be pretty familiar with his handwriting?"

"I know it as well as I do my own."

"Fine!" exclaimed the reporter, suddenly producing a letter. "That being the case, old man, take a good look at this and let me know whether you recognize the fist?"

The man studied the script closely, and a look of astonishment came to his face. "It is Felix's handwriting!" he declared positively.

"Good!" exclaimed Gale exultantly. "Now, see here: I'm going to give you a chance to make some easy money. I've got several more of these letters here, and I want them translated. I understand enough Spanish to get an idea what they're about, but I want a good translation. There's ten dollars— American money—in it for you if you want to undertake the job."

President Felix's former secretary nodded eagerly, and, taking a fountain pen and a notebook, which Gale handed him, rapidly wrote out an English translation of the correspondence.

"Much obliged," said Gale. "You'll get the ten dollars in a couple of days— provided you keep quiet about it. I don't want anybody to know about these letters just yet."

The next morning the New York *Daily News* published on its front page a story which bore the following heading:

"WIFE HEARS FROM MISSING PRESIDENT.

"Francisco Felix, Fugitive President of Baracoa, Sends Wife Cheering Epistles From Gay Paree.—Weird Rumor Knocked On Head.—*Daily News* Staff Correspondent at San Cristobal Unearths Interesting Correspondence Which Proves Absurdity of Charge that Felix Was Victim of Portiforo Conspiracy."

This, of course, did not escape the eagle eye of the New York correspondent of the San Cristobal *Herald*, whose chief duty was to go through each issue of the New York newspapers and pick out all stories which were likely to be of interest to the citizens of Baracoa. Thus it came about that five hours after that issue of the *Daily News* appeared on the streets of New York, the first edition of the San Cristobal *Herald*, with the same story, under a New York date line, spread all over its front page, was selling like hot cakes in the streets of the capital of Baracoa.

At about the same time a lengthy dispatch in cipher from the Baracoan consulate at New York arrived at the executive palace. It ended as follows:

"Upon investigation, I have the honor to report that this morning's article in the *News*, one of the most influential newspapers in the United States, has made a great impression upon the American people. There is already heard both here and in Washington considerable criticism of the President of the United States for having permitted a member of his cabinet to show such conspicuous friendship for the wife of Felix. Now that the woman's guilty knowledge of her husband's whereabouts has been proved, it is felt by the better class of citizens here, that the United States has been placed in an embarrassing position by the fact that while she was residing at the home of the United States attorney general she was in constant receipt of letters from the fugitive.

"I have the honor to report, also, that I am reliably informed that in addition to publishing its sensational story, the *News* has cabled secret instructions to its staff correspondent in Paris to begin immediately a search for Felix. The editor believes that the clews furnished by the postmark of the letters ought to make it an easy matter to find him."

That President Portiforo was not exactly vexed by this information was evident when he appeared in public later that day. As he rode through the streets in an open carriage, the people were able to get a good view of his features, and it was noted that he wore a grin broader than any that had appeared on his moonlike countenance since the day of his inauguration.

"I saw him this afternoon—I was walking along the Avenida Bolivar when the presidential equipage rolled past—and his expression reminded me of the cat just after swallowing the canary," the Camera Chap remarked laughingly to Virginia Throgmorton, whom he met by appointment that afternoon at the usual trysting place. "It looks as if our little ruse had the desired effect."

"It was tremendously clever of you to think of it, Mr. Hawley," the girl said enthusiastically. "Your ingenuity in all probability has saved President Felix's life. It isn't likely that Portiforo will feel so much like resorting to desperate measures now."

"Let us hope not," Hawley responded quietly.

Something in his tone caused the girl to regard him with great concern. "Has anything happened to make you believe the contrary?" she asked quickly.

"I don't know," the Camera Chap answered, with a frown. "I heard a report at the Red Cross Hospital this afternoon which I don't like. They say there that General Replife, the minister of war, has suffered a relapse, and is not expected to live another twenty-four hours."

"And you think," said Virginia fearfully, "that if Replife dies Portiforo may decide that it would suit his purposes to get rid of poor President Felix despite the reassuring news from New York?"

Hawley shrugged his shoulders. "At all events, it will be as well for us not to take any chances," he said quietly. "You remember that plan for getting the picture that I was telling you about yesterday, Miss Throgmorton? Well, the time has come to carry it out. Under the circumstances we cannot afford to delay any longer." He lowered his voice. "I have decided to make the attempt to-night."

CHAPTER XXII.
HIS PLAN.

"I have decided to make the attempt to-night," the Camera Chap repeated, looking earnestly at the daughter of the American minister to Baracoa. "The more I think about my scheme, the more convinced I am of its practicability."

"And you will take me as your assistant?" Virginia inquired eagerly.

Hawley hesitated. "Well, I don't know about that. There would be some danger, and I don't feel like letting you run any risk. Of course," he added wistfully, "the danger wouldn't be so very great. No matter how the venture should turn out, I don't think they would dare to harm you. The fact that you are a woman, and the daughter of the United States minister, ought to be——"

"Never mind the danger," the plucky girl broke in impatiently. "As I told you yesterday, nothing could please me more than to have a chance to help my unhappy friends, Señora Felix and her husband. I'd gladly make any sacrifice for them. I shall hold you to your promise, Mr. Hawley. As a man of your word, you've got to take me with you."

Hawley laughed. "I don't think I quite promised; I merely said that I would consider your application, Miss Throgmorton. However, I guess I've got to take advantage of your kind offer. I've got to have an assistant, and, while a man might do, a woman partner would add greatly to the chances of success—especially when she is beautiful enough to——"

Virginia stopped him with a gesture of disapproval. "This is no time for frivolous compliments, Mr. Hawley," she said severely, a faint tinge of pink making itself evident beneath her fair skin. "There is too much at stake for that."

"I assure you that I had no intention of being frivolous, Miss Throgmorton—or of paying you compliments, either," the Camera Chap explained hastily. "It is a fact that I am counting a great deal on your good looks as an asset in this venture."

Virginia appeared somewhat mollified by this explanation. "Tell me your plan, Mr. Hawley," she requested. "Now that it is settled that I am to have a part in it, isn't it only fair that you should take me into your confidence as to what you're going to do?"

"It surely is," Hawley agreed. "I was going to tell you all about it, anyway, only I deemed it advisable to keep the details to myself until I was ready to carry it out.

"It is very simple," he continued, his face lighting up. "In fact, I can't understand why the idea didn't hit me long ago. The inspiration came to me like a flash, the other day, as I was cruising in the motor boat in the vicinity of El Torro, watching the sentry pacing up and down outside the window of Felix's cell, and tying bowknots in my brain trying to conceive of a way of getting rid of him. That's been the big problem all along, of course—how to get past the sentry. If I could devise a way of luring him from his post for a few minutes, it would be a simple matter to get my snapshot of Felix in his cell."

"And you have found a way of doing that?" the girl asked eagerly.

"I believe I have. All that we've got to do is to take a tip from the New York underworld."

Virginia looked at him in bewilderment, but when she heard the plan he unfolded, she uttered an exclamation of delight. "It does sound good!" she declared. "You are absolutely the most ingenious man I have ever met."

Hawley regarded her quizzically. "This is no time for frivolous compliments, Miss Throgmorton," he said, with mock indignation. "There is too much at stake for that."

The girl laughed at the way he had turned the tables on her. Then, suddenly, her smooth brow puckered into a puzzled frown. "But there is one thing about your plan which I don't quite understand," she told him. "How do you expect to make your escape from the fortress after you get the snapshot? You cannot, of course, use the same boat I'm going to use, and it seems to me that a second boat would be out of the question."

"Of course it would," her companion agreed. "There's only one way that I can see of solving that difficulty: Since I can't travel on the water, I shall have to travel in it."

Virginia looked at him in horrified amazement. "Surely you're not thinking of trying to swim back?" she gasped.

"I guess that's what I'll have to do," was the cheerful reply. "However, there won't be any trouble about that. I'm a pretty good swimmer."

Virginia shook her head. "You must give up that idea," she said firmly. "It would be madness. You couldn't live ten minutes in those waters, Mr. Hawley. Don't you know that Puerto Cabero harbor is full of sharks?"

In spite of himself, the Camera Chap grew serious at this announcement. The presence of sharks in the bay was a detail which had escaped his attention when he had formulated his plans. The prospect was decidedly disturbing. Then, suddenly, his face lighted up. "Oh, well," he said, with a characteristic shrug, "I've read somewhere that it's all a fake about sharks being man-eaters. Anyway, Miss Throgmorton, you've got an exaggerated idea of the situation. I'm not thinking of swimming the whole width of the bay. All I'll have to do is to strike out for the battleship."

"The battleship?" the girl echoed, her eyebrows arching.

Hawley laughed. "By Jove! If I haven't forgotten to mention the most important detail of all. Evidently you do not know that the United States battleship *Kearsarge* steamed into the harbor this afternoon, and is now anchored a quarter of a mile off El Torro. That's another reason why I feel confident that our little venture is going to be a success."

CHAPTER XXIII.
UNDER SEALED ORDERS.

Although the arrival of the *Kearsarge* was news to Virginia, the visit of the huge gray fighting machine was no surprise to Minister Throgmorton. For some reason he had failed to mention the matter to his daughter, but a few days previously he had been officially notified by the state department at Washington that the warship was due to arrive in Baracoan waters on a "friendly visit."

This information he had formally conveyed to President Portiforo. The latter was profuse in his expressions of appreciation of this courtesy. He bade the representative of the United States assure his government that a cordial welcome would be given to the *Kearsarge's* officers and crew.

"But what does it mean?" he demanded informally of his friend Throgmorton. "What purpose has Washington in view? United States warships have visited us before, of course, for the reason stated; but I cannot help entertaining a suspicion that your government has some special motive in sending a battleship here at this time."

To this the United States minister had shrugged his shoulders. "If there is any such motive, my government has not seen fit to take me into its confidence concerning it," he answered. "However, Mr. President, if the presence of the *Kearsarge* in Puerto Cabero harbor is objectionable to you, I am confident that I have only to notify the state department to that effect, and Captain Cortrell will receive orders to sail before the vessel weighs anchor."

Portiforo, who, with a few exceptions, entertained a cordial dislike for gringos in general, and the citizens of the United States in particular, felt a strong inclination to have this brought about, but he was diplomat enough not to follow his wishes in the matter. "I wouldn't think of being so discourteous to our sister republic," he said. "Besides, I have no objection to the *Kearsarge's* visit, provided she does nothing to disrupt the amity existing between our two nations. Have you any idea how long she is to stay here?"

Throgmorton shook his head. "My advices do not state that," he said. "If you wish, I can cable Washington that you would like to be enlightened on that point."

"Certainly not," the other rejoined hastily. "It is quite immaterial to me, my dear Throgmorton, how long she remains. Besides, no doubt her commander will be able to tell us what his orders are in that respect." An anxious expression came to his face. "What kind of a man is this Captain Cortrell?" he inquired. "Can you tell me anything about him?"

"He's one of the most competent officers in the United States navy," the minister informed him. "He was graduated from Annapolis at the head of his class, and——"

"But his personality?" Portiforo interrupted impatiently. "I don't care anything about his naval record. Does he impress you as being a conservative man, or—to use an expression, of your country—the kind that would take chances? If you will pardon me for saying so, I believe that some of your naval officers have in past instances proved themselves to be somewhat lacking in discretion and a proper regard for the niceties of international law."

"Captain Cortrell is not that kind," Minister Throgmorton replied, with a smile. "He has a reputation for being one of the most cautious and conservative commanders in our navy, and he knows more international law than half our statesmen. You need have no fear, Mr. President, that he will commit any indiscretion which would disrupt the pleasant relations existing between our respective governments."

Somewhat reassured, the President of Baracoa made preparations to receive the visiting warship with fitting honors, and the guns of El Torro fortress thundered a vociferous welcome as the big gray ironclad steamed up the bay.

The Camera Chap was cruising in the harbor in his motor boat when the *Kearsarge* arrived. With keen interest he watched the colossal fighting machine come to anchor. A thrill of joy and pride shot through him as his eyes feasted on her grim gray outline, and there came to his ears the strains of the ship's band crashing out "The Star-spangled Banner."

Remembering his conversation with the president, in which the latter had given him clearly to understand that, win or lose, he could expect no help from the United States government, he felt that he had no reason to believe that the arrival of the battleship had anything to do with himself and his mission; yet he could not help hoping that such was the case—that something had occurred to change the presidential mind as to the impossibility of governmental succor being extended to him. Not that he craved such protection for himself; he was quite willing to take his chances, and abide by the consequences of the adventure; but he was in hopes that the arrival of the *Kearsarge* at Puerto Cabero might have something to do with a plan to protect Felix from Portiforo's vengeance. This desire caused him to seek admission to the battleship almost as soon as she had dropped anchor.

As he climbed the starboard gangway, a natty young officer stared hard at him, and exclaimed:

"I beg your pardon, but isn't your name Hawley?"

"It is," the Camera Chap replied, with a smile. "And you are Ensign Ridder, unless I am very much mistaken."

"Lieutenant Ridder," the other corrected pleasantly, with some pride. "But I was an ensign the last time we met. That was three years ago, when I was attached to the Brooklyn Navy Yard." His face broke into a broad grin. "I shall never forget, old man, how you came to my rescue that night down in Chinatown, when that gang had me backed up against the wall, and was——" He stopped short, suddenly realizing that this was scarcely the time or place to indulge in personal reminiscences. "I beg your pardon," he said soberly. "Perhaps you wish to see somebody on board?"

"I'd like to have a talk with the captain, if he isn't too busy," the Camera Chap answered.

"He's pretty busy, but I think he'll see you," said Lieutenant Ridder, emphasizing the pronoun. "As a matter of fact," he added, "he's expecting you."

"Expecting me!" Hawley echoed, thrilling with joy as he realized the significance of this announcement.

"He's given orders that if a man named Hawley should happen to come aboard, he's to be taken to his cabin at once," the naval officer confided in a whisper.

"Great!" exclaimed the Camera Chap. "That's the best news I've heard in a long while."

Thanks to his acquaintance with Lieutenant Ridder, the visitor had no trouble in establishing his identity to the satisfaction of the battleship's commander.

"I am glad to meet you, Mr. Hawley," the latter said. Then, abruptly: "I believe you were to bring a photograph. Have you got it?"

"Not yet, captain," the Camera Chap replied, "but I expect to get it soon, and——"

The commander of the battleship cut him short with an impatient gesture. It may have been his imagination, but Hawley fancied that the expression on his weather-beaten face was one of keen disappointment. "My orders say nothing about expectations, sir," he said gruffly. "Whenever you get that snapshot, Mr. Hawley," he added, "I shall be glad to see you again."

The Camera Chap did not attempt to ask any questions. He could tell from the taciturn old sea dog's manner that they would not be answered. Besides, he had found out what he wished to know. From the reference the captain had made to his orders, he felt absolutely sure, now, that the arrival of the warship was more than a coincidence—that the huge mass of steel, manned by as sturdy a crew as ever trod a deck, and bristling with guns powerful enough to smash El Torro fortress to smithereens, and reduce Puerto Cabero to ruins, was there to help in some way to right a great wrong.

It was then that he had made up his mind to carry out that same night the daring plan which he had afterward described to Virginia Throgmorton. But he did not tell his fair ally of his visit to the battleship. There were reasons why he deemed it wise to keep that incident a secret even from her.

As his visitor walked out of his cabin, Captain Cortrell took from a drawer of his desk a bulky envelope, and regarded it with speculative interest.

This envelope was sealed, and Captain Cortrell himself had never seen its contents. His verbal instructions were to anchor in Puerto Cabero harbor, and to remain there until further orders. The sealed envelope was not to be opened unless he should receive a visit from a man who could identify himself as a New York newspaper man named Frank Hawley. In the event of such an identification being established, the commander was to demand of his visitor whether he had brought a certain photograph. If the reply was in the affirmative, and the photograph forthcoming, Captain Cortrell was then to open the sealed envelope immediately, and compare the photograph it contained with the snapshot which his visitor had brought. If he was satisfied that the original of both pictures was the same, he was to proceed to carry out forthwith the written instructions which accompanied the picture.

What these secret orders were, the commander of the battleship had not the remotest idea; nor was he aware whose photograph was inside the envelope. It was felt by his superiors that there was no need for him to know these things until the time to act arrived. He did know, however, that the contents of the envelope had been placed there by the President of the United States himself.

Captain Cortrell was not naturally a curious man. It was largely because the bump of inquisitiveness was missing from his cranium that he had been selected for this mysterious mission; but when he had told his visitor that he was glad to meet him, he had never in his life spoken more earnestly, for his fingers were just itching to open that envelope. He had been wondering greatly, too, what manner of chap this young man named Hawley must be, that the head of the nation was willing to go to so much trouble on his account. It was the first time in his experience that he had heard of a United States battleship being dispatched under sealed orders to foreign waters to aid a newspaper photographer in his work. He had looked forward with eagerness to the time when the president's photographic envoy should choose to put in an appearance. For his instructions did not permit him to seek the latter out. He must wait until he came aboard of his own initiative. Evidently it had been taken for granted at the White House that the Camera Chap would come to the battleship without an invitation being extended to him. The logical mind responsible for these arrangements had foreseen that in the event of his landing the photographic evidence of Portiforo's rascality, it would naturally occur to him to seek refuge immediately in the safest place for him within a thousand miles of San Cristobal—the deck of a ship of war flying the Stars and Stripes.

CHAPTER XXIV.
THE SNAPSHOT.

The night which Hawley and Virginia had selected for their assault upon El Torro proved an ideal one for their purpose; for the moon was obscured most of the time by a steady procession of dark clouds which made the waters of the harbor as black as ink, save for an occasional phosphorescent streak on the surface of the wavelets, the sight of which made the girl shudder.

"I'm afraid there are many sharks in the bay to-night," she whispered fearfully to the Camera Chap, as he cast loose the painter of the launch, and took the oars—they had decided to row at the start, instead of using the motor, for fear that the noise of the latter might attract attention on shore.

"I guess it's only your imagination which makes you think that, Miss Throgmorton," Hawley responded cheerfully. "Of course," he added solicitously, "if you're really alarmed, we'll turn back this minute; but there's no danger so far as the sharks are concerned. They won't come near the boat."

Virginia gave him an indignant glance. "Of course, I know that they won't come near the boat," she said. "Do you suppose that I am scared on my own account? It was to your danger that I was referring. I really don't think that I have any right to let you do this thing, Mr. Hawley. Much as I would like to see poor President Felix freed, and my dear friend the señora made happy, it scarcely seems fair to encourage you to run such a terrible risk. To think of you attempting to swim in that water makes my blood run cold."

"Then I beg you not to think of it," he said laughingly. "Turn your attention to the sky instead. Did you ever see such a black night? I haven't, since I've been in Baracoa. It certainly looks as if we've got our luck with us. I haven't much doubt, now, that I'll be able to get up to the fortress unobserved."

All the while he was talking, he was rowing, his strong arms pulling at the oars so vigorously that the motor boat moved through the water almost as easily as if it had been built to be propelled in that manner. But presently he stopped rowing, and shipped his oars. "Guess we can start the motor, now," he remarked; "we're far enough from the shore to escape attention. See those lights twinkling over yonder? That's the *Kearsarge*. And those two little lights to the east of her are on El Torro. Notice how near to the fortress she is anchored. You see, I shan't have much of a swim, after all."

Virginia smiled at him reproachfully. "Do you think I am as easily deceived as all that? Those lights may not look far apart, from here, but I happen to know that the distance between the battleship and the fortress is nearly half a mile. However, Mr. Hawley, I'm not going to try to persuade you to give up this mad undertaking, because I realize that I stand no chance of making you listen to reason." She sighed. "It does seem unfair, though, that you should be running all the risk, while I——"

"All the risk!" Hawley interrupted protestingly. "Well, I like that! I suppose you're not running any risk at all? Why, you plucky girl!" he exclaimed, deep admiration in his tone. "As a matter of fact, you're doing the lion's share of the work. If our efforts to-night result in setting President Felix free, he'll have you to thank for it more than anybody."

"Nonsense!" the girl protested, much pleased, nevertheless, by his praise. "You know very well that I shan't be in the slightest danger. Portiforo can't do anything to me, even when he finds out the trick I've played his soldiers. If you thought that he could, you would never have taken me as your assistant. Don't you suppose that I realize that?"

"But it's going to get you into trouble with your father," Hawley reminded her dryly. "I don't imagine that Minister Throgmorton is going to be exactly pleased when he hears of his daughter's escapade—especially when he finds out that her fellow conspirator is a *Sentinel* man."

"Yes; I suppose my father will be angry," Virginia agreed demurely. "However, that can't be helped. I never have been able to understand his great friendship for Portiforo," she went on, frowning. "It is a mystery to me why he is so persistently blind to the grossness of that tyrant. Possibly," she suggested archly, "it is because Portiforo flatters him. Father is very susceptible to flattery."

"Probably that is the reason," the Camera Chap acquiesced. "Think you'll be able to manage this boat all right after I leave you?" he inquired anxiously. "She runs very smoothly, and all you've got to do, you know, is to keep her headed straight for the fortress landing.

"That will be easy," she assured him. "Fortunately I've had some experience with motor boats."

"And you haven't forgotten your instructions? You know just what you are to do after you land? Remember, everything depends upon your ability to keep the attention of the sentry focused on you until after I've got my picture."

"Don't worry about that," said Virginia confidently. "He'll have to be an automaton if he's able to turn a deaf ear to my heart-rending screams of distress."

Hawley, busy with the motor, echoed her laugh. A little later the launch, running now under its own power, had drawn so near to the *Kearsarge* that they could hear her bells striking the hour. The Camera Chap abruptly changed their course. "We don't want to get any nearer to the warship," he explained to his companion. "They might take it into their heads, you know, to throw a searchlight on us, and just at present we're not at all eager to bask in the limelight."

Virginia gazed wistfully at the shadowy outline of the big vessel. "If only we could get them to help us," she murmured. "With a hundred sturdy bluejackets from that ship, we could take the fortress and bring back President Felix himself, instead of merely his photograph."

"A hundred!" exclaimed Hawley, with a laugh. "I venture to say that half a dozen would be enough. But I'm afraid that's out of the question. For the present I guess we'll have to be content with the picture."

"If we get it," said the girl, in a sudden fit of depression.

"We're going to get it," the Camera Chap declared confidently.

The motor boat was heading, now, straight for the fortress. Presently Hawley slackened her speed and motioned to Virginia to take his place at the wheel. "I guess the psychological moment has arrived," he announced. "We won't risk going any nearer." He took off his coat and shoes, and threw them overboard. Then he fastened around his waist a belt to which was attached a water-tight bag, which contained his photographic apparatus.

"Au revoir," he said lightly, extending his hand to the girl. "Sure you don't feel scared?"

"Not a bit—at least, not on my own account," she answered, pressing his hand with a warmth which in his opinion more than compensated him for any risk he was about to run. "Please be careful, Mr. Hawley. If anything should happen to you——"

"Nothing will," he assured her. "Nothing ever happens to me. I guess I was born under a lucky star."

The moon had emerged from behind a black cloud, and he ducked hastily to the bottom of the boat, fearing that he would be seen from the fortress. For half a minute he remained there; then, as another fleeting cloud once more plunged the sky in darkness, he left his hiding place and poised himself on the boat's gunwale.

"Try to manage to make a wide sweep so as to give me a chance to reach the shore about the same time you do," he said to Virginia.

The girl nodded. "But I don't like to see you venture among those horrid——" she began. Before she could finish the sentence, the Camera Chap had dived, entering the water so easily that she could scarcely hear the splash.

As he struck out for the shore, Virginia saw a phosphorescent streak in the water close beside him, and she uttered a scream of terror which was not prompted by her realization of the part she was to play.

A lone sentry at El Torro heard that scream, and, ceasing his pacing up and down his post, gazed out to sea with great curiosity.

Above the sound of the waves lapping the shore, he could hear the chug-chug-chug of a motor boat, first faint, then rapidly becoming more distinct. Realizing that a craft of some sort was approaching the fortress, he brought his rifle down from his shoulder to a horizontal position, and stood prepared to challenge the unseen visitor.

Then, suddenly, there came to his ears a repetition of the weird scream he had heard, followed by a series of screams in quick succession. The moon appeared from behind a cloud, and by its light he caught sight of a launch heading toward a point of the beach about two hundred feet to the east of where he stood. Simultaneously he became aware of the fact that the sole visible occupant of the boat was a woman, and that it was she who was responsible for the cries of terror or distress he had heard.

Now, fortunately for the Camera Chap and Virginia, and the righteous cause for which they strove, there was not in the whole army of Baracoa a more chivalrous man than this particular sentry. Naturally a man cast in such a sentimental mold was not the sort to turn a deaf ear to the call of beauty in distress. From where he stood he could not as yet see that the woman in the motor boat was beautiful, but he took that for granted.

Clubbing his rifle, he ran along the beach to the point where the launch was about to land. As he came near, he saw that he would not have to draw upon his imagination in order to class the craft's agitated occupant as young and very fair. With added zest he hastened to assist her to disembark.

"What is it, señorita?" he demanded sympathetically. "If you will tell me what has happened——"

"Oh!" gasped Virginia, stumbling out of the boat and into his arms, according to schedule. "Oh, it was terrible. I——" Her eyes closed, and she would have fallen if he had not held her.

According to the rules and regulations, it was his duty to summon the guard, but he was too busy just then to give thought to rules and regulations. He was struggling with the dead weight of the girl, who had become as limp and inanimate as a rag, when a tall, dark-faced young man, who wore the fatigue uniform of a captain, ran out of the fortress and approached the pair.

"What have we here?" he demanded sternly. Then, as his gaze rested on the girl's face: "Good heavens! It's Miss Throgmorton! What is the matter with her, Sanchez?"

"I think she has fainted, captain," the sentry replied, allowing his fair burden to drop gently to the sand in order that he might salute his superior officer. He pointed to the motor boat. "She came ashore in that, a minute ago."

"Alone?"

The sentry nodded. "She was screaming as though in great terror."

"It is strange—very strange," muttered Captain Ernesto Reyes. "I wonder if——"

He was interrupted by a dull report and a vivid flash of light which came from the beach, about four hundred feet from where they stood.

The sentry and his superior officer exchanged glances of mingled mystification and dismay. Leaving the girl, both of them started to run frantically toward the spot from which this startling interruption had come. Through the gloom they saw dimly a man step to the edge of the beach, and hurl himself into the water.

With an exclamation of joy, Virginia opened her eyes and rose to a sitting position. "Victory!" she murmured. "He has done it."

But a second later her exultation gave place to horror and dismay, as she heard the bark of a revolver. By the spurt of flame which accompanied the report, she saw Captain Reyes standing at the water's edge, shooting savagely at the fugitive.

CHAPTER XXV.
CAPTAIN CORTRELL'S ORDERS.

A short row of high bushes in front of the fortress had supplied the Camera Chap with a clew as to which was the window of President Felix's cell. Early in his investigation, he had learned from one of the natives of Puerto Cabero that this foliage was of recent planting. It had been put there two years previously, when Portiforo had first taken over the presidency, after the sensational disappearance of Felix.

Hawley had remarked that by its stage of development it appeared to be much more than two years old, and his informant had told him that the bushes had been transplanted from the Botanical Gardens by order of the president himself. Immediately the significance of this had suggested itself to him. He felt sure that they were intended to serve as a screen—to guard against the possibility of some curious person in the bay trying to get a glimpse of the occupant of the cell by means of powerful glasses, and he took it for granted that this precaution indicated that the occupant of that cell was the unhappy Felix.

Therefore, when he landed on the beach, he did not have to waste any time in hunting for the captive's cell. There was only one barred window behind this screen of foliage, and he hastily stepped up to it. By raising himself on tiptoe, he was just able to look into the cell, and he caught sight of a white-haired man seated at a rough wooden table, with his back toward the window, reading a book by the light of a sputtering candle.

"Señor Felix!" he whispered eagerly. "Señor Felix!"

The captive jumped up with an abruptness which upset the table, and extinguished the candle. "Who are you, and what do you wish?" Hawley heard him ask hoarsely.

"I am a friend—from the United States," the Camera Chap replied, busying himself with the waterproof bag attached to his waist. "I have come to help you, sir."

"To rescue me?" the other exclaimed, with pathetic eagerness.

"Eventually, yes; but all I can do now is to take your photograph," the Camera Chap explained. As he spoke, he tugged at one of the iron bars, with the hope that he might be able to wrench it from its fastening, in which case he would, indeed, have essayed a rescue; but, as he had feared, the iron was fastened too securely to the stone to render that possible.

"My photograph!" the occupant of the cell repeated, with a bitter laugh. "What mockery is this?"

"It isn't mockery. There are plans afoot to bring about your release, if the picture can be obtained," Hawley explained hurriedly. "I assure you, on my word of honor, that it means your liberty. Drag the table to the window and stand upon it so that your face is against the bars. Quick! There is no time to lose. I beg of you, President Felix, do as I say. You've got to trust me."

With prompt decision the captive complied with this request, and a few seconds later the snapshot was an accomplished fact. Then, for the first time, the Camera Chap found opportunity to glance toward the other end of the beach, where his fair ally was engaging the attention of the sentry. He espied two men rushing toward him, and, swiftly thrusting his camera into its receptacle, he turned and plunged into the sea.

Thus far the carrying out of his daring plan had been effected with an ease and simplicity which exceeded his most sanguine expectations.

As he had stated to Virginia, he had borrowed his idea from the underworld. That is to say, as he had cruised in Puerto Cabero Bay, cudgeling his brains in an effort to find a way of luring the sentry of El Torro from his post, there had come to his mind an effective trick which New York crooks often work when contemplating a robbery on a green policeman's beat.

He had never seen this trick done, but he had often heard it described by his friends on the force. They had told him that the wily rogues, in order to make sure of being able to commit their crime without danger of police interference, get some of the pals to start a street fight at the other end of the beat. Attracted by the noise of the brawl, the policeman rushes to the spot, and places the rowdies under arrest. And while he is marching his prisoners to the police station to answer to a charge of disorderly conduct, the burglars have a clear field.

The snapshot adventurer had reasoned that a ruse which was clever enough to fool a New York policeman ought to work equally as well on an El Torro sentry. For his study of the garrison of the fortress had convinced him that its members were not an overintelligent lot, and, as for discipline, it was a matter of common knowledge that the army of Baracoa was one of the worst-disciplined military bodies in the world.

The only thing which had bothered him had been the fact that, in order to get his picture, he would have to set off a flash light, which, of course, was bound to attract the attention of the sentry from Virginia to himself, and, probably, bring the whole garrison rushing out of the fortress. He hoped, however, that as soon as the flash light went off, and the picture was taken, it wouldn't make much difference how much attention he attracted, because he would be able to make his escape before any of them could get near enough to lay hands on him.

Now, as he saw Captain Reyes and the sentry rushing toward him, and threw himself into the sea before they were anywhere near him, it looked as if that hope was going to be fulfilled.

Pursued by the bullets of Captain Reyes, he dived to dodge the deadly hail, and swam under water while his breath lasted. Presently he rose to the surface, and struck out, with the long, vigorous stroke of an expert swimmer, for the battleship, whose lighted hull seemed just then to be miles away.

He encountered no obstacles in his course, and before he had any feeling of exhaustion, so finely trained was he for the task, his hand grasped the starboard accommodation ladder of the warship, and he lifted himself clear of the water.

Five minutes later, white-faced, and somewhat shaky in the legs, hatless and coatless, and dripping water from head to foot, he stood in the presence of the battleship's commander, who, recognizing him despite his disheveled appearance, stared at him wonderingly.

"You told me to come back to you, captain, as soon as I got the snapshot," the Camera Chap began.

Captain Cortrell's face lighted up. "Have you brought it?" he demanded eagerly.

"I have brought the plate. I haven't had a chance to develop it yet, so I don't know how it turned out, but I generally have pretty good luck with flash lights. Don't happen to have a photographic dark room aboard, do you, captain?"

The naval officer shook his head. "I guess we could fix you up a dark room easily enough, but we haven't the materials for developing a negative, if that's what you mean. I'm sorry that we haven't," he added, "for I don't mind confessing, Mr. Hawley, that I am impatient to see your picture."

"I will go ashore at once, develop the plate, and bring you back a print," the Camera Chap promised. "I have a complete outfit in my room at the hotel. But in the meantime, captain," he added anxiously, "if you have any instructions which concern me—as I feel confident you have——"

Captain Cortrell cut him short with a curt gesture. "Go ahead and get your plate developed," he said gruffly. "Whatever instructions I may have concerning you, sir, cannot be discussed until you have brought me the snapshot—a finished picture, not an invisible negative."

"But it isn't safe to wait until then. I am afraid you may be too late," the Camera Chap protested.

"Too late for what, sir?"

"To save President Felix. If you don't act promptly, I am afraid they will assassinate him. Every minute counts now."

A slightly bewildered expression came to the naval officer's face. His demeanor aroused Hawley's indignation. The latter suspected that his air of mystification was feigned, that his attitude must be due to an excess of caution.

"See here, Captain Cortrell!" he exclaimed impatiently; "there's no sense in our playing at cross-purposes with each other. There isn't time for anything of that sort. I am quite sure that you know who sent me to Baracoa, and what I am doing here——"

"I know nothing about it," the other interrupted, but Hawley impatiently waved aside the disclaimer.

"And therefore I have no hesitancy in talking plainly to you," he continued. "I don't know just what your orders are, but if they provide for any protection being extended to Felix—as I trust is the case—I assure you that no time is to be lost. If you land a force of men at the fortress at once you may be able to save him, but if you delay, I fear it will be fatal."

During this speech the bewildered expression passed from Captain Cortrell's face, and was replaced by one of great astonishment. "Am I to understand that the man whose photograph you were to bring me is Francisco Felix, the missing President of Baracoa?" he inquired excitedly.

"Why, of course. Didn't you know that?"

"And he is in El Torro fortress?"

"He was there—half an hour ago," the Camera Chap replied significantly. "It may be too late, even now, to save him, but if not, you must realize that we can't afford to beat about the bush. No doubt a report of my visit to the fortress, to-night, and the taking of the flash light, has already been sent to Portiforo. If so, he will probably resort at once to desperate measures."

The naval officer's face grew grim. "What do you expect me to do?" he inquired coolly.

The Camera Chap showed his astonishment at the question. "It seems to me that there is only one thing to do, captain—rescue Felix before

Portiforo's assassins can get to him. Why," he went on eagerly, "the thing could be done in ten minutes without any trouble at all. I don't know much about military tactics, but I've been studying the garrison of El Torro pretty closely for the past few days, and my observations make me feel confident that one boatload of your marines would be sufficient to take possession of the fortress without even a gun being fired. Or if you don't care to go quite as far as that," he added, "there is no need for your men to enter the fortress at all. They could rescue Felix from the outside—the same way that I got my picture. All that they'd have to do would be to step up to his window, break down the bars, and lift him through the opening."

The warship's commander smiled grimly. "Yes; I reckon it could be done," he said.

"And you will do it?"

The old sea dog hesitated. The Camera Chap saw a grim expression come to his weather-beaten face. It quickly passed away, however. "I am sorry, my boy," he said, real regret in his tone, "but, as I said before, I can do nothing until you have brought me the snapshot. You see," he explained, "I am here under sealed orders—I don't mind telling you that much in return for the information you have given me. In view of what I have learned from you, I now have what some of my junior officers would no doubt term 'a good-sized hunch,' as to the nature of those orders. I think it very likely that when the envelope is opened, it will be found to contain official instructions for me to proceed immediately to take the very action you urge."

"Then why not open it immediately?" the Camera Chap suggested impatiently.

"I am sorry, but that is out of the question. The conditions must first be complied with. I appreciate the danger of delay, my boy, but orders are orders. I would suggest that the best thing for you to do is to hurry ashore, get that picture finished, and bring it to me as quickly as possible. Then, provided my orders permit it, I will promise you prompt action."

Perceiving that argument would be useless, the Camera Chap proceeded to follow this advice. The commander of the *Kearsarge* placed a speedy steam launch at his disposal, and also suggested that it would be a good idea for him to have a naval escort when he went ashore. "We don't want to have any mishaps," the captain remarked dryly, "and it is just possible that circumstances might arise in which you would find it mighty convenient to be surrounded by an armed guard."

Hawley immediately grasped his point, for the possibility of an attempt being made ashore to wrest the precious picture from him had already suggested itself to his mind. "Thank you, captain; I shall be glad to take advantage of your kind offer," he said. "I think, however, that one of your men will be enough, if you can spare Lieutenant Ridder for a little while. He and I are old friends, and if he were along with me, I should feel perfectly safe."

This request met with a ready response, and a few minutes later Hawley and the husky young lieutenant were speeding toward the shore of Puerto Cabero.

As they landed from the launch, the Camera Chap caught sight of two men skulking in the shadow of the wharf, and when he and Ridder walked toward the railway station, he observed that these men stealthily followed them. By the light of a street lamp he was able to get a good look at their faces, and he recognized one of them instantly. It was his old acquaintance, Señor Lopez, the mysterious individual who had been his fellow passenger on board the steamship *Colombia*, and who had displayed such a keen interest in his movements. The Camera Chap had not seen the fellow since the day of their arrival at Puerto Cabero. He was not at all glad to see him, now. He had an uneasy suspicion that Lopez's presence at the wharf was no mere coincidence—that already the tidings of what had happened at the fortress had been flashed to the capital, and that the spy had been sent to await his landing.

Fearing for the safety of his precious snapshot, he was doubly glad, now, that he had brought Ridder along with him.

CHAPTER XXVI.
THE PLATE DEVELOPED.

A train was just about to pull out of the station, when Hawley and his companion arrived there. It was the last train to leave for the capital that night, and the Camera Chap congratulated himself upon his luck in catching it. If he had been half a minute later he might have found himself stranded in the seaport for the night, for at that hour it was difficult to find any kind of conveyance for hire, even a horse; in which case he would have been obliged to wait until morning before developing his plate.

As they jumped on the train, he glanced behind him, and saw that Lopez and his companion were evidently determined not to lose him, for they, too, got aboard, taking the precaution, however, of entering a car at the other end of the train.

If there had been time to take such a step, Hawley would have gone to the trouble of endeavoring to throw his shadowers off his trail before proceeding to his hotel, but, realizing the necessity of getting the picture finished and into the hands of the commander of the battleship without delay, he decided that he must run whatever risk lay in having them at his heels.

While the spies were only two in number, he had no fear of an attempt on their part to adopt violent tactics in order to get possession of the negative; he apprehended, however, that as soon as they reached the capital they might be joined by reënforcements, and with grim satisfaction he patted a pocket of the coat with which Captain Cortrell had supplied him from his own wardrobe, to replace the garment he had lost. In that pocket reposed a loaded forty-four. With this toy, plus the moral and physical support of his friend, Lieutenant Ridder, he felt confident that Portiforo was going to have quite a time getting that plate away from him, even though he sent a whole regiment to do the job.

As soon as he and the naval officer arrived at his room on the top floor of the Hotel Nacional, he took the precaution, after locking the door, of piling up all the furniture of the room against it. Having thus guarded against surprise in that direction, he stationed Ridder on the balcony outside the one window of the room. With the alert lieutenant crouching there, revolver in hand, he felt confident that there would be no invasion from that quarter.

As he had told Captain Cortrell, he had in his trunk a ruby lamp, and all the other materials necessary for developing a plate, and make a print from it by artificial light. It was not often that he did his own developing, but he had brought them with him, foreseeing the possibility of just such an emergency as the present one.

By the light of the ruby lamp, he opened the waterproof bag which contained his camera, and was relieved to find that, despite its exposure to the sea, not a drop of moisture had touched its contents. Removing the plate holder from the camera, he withdrew the negative and plunged it into the developing bath. With intense eagerness he leaned over the shallow hard-rubber tray, waiting for the first dim outline to show itself on the glass, probably more nervous than he had ever before been in his eventful life.

Five minutes later, the young naval officer on guard on the balcony heard an exclamation of dismay from within the room.

"What's the trouble?" Ridder whispered hoarsely. "Need any help in there?"

There was no answer, and an anxious expression came to his face. The shade of the window was drawn, and Hawley had warned him that under no circumstances must he disturb it while the work of developing the picture was in progress, as the admission of the slightest ray of moonlight into the room might spoil the negative. Still, he scarcely felt like waiting there when, evidently, something had happened to the Camera Chap.

"What's wrong in there?" he repeated, tapping impatiently against the glass. "May I come in, Hawley?"

The Camera Chap threw open the window. "Sure; come on in," he said. "There's no reason for you to stay out there any longer."

"The picture is finished?"

Hawley laughed ironically. "Yes, it's finished, all right—completely finished. Take a look at it." As he spoke he held up the square of wet glass.

"I don't know much about this sort of thing," said the navy man, taking the negative gingerly, and holding it against the light of the ruby lamp. "It's always been a mystery to me how you fellows can tell at a glance whether a negative is a good or a poor one. The few I've handled all looked pretty much alike to me. They all—why, hello! There doesn't seem to be anything on this plate. I can't see a blessed line. Anything wrong with it, old man?"

The Camera Chap smiled ruefully. "No, there's nothing wrong with it at all," he said. "It's a perfectly good plate—only, unfortunately, it's never been exposed."

"Never been exposed?" Ridder repeated, too ignorant of photographic terms to grasp immediately the full significance of this announcement. "Do you mean that the picture is spoiled?"

"I mean that the picture was never there," the Camera Chap replied. "Something was wrong with the shutter of my camera. It couldn't have been open when I set off the flash light. Can you beat that for tough luck?"

"Too bad," the lieutenant murmured. "I guess the old man will be disappointed when he hears this. I don't know what this picture business is all about, since neither of you has seen fit to take me into the secret, but I gathered from the skipper's manner that he was dead anxious to get the snapshot." He glanced at the Camera Chap anxiously. "Does this mishap make much difference, old man? Can't you take the picture over again?"

The question brought a sardonic smile to the other's face. "I suppose that's what I'll have to do—take it over again," he said presently, the smile giving place to an expression of grim resolution.

Just then they were interrupted by a knock at the door. The two men exchanged a questioning glance, and the Camera Chap's hand went to his coat pocket, and grasped the revolver it contained. Lieutenant Ridder's weapon was still in his hand.

But suddenly, as the knock was repeated, the Camera Chap's face relaxed, and his hand came empty out of his pocket. "Whoever it is, we might as well let them come in," he said, in an undertone to Ridder. "There is no reason to keep them out, now."

In a louder tone he demanded who was there, and there was a whispered consultation outside before anybody replied.

"It is a friend. Open the door, Señor Hawley. I must see you immediately," somebody answered.

The Camera Chap laughed. "Wait a minute, friend," he called, dragging the furniture from the door.

As he turned the key in the lock, the door flew open, and Señor Lopez stepped into the room. He was by no means alone. Behind him flocked a dozen men, who wore the uniform of the army of Baracoa. Each of them held a revolver in his right hand.

"There is your man," Lopez cried dramatically pointing to Hawley. Whereupon one of the soldiers, whose epaulets proclaimed him to be of higher rank than the others, stepped up to the Camera Chap and pressed the barrel of his weapon against his breast.

"I regret to have to inform you, señor, that you must accompany us at once," he said politely. "You are under arrest."

Hawley laughed lightly. "This is so sudden," he said. "Might I inquire, gentlemen, the nature of the charge against me?"

"I think that Señor Hawley can guess the nature of the charge against him," Lopez sneered. "If not, however, he will be fully informed later. Come, captain, hadn't you better search the prisoner?"

Up to this point Lieutenant Ridder had stood as though spellbound. Now, gun in hand, he stepped forward, contemptuously careless of the fact that eleven revolvers were pointed his way.

"This man is an American citizen," he exclaimed, ranging himself alongside the Camera Chap. "You're not going to take him away, and you're not going to search him, either. If you fellows are looking for trouble——"

With a laugh the Camera Chap cut him short. "It's no use, Ridder, old man," he said. "I guess you've got to let them take me. Put up that gun. As an officer of the United States navy you can't afford to mix up with this little unpleasantness."

CHAPTER XXVII.
A SERIOUS SITUATION.

Virginia Throgmorton's return from the fortress to the United States legation was almost as comfortable a proceeding as if she had been coming home from a social function. Captain Ernesto Reyes himself escorted her in the launch to Puerto Cabero. The last train to the capital had gone when they reached the station, but the gallant captain knew where a fast automobile could be obtained, and, pressing it into service, rode with her to the door of her home.

Captain Reyes' manner toward her was very sympathetic. If he had any suspicions of the part she had played in the Camera Chap's adventure, he did not betray them. Apparently he was completely deceived by the ingenuous story which she had narrated in order to account for her startling visit to the fortress.

This story, which was the Camera Chap's invention, was true enough—as far as it went. She explained that she had been out motor boating in the bay with a young man, a friend from the United States. The motor-boat trip had started out most delightfully, but just as the boat arrived in the vicinity of the fortress, her companion had spoiled the whole evening for her by suddenly falling or jumping overboard. What had become of him she did not know. She feared that he might have been killed by the harbor sharks. What had happened after that, Captain Reyes knew as well as she did; screaming with terror, she had headed the boat toward the fortress, and had fallen fainting into the arms of the sentry.

When Captain Reyes and, later, the commandant of the garrison, had asked her to tell the name of her man companion who had been unfortunate enough to fall overboard, she declared, with a blush, that she would rather not give that information, as the man was not in the good graces of her father, and she feared that she would get into trouble at home if the fact that she had been with him should come out.

Greatly to her astonishment, they had appeared to be satisfied with this ingenuous explanation which she and Hawley had expected would prove to be the weakest part of her story. The Camera Chap had instructed her that if this evasion should prove ineffectual, and the inquisitors should insist upon her telling the name of her escort, she was finally to give them the information, since her refusal to do so might get her into trouble. Virginia had secretly resolved to disregard her ally's instructions in this respect. She had made up her mind that she would languish in a Baracoan dungeon for the rest of her days before she would mention the Camera Chap's name. But, fortunately, it did not come to that. The commandant said courteously that he would respect Miss Throgmorton's wishes in the matter, and not force her to make any revelations which were embarrassing to her.

Later on, Virginia learned the explanation of this astonishing forbearance, but it did not occur to her, then, that the reason they did not press her for the name of her companion might be that the name was known to them already.

Expressing deep sympathy for her alarming experience, the gallant commandant of El Torro had offered her refreshments, and then assigned Captain Reyes to escort her home.

Early the next morning, Virginia sent a trusted messenger to the Hotel Nacional, with a note for Hawley. The messenger was instructed to bring back the note to her if the Camera Chap was not there. The girl realized the imprudence of this act, but she felt that she must know without delay what had become of the daring man of whose fate she was in absolute ignorance. Half an hour later her messenger, an old negro manservant, whom her father had brought with him from the United States, and who had been in the service of the Throgmortons since Virginia's birth, returned to the embassy and handed back her note.

"He is not there?" she exclaimed. "Hasn't he been back to the hotel since last night?"

The old servant nodded. "Yes; he has been back, Miss Virginia; but he is not there, now," he whispered. "He has been arrested. The clerk informed me that soldiers came to Mr. Hawley's room late last night and took him away to the arsenal."

Virginia's first sensation upon hearing this was one of intense relief. The situation was bad enough, to be sure, but the thought of the Camera Chap being in a prison cell was not nearly so disquieting as the fear that he might have been drowned or killed.

"Arrested!" she cried. "On what charge, Uncle Peter?"

The old negro shook his head. "I couldn't find out what they done accuse him of, Miss Virginia," he replied. "The clerk didn't know."

She did not have to wait long, however, to be informed on this point, for just then Gale entered the room. He appeared to be greatly excited.

"Heard the news, Virginia?" he asked. "A friend of yours was arrested last night."

"A friend of mine?" the girl echoed, with an inflection of wonder. "Who was that?"

The reporter grinned. "A young man named Frank Hawley, sometimes known as the Camera Chap," he announced. "From what I hear, he's in pretty bad."

"Indeed!" Virginia exclaimed, arching her eyebrows. "What has he done?"

Gale's grin broadened. "They accuse him of being a spy," he declared.

"A spy!" cried the girl, with a nervous laugh. "Why, how perfectly absurd. Surely he will have no difficulty in disproving that charge."

"Think so?" the reporter rejoined, a vestige of a sneer in his tone. "Well, I'm not so sure of that. It looks to me as if they've got the goods on him. He went out to the fortress last night and took a flash-light photograph of the fortifications. That's a pretty serious business."

"Flash light of the fortifications!" Virginia cried impulsively. "Is that what they think he was after?"

She regretted the words as soon as they were out of her mouth, and would have given a great deal to be able to recall them, as she observed the astonished expression which came to the man's face.

"What do you mean by that?" he demanded sharply. "Have you any reason to think that he was after anything else?"

The girl shrugged her shoulders. "How should I know what he was after?" she said indignantly. "What I meant was, that I scarcely thought it possible that he would have gone there for that reason. Mr. Hawley isn't a spy; he is a newspaper man. It is much more logical to suppose that if he took any picture at all, it was a photograph of the fortress for publication in his paper." A shade flitted across her face. "What does he say?" she demanded, striving desperately to keep all trace of anxiety out of her voice. "What explanation does he give?"

"That's the queer part of it," the reporter replied. "He won't give any explanation at all. They tell me that he's as tight-mouthed as a Wall Street magnate before a congressional investigation committee. To all questions they put to him last night he replied that he refused to answer, by advice of counsel. The idiot seems to take his arrest as a joke."

An expression of admiration came to Virginia's pretty face. She felt sure that she understood the reason for the Camera Chap's uncommunicative attitude. It was not with an idea of making things easier for himself, she knew, that he had refused to answer their questions. It was because he was determined to make no statement which might lead Portiforo to suspect the truth, with disastrous results for the unfortunate captive of El Torro.

"But, take it from me, he'll soon find that it's no joke," Gale went on, a malicious glint in his eyes. "He'll be lucky if he gets off with a prison sentence. The chances are that they'll back him up against a stone wall, with a handkerchief over his eyes and a firing squad in front of him. That's the treatment they generally hand out to spies."

Virginia turned pale. "They wouldn't dare do that!" she gasped. "Even Portiforo would be afraid to go so far with a citizen of the United States."

"I don't know about that," Gale rejoined. "It's been done before, you know. When a man's convicted of being a spy, they can do as they please with him, and his government is powerless to interfere. That's international law. Surely you, the daughter of a diplomat, ought to know that."

Virginia did know that, and an expression of horror came to her eyes. Then, suddenly, her face lighted up. "You are exaggerating the situation, Mr. Gale," she said, with a scornful laugh. "They don't shoot spies in times of peace. If you are such an authority on international law, you ought to know that. It is only when there is war that they adopt such stern measures."

"Very true," the reporter returned, with a grin. "But evidently, my dear Virginia, you are not aware that the Republic of Baracoa happens to be in a state of war at the present moment. I heard, this morning, that Rodriguez, who broke out of jail the other day, reached the hills yesterday, and raised the standard of revolt. And they accuse Hawley of being mixed up with the revolutionary party. So you see, I am not exaggerating the seriousness of his plight."

CHAPTER XXVIII.
THE PRISONER.

The soft-footed man with the wolflike smile, known as Señor Lopez, was elated over the arrest of that adventurous man, the Camera Chap, and warmly congratulated himself upon the stroke of luck which had enabled him to bring it about so speedily, for it had been a mere coincidence that he happened to be standing near the dock, earlier that evening, when Hawley, accompanied by a young woman whom the spy immediately recognized as the daughter of the American minister, approached the water's edge and furtively embarked in a motor boat.

His curiosity aroused, Lopez would have followed the pair, but was prevented from doing so by his failure to obtain a craft in time; so he had to content himself for the time being with speculating as to the motive of this evidently secret expedition. At first he had supposed that they were bound for the American warship, but later the possibility that the fortress might be their goal had suggested itself to his mind. As soon as this suspicion occurred to him he sent a note to the commandant of the fortress warning him to keep a sharp lookout for the pair; but by the time his messenger reached the fortress Hawley had already been there, taken his snapshot, and escaped by throwing himself into the sea.

Lopez's note had arrived just as the commandant and Captain Reyes were questioning Virginia as to the identity of her mysterious companion, and it was for this reason that they had astonished the girl by their apparent courtesy in not pressing her to give them the information they desired.

When Lopez's messenger returned to him with a brief reply from the commandant stating what had occurred at the fortress, the spy decided to wait at the dock in the hope that later on the snapshot adventurer would return in one of the battleship's launches; for he was shrewd enough to suspect that Hawley's motive in throwing himself into the sea was to swim out to the *Kearsarge*.

Possessed of the patience of a cat, he would have waited there all night if necessary, but such a display of endurance was not required of him, for shortly afterward a gray launch dashed up to the pier and two young men came ashore. Recognizing one of them as the man he was waiting for, the spy trailed the pair to San Cristobal, and thence to the Hotel Nacional. Then he hurried to the nearest barracks, provided himself with a military escort, and returned to make the arrest.

After the soldiers had taken Hawley away Lopez spent some time in making a thorough search of the latter's room at the Hotel Nacional. Then he went to the arsenal to have a talk with the prisoner.

The cell in which the Camera Chap was confined did not exactly measure up to the standard of luxury of a first-class hotel. The floor was of cement, hard and cold, and had every appearance of not having been cleaned since the place was built. There was no furniture, save a rusty iron cot which was attached to the wall. This couch, which was supposed to serve both as bed and chair, was without pillow or mattress. If the prisoner wished to sleep he would have to get used to stretching himself on the unyielding iron slats. But these physical discomforts did not appear to have a depressing effect upon the present occupant of the dungeon, judging by the cheerful smile with which he greeted Lopez when the latter stepped softly up to the bars.

"I suppose here's where I get a chance to study at first-hand the Baracoan method of administering the third degree," he remarked carelessly.

The visitor shrugged his shoulders. "I desire merely to ask Señor Hawley a few questions," he announced. "I hope for his sake that he will find it convenient to answer them."

"Well, you might submit a sample question," the prisoner replied. "I'll be able to tell you better, then, what chance you stand of having your curiosity satisfied."

Lopez bowed. "To begin with, what have you done with the picture you took to-night?"

"Why, it seems to me that you can answer that question yourself. I saw you take the plate from the table and put it in your pocket before your army took me out of the room."

His visitor looked at him searchingly. "You refer to the plate that was spoiled, señor? Was that the only snapshot you took?"

"It was, on my word of honor," Hawley answered with intense earnestness. He had no wish to evade this question; on the contrary he was most anxious to have his interrogator know that there was no other picture.

"And this spoiled plate—what does it represent? If Señor Hawley had been successful with his camera what would the plate have shown?"

The Camera Chap smiled. "It seems to me that you're asking a hypothetical question," he said. "Yes, decidely hypothetical."

Lopez shrugged his expressive shoulders again. "It is Señor Hawley's privilege to answer or not as he sees fit, but," he added, "I must warn him that if he refuses to tell why he went to the fortress to-night we shall be compelled to draw our own conclusions from his silence."

"That'll be all right," Hawley rejoined cheerfully. "Have you any objections to dropping me a hint as to what those conclusions may be?"

"Not the slightest. Unless the señor is prepared to give us an explanation more favorable to himself we shall assume that he went there to get photographs of the fortifications—that he is a spy in the service of the insurrectos."

"An insurrecto spy! Well, of all the——" the president's photographic envoy began. Then he abruptly cut himself short as the advantages of having this interpretation placed upon his act suddenly occurred to him— advantages to others, although possibly not to himself.

"And no doubt Señor Hawley is aware of what happens to those who are convicted on that serious charge," his visitor suggested quietly.

The prisoner imitated the other's shrug. "Oh, well, I guess I'll be able to stand it," he said optimistically. "I can't truthfully say that the accommodations of this hostelry are pleasant, but no doubt I shan't find them so bad after I get used to them."

"I am afraid the señor is laboring under a slight misapprehension," he remarked. "In the event of his conviction he would have no chance to get used to these accommodations. He would be tried under martial law, and— under martial law a spy's punishment is not imprisonment."

The Camera Chap looked uncomfortable as he caught the significance of this remark, but almost immediately he regained his composure. "Well, you've got to convict me first," he remarked confidently. "You can't hang a man on suspicion alone—at least, you can't do it if that man happens to be a citizen of the U. S. A. If you dare to convict me without sufficient proof I venture to predict that something is going to happen to Baracoa."

The assurance with which he said this was not wholly feigned. While he realized that in the event of his guilt being proven his government would be powerless to protect him, he felt sure that Washington would demand the strongest kind of proof before they would permit the sentence to be carried out. And he had a shrewd suspicion that the enemy had only a circumstantial case against him. He felt positive that in the gloom it had been impossible for Captain Reyes or the sentry to recognize him, so that unless Virginia Throgmorton had been compelled to reveal his identity there was no direct evidence that it was actually he who was the mysterious photographer who had visited El Torro.

"Señor Hawley can rest assured that we shall be able to produce sufficient proof of his guilt," Lopez boasted. "To begin with, we can show that he stands high in the confidence of the insurrectos."

"Indeed!" the prisoner exclaimed, carefully weighing this statement. "Might I inquire how you expect to prove that?"

"By the fact that he was in conference with one of their most active leaders, the other day. I refer to the infamous Doctor Gaspard Bonsal. I presume, señor, that you will not attempt to deny that you visited him when I tell you that you were seen surreptitiously leaving his house on the night of his arrest."

In spite of himself the Camera Chap was unable to avoid a start of astonishment, for until that moment the fact that his visit to the venerable physician was known to the enemy had not entered his mind.

"If I was seen, how is it that I, too, was not arrested?" he demanded.

Once more there was a display of gestures and shrugs. "I believe there is a saying in the señor's own beautiful language to the effect that it is sometimes advisable to give a rogue plenty of rope in order that he may bring about his own hanging."

"Who claims to have seen me?"

"I myself had that honor," Lopez answered, with a bow.

"By Jove!" exclaimed the prisoner, with an ironical laugh, "you certainly are the busy little man. Nothing seems to escape those eagle eyes of yours. But, after all, the fact that you saw me leaving a physician's house doesn't strike me as being very incriminating. How do you know I didn't go there to consult him professionally?"

"If Señor Hawley can prove that such was the case it would undoubtedly be to his advantage," Lopez responded. "But, of course, in that event, his testimony would have to agree with that of the lady."

"The lady?" A shade of anxiety flitted across the snapshot adventurer's face.

"I refer to the lady who came out of Doctor Bonsal's house that night with Señor Hawley and entered the automobile which was waiting for her at the garden gate. Señora Felix was heavily veiled, but that disguise was not sufficient to prevent me from recognizing her."

Portiforo's spy laughed maliciously at the prisoner's evident discomfiture. "And she is not the only fair witness we shall have at the trial in the event of Señor Hawley's insisting that he is not an insurrecto spy," he announced.

"The government of Baracoa would regret exceedingly having to put the daughter of the United States minister to any inconvenience, but if Señor Hawley's attitude makes the testimony of these ladies necessary——"

"Their testimony won't be necessary," Hawley interrupted grimly. "Whatever happens, we'll leave the women entirely out of this business."

Lopez bowed. "Señor Hawley has decided most chivalrously." With this remark, evidently well satisfied with the result of their conversation, he turned on his heels and abruptly left the prisoner to his own thoughts.

Those thoughts were not pleasant ones. For some time the president's photographic envoy sat on the edge of his iron cot, his hands supporting his chin, reflecting moodily on the situation. He realized that he was confronted by the most serious predicament of his career. If he revealed the real motive of his expedition to the fortress, it would, of course, clear him of the charge of being a revolutionary spy. They couldn't do much to an American newspaper photographer for attempting to take a snapshot of a political prisoner. They would be compelled to let him off with a slight punishment. But he had not the slightest intention of making such a revelation. From the demeanor of Lopez he had an uneasy suspicion that the truth was already known to that perspicacious person, and that this threat of condemning him as a spy had been made with the idea of forcing him to show his hand. Still, there was a chance that he might be mistaken, that in spite of all that had happened Portiforo and his fellow conspirators might still be under the impression that their secret was safe, and while there was that chance Hawley did not feel at liberty to betray the confidence of the President of the United States and imperil the life of Felix in order to save his own neck.

He realized that Lopez had not exaggerated the peril which he faced, for he knew that under martial law, capital punishment is the fate of a spy; and as Rodriguez, since his escape from prison, had fled to the hills and started an incipient revolution, he believed that it was under martial law that he would be tried. That his government would see that he had a fair trial he felt confident, but as his lips were sealed by this threat to call Virginia and Señora Felix as witnesses if he sought to make his accusers prove their charge, he already looked upon himself as doomed.

"I guess I'm up against it," he mused grimly. "It looks as if friend Portiforo holds all the trump cards."

CHAPTER XXIX.
A VAIN APPEAL.

Greatly alarmed by what Gale had told her concerning the Camera Chap's peril, Virginia lost no time in seeking an interview with her father. She found the latter seated in his library engaged in the preparation of a long dispatch to Washington. He looked up from his cipher code with a frown as she entered.

"Some other time, my dear; I am exceedingly busy just now," he protested. "This dispatch has got to be sent off at once."

"But I can't wait," the girl announced. "The business I want to talk over with you is more important than what you are doing. Unless," she added, with a flash of intuition, "that telegram you are writing concerns the arrest of Mr. Hawley."

The United States minister swung around in his swivel chair and regarded his daughter with surprise. "How on earth did you guess that?" he demanded.

"Then it is about Mr. Hawley!" the girl exclaimed joyously. "You are cabling the state department that you are going to get him out of prison immediately?"

Minister Throgmorton shook his head. "On the contrary, my dear, I am informing Washington that we can do nothing for him, except to make sure that he gets a fair trial," he said coldly. "The young man has only himself to blame for his predicament. If he is guilty of the serious offense with which he is charged—and I am given to understand that the government of Baracoa has the strongest kind of a case against him—he must suffer the consequences. The United States government cannot afford to affront a friendly nation by acting in behalf of a mercenary adventurer who has been caught red-handed as a spy for the revolutionists."

"But Mr. Hawley isn't a mercenary adventurer," Virginia protested. "Nor is he a revolutionary spy. I happen to know that he——" She stopped short, suddenly realizing the danger of completing what she had started out to say. In her zeal to save her plucky friend, she had been about to take her father into her confidence concerning the worthy mission which had brought the snapshot wizard to Baracoa, but just in time she recalled that she had made a promise to Hawley that, no matter what happened, she would not give away his secret.

Observing her hesitancy, Throgmorton looked at her keenly. "You happen to know that he is—what?" he demanded sharply.

"I happen to know that he is a newspaper man," the girl replied evasively.

"A *Sentinel* man, you mean," the diplomat rejoined tartly. "That certainly is nothing in his favor. My own experience with that sensational sheet has been quite sufficient to convince me that everybody connected with it is capable of almost anything."

Virginia's blue eyes flashed indignantly. "And that is why you are taking this attitude toward Mr. Hawley," she said bitterly. "Just because the paper he represents has been unkind to you in its editorial columns you have made up your mind not to interfere in his behalf. It is incredible to me, father, that you could be as small as that."

The diplomat frowned. "I think you forget yourself, my dear Virginia," he said with dignity. "Your insinuation is not only disrespectful, it is preposterous. I hope that I am conscientious enough not to allow my personal prejudices to influence me in the discharge of my duty. By the way," he added sharply, "might I inquire why you appear to be so greatly interested in the fate of this spy? Surely it cannot be possible that you number him among your friends?"

"I do," the girl answered warmly. "He is the bravest, most unselfish man I have ever met, and I am proud to be able to say that he is my friend. And what's more," she added, a light of determination in her blue eyes, "whether you will do anything for him or not, he's not going to be made the victim of Portiforo's vengeance if I can help it."

Her father's frown deepened. "My dear child, you are talking most intemperately. The object of your misplaced sympathy is not going to be made the victim of anybody's vengeance. You can rest assured, as I said before, that he will have a fair and impartial trial. As the representative of his country I shall see to that. And that is all that he or any other fair-minded person could expect me to do for him."

"It isn't all," the girl protested. "There needn't be any trial at all if you don't wish it. You have sufficient personal influence with the Portiforo administration to have him set free even though he were guilty."

Minister Throgmorton shrugged his shoulders. "I fear that you overestimate my power, my dear," he said deprecatingly. "However, even if I had sufficient influence, I don't think I should feel justified in using it in that way. The prisoner's demeanor is scarcely such as to entitle him to clemency. His bearing toward the authorities is almost defiant; and, as for his attitude toward me——"

Virginia interrupted him with an excited exclamation. "You have been to see him?" she inquired eagerly.

"Yes; I called at the arsenal immediately after his arrest. I deemed it my duty to interview him." He paused, and an expression of annoyance came to his face. "But I could get absolutely nothing out of him. The fellow was almost contemptuous in his refusal to answer my questions. No; I certainly shouldn't feel like doing any more than my duty calls for to help him."

After some further pleading and argument, Virginia went out of the room convinced that so far as her father was concerned the Camera Chap was a doomed man. For a while she was in despair; then an idea came to her which caused her to order the touring car and journey therein to Puerto Cabero. Arrived at the seaport, she went down to the wharf which the *Kearsarge's* launches were using for a landing. One of the battleship's graceful little fifty-footers had just come in with a liberty party of jackies. Virginia addressed a natty young officer in charge of the men. "Is this boat going right back to the battleship?" she inquired.

"In a few minutes, miss. Do you wish to go?"

"If Captain Cortrell is there. I must see him immediately."

The officer replied that she would find the commanding officer in his cabin, and a few minutes later Virginia was speeding over the water toward the big gray fighter. As she reached the warship's side and stepped to the main deck her hopes suddenly soared. The sight of the guns protruding from the grim turrets, and the sturdy, white-jacketed boys from her own land swarming over the decks, was decidedly reassuring. Somehow, in spite of what her father had said, she could not believe that the ruler of a "fussy little banana republic"—as she was wont to refer contemptuously to Baracoa—would dare to go to extreme lengths with a citizen of a country powerful enough to own such engines of destruction as this.

When the officer of the deck learned her identity he conducted her at once to the commanding officer's cabin. Captain Cortrell had already met her at the embassy when he had called there to pay his respects to her father. The smile which came now to his weather-beaten countenance betokened how delighted he was to renew the acquaintance; for grim old sea dog though he was, he was always glad to see a pretty face aboard his vessel, especially when that pretty face belonged to one of his own countrywomen. His smile abruptly disappeared, however, when he learned the object of Virginia's visit, and he shook his grizzled head sadly.

"I regret to say, Miss Throgmorton, that I am powerless to do anything. I sympathize greatly with Mr. Hawley, and, unofficially, would do anything in my power to help him, but you must realize that officially my hands are tied."

"I don't realize anything of the sort!" Virginia cried impetuously. "If you were to go to Portiforo and tell him that unless he releases your countryman immediately the *Kearsarge's* guns will wipe Baracoa off the map, I am confident that he would be impressed."

Captain Cortrell received this suggestion with a laugh, but that the girl had struck a responsive chord within him was evident by the glint which came to his eyes. "I don't mind admitting that such a step is exactly the one I'd like to take," he confided to her. "But, of course, it is quite out of the question. You must see that. Your father is in command of the situation here. I could not presume to go over the head of the United States minister."

"This is no time for red tape," the girl protested. "What does it matter whose head you go over when the life of a brave man is in danger?" Her voice suddenly became softly coaxing. "I feel sure you, too, are a brave man, Captain Cortrell. Why not take the chance? Other American commanders have taken chances."

The naval officer cut her short with another laugh. "I hate to forfeit your good opinion, Miss Throgmorton," he said dryly, "but I am afraid I can't let you tempt me to be guilty of such a gross breach of discipline. Why not try that line of argument on your father?" he suggested. "I will promise you this much—if you can persuade him to make a formal request to me to take steps to bring about Mr. Hawley's release, I will proceed to take whatever action may be necessary, immediately, without waiting to hear from Washington."

Virginia shook her head. "I know my father's disposition too well to have any hope of being able to change his mind once it is made up," she said. Then, suddenly her face brightened. "Well, anyway, I suppose it won't do any harm to try," she exclaimed. Without telling Captain Cortrell of the new idea which had come to her, she hurried from the warship and back to San Cristobal.

CHAPTER XXX.
LOYAL FRIENDS.

Minister Throgmorton was still in his library when Virginia returned. He had sent his report to Washington and had just received a reply. He was in the act of opening this dispatch when his daughter entered the room.

"Father, are you aware that Mr. Hawley was not alone when he went to take the snapshot at the fortress last night?" she began abruptly.

The diplomat nodded. "I am informed that he had a woman confederate with him. But, really, my dear girl——"

"You have been correctly informed," Virginia quickly interrupted. "But did they tell you who the woman was?"

Her father looked at her searchingly. "No, they did not. Do you know?"

"I do; and I think that you ought to know, too, before you fully make up your mind that it will be impossible to use your influence with the government to prevent this case from coming to trial. Surely you wouldn't want your own daughter to be convicted as accessory before the fact?"

"My own daughter! Why, what do you mean? It can't be possible that you——" He stopped short, and a look of alarm came to his face.

"Yes; it was I," the girl announced, her voice as calm as if she had been telling him of a visit to her milliner. "I accompanied Mr. Hawley to the fortress last night, and helped him to get his snapshot. You might as well hear the truth now, for you are bound to learn it later on when I am brought to trial. For," she added, with determination, "I have fully decided that I must confess my part in the adventure. It would not be honorable for me to remain silent and let Mr. Hawley suffer alone, when I am fully as guilty as he."

Her father smiled incredulously. "I hate to doubt your word, Virginia, but I am inclined to believe that you are inventing this story in the vain hope of frightening me into helping the rascal."

"If you doubt me," said Virginia indignantly, "you have only to make inquiries at the fortress. Ask the commandant, or Captain Reyes; they can tell you that I was there. I told them a story which threw them off the track as to my part in the adventure and caused them to let me go, but when they hear my confession they will have no doubt as to its truth."

A troubled expression came to the minister's face. He got up and paced the room in agitation. "What made you do it?" he demanded presently. "What motive could you have for assisting this spy?"

Virginia shrugged her shoulders. "He couldn't get his snapshot without an assistant, so I volunteered my services. The excitement of the adventure appealed to me. Things have been so slow around here lately."

Her father scowled. "Do you realize the position you have put me in?" he exclaimed angrily. "The daughter of the United States minister mixed up in a conspiracy against the government of a friendly power! It is intolerable. It is liable to cause international complications. It may result in my recall."

"It needn't do either of these things, if only you could see your way to do as I have suggested—use your influence with the government here to have Mr. Hawley set free without a trial. I'm sure everything will be all right so far as I am concerned."

Minister Throgmorton scowled again. "That is quite out of the question," he began. Then he happened to glance at the cablegram in his hand which he had been about to read when his daughter had interrupted him. The message, which was in cipher, was very brief. Translated it read as follows:

"You must make every fair and legitimate effort, at your discretion, to obtain Hawley's release."

The United States representative did not have to consult his code book for the identification of the name which was signed to the message. He knew that it was the personal cipher of the President of the United States.

As he was working out the translation his daughter took a step toward the door. With an intuitive apprehension of her purpose he looked up from his desk. "Where are you going, Virginia?" he asked uneasily.

"To give myself up to the authorities," the girl answered, a resolute tilt to her chin. "I have fully made up my mind that if Mr. Hawley is going to suffer I am going to share his punishment with him."

"You are going to do nothing of the sort," her harassed parent declared peremptorily. He got up from his chair and took his hat and cane. "Wait here," he commanded. "I am going out for a little while. I forbid you to leave the house until I return."

"Very well, father," the girl meekly assented. Her blue eyes twinkled as she spoke. Something about the envoy's manner caused her to believe that she could guess his destination.

A few minutes after he had gone a young man visited the embassy. He wore the uniform of a lieutenant of the United States navy. He wore also an exceedingly perturbed expression. From the card which the servant brought, Virginia learned that the visitor's name was Ridder, and that he was attached to the battleship *Kearsarge*. The servant announced that the young man desired an audience with the United States minister, but the girl, hoping that his business might have something to do with the Camera Chap, ordered that he be shown into the library.

"My father is not in just now," she announced. "Is there anything I can do for you?"

"I'm afraid, not," Lieutenant Ridder replied. "I have come to see your father about a friend of mine who was arrested last night."

"Mr. Hawley?"

"Yes; do you know if anything is being done for him? I am anxious to know whether my telegram has already brought results."

"Your telegram?" Virginia exclaimed with eager curiosity.

"Last night when a mob of chocolate soldiers marched into the hotel and arrested my friend," the naval officer explained, "I sent a dispatch to the managing editor of the New York *Sentinel*, notifying him of what had happened. I figured that he might have a pull with Washington."

"What a clever idea!" exclaimed Virginia, looking at him admiringly. "That scheme never even entered my mind. Did you get a reply?"

"Yes; he assured me that he will do everything in his power to stir up Washington. I was in hopes that he might have succeeded in getting the state department to send word to Minister Throgmorton to demand Hawley's release."

"My father received an official dispatch a short time ago," Virginia informed him, "but of course I don't know what it contained. Are you a very great friend of Mr. Hawley's?" she inquired.

Lieutenant Ridder smiled. "Well, that depends on what you mean by friend. We've only met a few times, but—well, you see, he saved my life once. That was the first time we met. A gang of toughs had me down and pretty nearly out. They would have finished me, I guess, if Hawley hadn't come along. There were at least six of them, but he sailed into the bunch and routed them all. He's the gamest, whitest chap I've ever met, and now that he's in trouble I'd go the limit to help him."

Virginia regarded him with interest. "I wonder just how far you really would go," she said, a challenge in her tone. "If all other measures failed, would you be willing to land a rescue party to the jail and get him out by force?"

The naval officer smiled sheepishly. "Are you a mind reader, Miss Throgmorton? Ever since last night," he confided to her, "I've been figuring whether that very thing couldn't be done, if things should come to a pinch. I know I could pick out at least a dozen men on the *Kearsarge* who would be eager to help me. The only difficulty is that if I took them in on the scheme it would get them into trouble."

"It would get you into trouble, too," the girl reminded him. "I am afraid that, at the very least, it would cost you your commission."

Ridder smiled. "Possibly it would," he said simply, "but—well, didn't Hawley risk more than that when he sailed into that bunch down in Chinatown and saved me from being beaten to death? As I said before, I'm willing to go the limit to help him."

"I feel sure that you would," said Virginia, noting with admiration the breadth of his shoulders and the strong set of his jaw. "Mr. Hawley is indeed fortunate to have such a loyal friend so near at hand. Let us hope, however," she added, "that such desperate measures will not be necessary. I have an idea, Mr. Ridder, that my father has gone now to the national palace to interview President Portiforo on behalf of our friend. When he returns he may have good news for us."

CHAPTER XXXI.
PORTIFORO'S WAY.

As he told Virginia, Minister Throgmorton had been to the arsenal early that morning to talk with the Camera Chap, but the interview was brief. Finding the prisoner evasive and uncommunicative, the United States representative had left in a rage, mistaking Hawley's attitude for brazen indifference to his fate.

With the exception of this visitor and Lopez, the prisoner was permitted to receive no callers. Lieutenant Ridder, who had visited the arsenal shortly after his friend's arrest and demanded to see him, was politely but firmly informed that, according to the rules and regulations, Señor Hawley, by the nature of the charge against him, was strictly denied visitors, and although the naval officer resorted to both pleading and threats, he was unable to change this decision.

Although Hawley was by no means an unsociable man, he was glad that this rule was in force, for ever since his arrest he had feared that Virginia Throgmorton might be indiscreet enough to come to see him. Even as it was, knowing the girl's loyal and impulsive nature, he was afraid that she might manage, by the use of her father's influence, to obtain the necessary permission to visit him. Such an interview, he felt sure, would be disastrous, for he had no doubt that every word that passed between them would be eagerly listened to by Portiforo's spies.

Consequently, when late that afternoon he heard footsteps in the cement-walled courtyard upon which the door of his dungeon opened, and, peering through the bars, caught sight of the figure of a woman approaching his cell, his heart skipped a couple of beats. The woman, who was flanked on either side by a uniformed official, wore a heavy veil, but as she drew near she threw aside this covering, and an involuntary exclamation of dismay escaped from the Camera Chap's lips as he caught sight of her features.

The visitor was not Virginia. Recognizing that pathetic, haggard face at first glance, the prisoner would have been relieved at that moment to have seen the daughter of the United States minister standing there in her place; for if Virginia's visit to the jail would have been an unwise step, the presence of this woman was a hundred times more so. He marveled at the madness which had caused Señora Felix to come to see him—for he supposed at first that it was on his account that she was there.

Greatly to his surprise and relief, however, the señora and her companions passed his cell without even a glance at him. As she went by he observed that tears were streaming down her cheeks and that her frail form was trembling with emotion.

They halted at a cell on the same tier, a few yards away, and the two officials withdrew a short distance, leaving the woman to talk with its occupant through the bars. The Camera Chap could not see her now, but he heard her burst suddenly into a fit of violent sobbing. Then he heard a man say soothingly: "Courage, señora! I entreat you to be calm, my dear friend. Surely you who have faced all your tribulations with such sublime bravery are not going to break down now."

At the sound of that patient, softly modulated voice, Hawley gave a start of surprise. He felt positive that he recognized it as the voice of Doctor Gaspard Bonsal. Until that moment he had been unaware of the identity of any of his fellow captives, and the possibility that the venerable physician might be confined in the arsenal jail had not occurred to him, for he had heard that he had been sent to El Torro.

Although, under other circumstances, he would have been averse to playing the rôle of eavesdropper, he could not help now straining his ears in an effort to catch the conversation which passed between the señora and her devoted old friend, for he had an uneasy suspicion of what her visit and her great grief portended. They spoke mostly in such low tones that what they said did not reach him, but once Doctor Bonsal unconsciously raised his voice, and the Camera Chap heard him say. "I am old, my child, and what happens to me does not matter. We must accept the situation with philosophy."

"If only I could do something," the woman sobbed. "I have been to Portiforo and pleaded with him, but it was no use. He would not listen. That tyrant——"

She stopped short at a remonstrance from the physician, spoken in a voice so low that Hawley could not catch the words. Almost immediately after that the two officials stepped up to the señora and gruffly informed her that it was time for her to withdraw. The Camera Chap heard her plead with them to be allowed to have a few more words with the prisoner, but the request was refused, and, sobbing violently, she was literally dragged from in front of the barred door.

The next morning Hawley's fears for the old physician were confirmed in a startling manner. At sunrise the tramp of many feet resounded on the stone floor of the courtyard, and he heard a hoarse voice exclaim: "*Adelante!*" Knowing that this order was the Spanish equivalent for "Forward, march!"

he was not surprised, upon jumping from his bed and gazing through the bars, to see a file of soldiers in the courtyard. There were about twenty of them. At the command of the officer they ranged themselves at one end of the yard and stood at attention, as unconcerned as though they had come there to perform their usual morning drill. Presently Hawley heard voices to the right of his cell. "Are you ready?" somebody asked. Then, in a voice which thrilled the listener, Doctor Bonsal answered unfalteringly: "I am ready."

A gate creaked on its hinges, and the venerable prisoner, his head held high, his shoulders squared, walked past the Camera Chap's door, an army officer in dress uniform on each side of him.

Like a man in a dream, the snapshot adventurer gazed upon the scene that followed. He saw the officers place their victim with his back to the cement wall of the courtyard, and tie a handkerchief over his eyes. He saw them step back, and heard one of them give an order which caused the long line of gleaming rifle barrels at the other end of the yard to rise with a precision that seemed almost automatic. In another minute the tragedy was over, and in ten minutes the courtyard was clear, and the routine of the prison was resumed.

Hawley was horrified at what he had witnessed, but his predominant emotion was one of violent rage. "If ever I get out of here," he murmured, "I'll make Portiforo pay for this." Then he smiled grimly as the thought came to him that instead of getting out, the chances were that before long he himself would be in the same position as the ill-fated Doctor Bonsal.

Presently two men came to his cell and threw open the door. "Señor," one of them said politely, "we must request you to be good enough to accompany us."

CHAPTER XXXII.
OLD SCORES.

Since the publication in the New York *Daily News* of the letters of the missing President Felix to his wife, Gale had stood high in the favor of Portiforo. The latter had sent for the reporter and assured him of his deep appreciation of the service he had rendered the government of Baracoa by disposing so effectively of the unpleasant rumors concerning Felix, the circulation of which had been a source of distress to him, Portiforo, and the high-minded patriotic gentlemen connected with his administration. Incidentally he had told Gale that the latchstring of the national palace was at all times out for him.

On the day that he learned of the Camera Chap's arrest, Gale decided to take advantage of this standing invitation. He deemed it his duty to have a chat with the president concerning the prisoner. He found Portiforo not at all unwilling to talk on that subject.

"In fact, Señor Gale, if you had not come, I was about to send for you for that very purpose," said the president, when his visitor had made known the object of his call. "I am desirous of getting some information about that misguided young man, and since you and he are members of the same profession, you ought to be able to tell me what I want to know. I am informed," he went on, somewhat anxiously, "that this man Hawley is quite a big figure in American journalism—a sort of a celebrity."

Gale laughed disdainfully. "I don't know where you could have got hold of that idea, Señor Presidente. A celebrity, eh? Well, that's pretty good!"

He spoke with malicious emphasis, for he believed that he understood his questioner's motive in seeking to ascertain the status of the Camera Chap in the newspaper world. If he was convinced that Hawley was a man of prominence in his own country he would probably hesitate to go to extremes with him for fear of bringing upon himself the wrath of the American people. If, on the other hand, he was led to believe that the prisoner was a person of no great importance, the latter was likely to receive scant consideration from him.

Realizing that here was an opportunity to settle old scores with his rival, Gale eagerly availed himself of it. "You can take it from me, Señor Presidente," he declared, "that Hawley is nothing but a plain, ordinary camera man, and in the newspaper business camera men don't rank very high. We reporters rather look down on them."

The president looked surprised. "Then it isn't true that he gets an enormous salary, and that his brilliant exploits have made him so famous that even the President of the United States has been known to employ his services in diplomatic work?" As Portiforo asked the question he looked keenly at the reporter.

"Certainly not," the latter answered. "Who's been filling you up with such trash as that? The President of the United States doesn't employ newspaper men for diplomatic work," he added, unaware of the good turn he was really doing the man he desired to injure. "There are lots of secret-service men who understand how to use a camera. If the president required any photographic work of a diplomatic nature, he'd employ one of them, of course."

Portiforo was considerably impressed by the logic of this argument. For a few seconds he puffed reflectively on his cigar. "Do you happen to know, Señor Gale, why Hawley came to Baracoa?" he inquired suddenly. "The real reason, I mean. Did anybody send him, or did he come here of his own accord?"

It was on the tip of the reporter's tongue to tell his questioner the truth about Hawley's mission so far as he knew it, for he realized that such information was not likely to prejudice Portiforo in the prisoner's favor. But fortunately for the cause for which his rival had made such sacrifices, he did not yield to this impulse. On second thought he decided that more was to be gained by supporting the accusation that the Camera Chap was an insurrecto spy.

"Yes, I do happen to know why he came to Baracoa, Señor Presidente," he answered. "He came here of his own accord to help the revolutionists. He made no secret of his purpose in New York. He boasted to several of the men on Park Row of his friendship for that rascal Rodriguez. He said that there was going to be a revolution in Baracoa and that he was going to help things along with his camera. You are aware, of course, that he and Rodriguez left New York together and arrived here on the same boat?"

Portiforo nodded. "Yes; that significant fact naturally did not escape our notice. Still——" he paused, and a puzzled frown darkened his beefy countenance—"what you have told me is most interesting, Señor Gale," he said, leaving unspoken the thought that had been in his mind. "I am deeply indebted to you for the information you have given. It has enabled me to decide what course I shall pursue regarding that wretched young man."

"I am glad of that," said the reporter, a glint in his eyes. "You can go as far as you like with him, Señor Presidente, without any fear of angering the government of my country."

The president smiled sardonically. "It seems to me, my dear friend, that you are not exactly fond of your countryman."

"I must admit that I haven't any use for him," the other responded. "But I am not alone in my prejudice. Every self-respecting newspaper man in New York who has had dealing with the fellow feels the same way about him. We regard him as one of the black sheep of our profession."

Portiforo appeared pleased to hear this. "If that is the way your brother journalists regard him I presume that his fate will not cause a great outcry from the press which is so influential in your country?"

"Of course it won't," the newspaper man eagerly assured him. "The scamp has been mixed up in so many shady transactions that we've all been expecting to see him come to a bad end. Of course, you must expect that his own paper, the *Sentinel*, will try to stir up a fuss about him; but, then, nobody pays any attention to what that sensational sheet says or does."

Portiforo expressed surprise at this. "I had been under the impression that the New York *Sentinel* was one of the most influential journals in the United States," he said.

"You have been misinformed," Gale returned. "It has a fair-sized circulation, but its readers consist mostly of the more unintelligent classes." He leaned forward in his chair. "You can take it from me, Señor Presidente, that if that rascally camera man gets his deserts the better portion of our press will heartily approve of what you have done as soon as the facts become known. And I shall make it my business to see that the facts are known," he added significantly. "I am returning to the United States on next Wednesday's boat—my editor has sent me word that he positively cannot get along without me any longer—and when I get to New York it will give me great pleasure to combat with my pen any adverse sentiment which the *Sentinel* may try to create against your government."

"That is most kind of you, my dear Señor Gale," the president declared gratefully. "You are indeed a true friend of Baracoa. With such a distinguished journalist enlisted on the side of truth I have no fear of being misunderstood by the people of your great nation."

He slipped from one of his pudgy fingers a massive gold ring set with a huge diamond. "Since you are about to leave us," he said, handing the piece of jewelry to his visitor, "I beg you to accept this as a small token of my esteem and gratitude."

Gale left the palace well satisfied with the result of his visit. "Guess the boys on Park Row will think this is pretty poor." He chuckled, gazing at the gem which glistened on his finger with all the pleasure of a woman. But what pleased him much more than the president's valuable gift was the thought of what influence his conversation with Portiforo was likely to have upon the fate of the man whom he hated more than anybody else in the world. "I rather think I've settled Frank Hawley's hash," he told himself delightedly.

Shortly after Gale's departure from the palace, Minister Throgmorton arrived, and was closeted with the president for over an hour. The interview was at times a stormy one. It was as a result of that conference that the Camera Chap, the next morning, was visited by two men who threw open the door of his cell and bade him accompany them.

CHAPTER XXXIII.
AT THE PALACE.

Hawley believed that almost anything outrageous was possible after the terrible scene he had witnessed in the courtyard of the jail, and he accompanied his own visitors with some misgivings, which, however, he took pains to conceal from them.

"If you don't mind," he said, with well-simulated carelessness, as they invited him to enter an automobile with a closed top which was standing outside the jail, "I'd like to know where you're taking me? I'm naturally of a rather curious disposition."

"To the national palace, señor," one of the men answered. "The president sent us for you."

The prisoner's face grew grim. He thought he could guess the reason for this summons. Disappointed at Lopez's inability to get the truth about the snapshot expedition, Portiforo was going to try his own skill as a cross-examiner. The Camera Chap had no doubt that the president of Baracoa was a past master at the gentle art of administering the third degree, but he was fully resolved that if Portiforo hoped to get anything out of him he was going to be greatly disappointed.

Arriving at the palace in a decidedly belligerent mood, which was intensified by his contempt for the man of whose brutality he had just had such startling evidence, he was somewhat astonished by the graciousness with which he was received. Portiforo was seated in the audience chamber, a large room furnished in massive mahogany and hung with rich Oriental draperies. Near the president sat Minister Throgmorton, whose scowling face was in sharp contrast to the smile which illuminated the former's rubicund countenance. The only other person present was a dark-skinned young man who sat at a big writing table in the center of the room, chewing the end of a pencil, with a stenographer's notebook before him.

"So this is Señor Hawley," Portiforo began quizzically, when the Camera Chap's two guides had conducted him to a position in front of the massive, thronelike chair in which the first gentleman of Baracoa lolled. "So this is the adventurous young man whose discretion, I fear, is not always as great as his valor."

To this the prisoner did not deem it worth while to make any reply. He merely looked straight into the tyrant's beady eyes, his muscles tense, his mouth set in a straight line.

"I am always glad to gaze upon genius," Portiforo continued, without a vestige of irony in his tone, "and I am informed, Señor Hawley, that you are such a great man in your line that even the President of the United States has honored you by providing work for your camera."

Grasping the significance of this question, and conscious of the fact that the other's gaze was riveted searchingly upon his face, Hawley was keenly on his guard. "I have had the honor of photographing the President of the United States, if that is what you mean," he replied coldly.

His evident miscomprehension of the question seemed to please Portiforo.

"No; that was not quite what I meant," the latter said, after a slight pause. "However, we will let it go at that. I presume, señor," he continued, "you are wondering why I sent for you?"

The Camera Chap shrugged his shoulders.

"Perhaps you are in hopes that this summons may mean that, in spite of the seriousness of your offense, you are to receive mercy?"

"Mercy!" Hawley exclaimed, with an ironical laugh. "No, I scarcely expect that, sir—after the scene I witnessed in the prison yard this morning. I hardly think you know what mercy means."

Minister Throgmorton's scowl deepened, but the president's face did not lose its smile as he turned to the stenographer at the table, who had already started to make a record of the conversation. "I don't think you need put that down, Garcia," he said good-humoredly. "I feel confident that Señor Hawley will wish to withdraw that remark later on."

He addressed himself once more to the man before him. "I presume, señor, you refer to the execution of the traitor Bonsal. That was indeed a sad affair, and I regret that you should have been compelled to behold it. I think, however, that you are unjust in calling it an outrage. The unhappy man met only his just deserts. He was found guilty, after a fair trial, of conspiring against the government of his adopted country. His fate was the fate which all traitors must expect." His small eyes twinkled. "Perhaps, however, you will change your mind about my ignorance of the meaning of the word mercy," he said dryly, "when I tell you that, in spite of the seriousness of your own offense, I have decided to let you go free."

The Camera Chap gave a start of surprise.

"The worthy representative of your country here," Portiforo continued, with a bow in the direction of the envoy, "has been kind enough to exert his personal influence in your behalf. While he fully agrees with me that officially he has absolutely no rights in the matter—that the nature of your crime puts you outside the protection of your government and permits us to do with you as we see fit, my esteem for Señor Throgmorton is so great that I have decided to grant his request to set you free, since he has asked it of me as a personal favor to him."

The prisoner, scarcely able to believe that what he heard was true, turned with a grateful smile to the American diplomat. "This is very good of you, sir," he began.

Minister Throgmorton silenced him with a curt gesture. "You can spare me your thanks," he said, his face still maintaining its frozen expression. "I want you to understand clearly that my intercession is not prompted by any sympathy for you. On the contrary, I feel that whatever sentence the court might see fit to pass upon you would be no more than you richly deserve. I consider you, sir, a disgrace to your country and to the honorable profession which has the misfortune to number you among its members. My action in procuring your pardon is due entirely to—er—to other reasons."

The president smiled appreciatively, and his glance, wandering over to the table, noted that the official stenographer was taking down every word of this caustic speech.

"You will observe, Señor Hawley," he remarked pointedly, "that were your own countryman in my place, you could scarcely expect to receive the leniency which I am showing you. Perhaps, now, you are ready to withdraw the intemperate remark you made a little while ago about my mercy?"

The Camera Chap smiled shrewdly. "I think I had better wait until I have heard the conditions on which I am to get my release. I suppose there will be conditions?"

"The only condition," said Portiforo, frowning at this cold response, "is that you get out of this country immediately. We will give you until to-morrow. There is a boat leaving for New York in the morning. If you are caught on Baracoan soil after that—well, what you saw take place in the prison yard this morning ought to give you a graphic idea of what you will have to expect."

Hawley opened his mouth as though about to say something, but changed his mind and merely bowed.

"And I warn you that next time," said Minister Throgmorton sharply, "if you expect any help from me you are going to be disappointed."

Portiforo chuckled. "I feel confident that there isn't going to be any next time, eh, Mr. Hawley? As a man of common sense, you are no doubt fully convinced of the inadvisability of doing any more camera work in Baracoa."

"Could I stay if I were to give you my word that I wouldn't use my camera while in this country?" the snapshot adventurer inquired.

The president grinned and shook his head. "Señor Hawley is such a great camera enthusiast that we should have cause to fear that he might be tempted to forget such a promise," he said dryly. "No; greatly as I regret having to be so inhospitable, we must insist upon your leaving Baracoa."

The Camera Chap bowed. "Very well, sir; I shall sail on to-morrow's boat," he said. His air was so much like that of one who feels that he is driving a hard bargain, that Minister Throgmorton commented upon it angrily. "Anybody would think that you weren't satisfied!" he exclaimed. "You are without exception the most impertinent and ungrateful fellow I have ever met."

"I am sorry if I appear that way," Hawley responded simply. "I assure you, sir, that I am not ungrateful to you and Señor Portiforo for this unexpected clemency."

The president chuckled. "There is one other person to whom you are indebted for your good fortune," he announced dryly.

"Who is that?"

"Your brother journalist, Señor Gale. He was here yesterday to see me concerning you."

"To intercede for me?" Hawley exclaimed, scarcely able to conceal his astonishment.

Portiforo smiled. "He gave me some information concerning you which had a great influence upon me," he said vaguely. "In fact, if it had not been for the arguments he advanced, I don't think I should have decided to grant you freedom, even to oblige my dear friend Señor Throgmorton."

CHAPTER XXXIV.
BLUE SPECTACLES.

When Gale told Virginia Throgmorton that he had a cablegram from his office asking him to return to New York and report for duty immediately, the girl received the tidings with an equanimity which was not at all flattering to his pride.

"Won't you be sorry to see me go?" he queried. Although his host's pretty daughter had taken no pains to conceal her dislike for him, his egotism was so strong that he found it difficult to believe that he really was not in her good graces.

"I think I shall be able to survive the blow," Virginia answered lightly.

The reporter frowned. "You didn't feel that way about me when I first came here, Virginia," he said reproachfully. "You and I got along together famously at first. It was only when that scamp Hawley first showed his face in San Cristobal that I began to lose my pull with you."

Virginia gave him a scornful glance. "Mr. Hawley isn't a scamp," she replied indignantly. "And he didn't have anything to do with your losing your pull with me, as you term it. I had already found you out before he arrived."

"Well, it's a mystery to me why you seem to be so strong for that fellow," Gale protested, ignoring the last part of her remark. "I should think, after the trick he played you with those Felix letters, you wouldn't have any use for him."

The girl stared at him wonderingly. "Have you the effrontery to keep on claiming that Mr. Hawley stole those letters from my desk, when they appeared in your own paper!" she exclaimed.

"That's easily explained," he rejoined coolly. "He sold the letters to my paper. He didn't dare sell them to his own, for fear that if he did the crime would be traced straight to him. A fellow with as little conscience as he has wouldn't hesitate to scoop his own sheet in order to make a few dollars. If you don't think he was the thief," he added audaciously, "who do you suppose was?"

"If I wished to name the thief, I feel confident that I could do so," Virginia returned disdainfully.

Gale's expression was one of injured innocence. "From your tone, I almost think that you suspect me," he said. "That's pretty tough, Virginia—giving that crook the benefit of the doubt in preference to me. Since you persist in being so cruel," he went on plaintively, "I am almost glad to go back to New York. Without your friendship, San Cristobal is a dull burg." His eyes gleamed spitefully. "My only regret at having to leave Baracoa at this time is that I shan't be here to see that rascally Camera Chap stood up in front of a firing squad."

With this kindly remark he went out to see about booking his passage home. As he drew near the steamship office he received the greatest surprise of his life. Two men were just coming out of the place. One of them wore the uniform of a lieutenant in the United States navy. The other, who was in civilian garb, was a tall, slim young man whose pale face offered a striking contrast to his companion's ruddy countenance. Gale stared at the latter with as much amazement as if he had been gazing upon a ghost, and his surprise was not diminished when the tall man, recognizing him, came eagerly toward him with his hand outstretched and a smile upon his lips.

"I want to thank you, old man, for what you've done for me," he said warmly.

"Thank you!" the reporter couldn't help exclaiming blankly.

"I understand that it is largely to you that I owe my freedom. It was mighty white of you, Gale, to go to Portiforo on my behalf. I shan't forget it in a hurry."

Gale felt somewhat uncomfortable, suspecting that what he heard must be irony. But there was no mistaking the sincerity of the other's manner, and, as soon as he was convinced of this, the *News* man grasped the outstretched hand with well-simulated cordiality. He was greatly puzzled by this queer situation, but, possessing remarkable rallying powers, he quickly recovered his self-possession. "Don't mention it, Hawley, old fellow," he said, "I am glad to see you free. Who told you that I had a hand in getting you out?" he inquired, his manner implying that he would greatly have preferred to have his good act shrouded in anonymity.

"Portiforo told me," was the amazing answer.

"The deuce!" Gale muttered. "I can't understand why he should have told you that?"

"Isn't it true?" the other exclaimed, in an astonished tone.

The reporter smiled. "Oh, yes; it's true enough. When I heard about your being in trouble, I figured that my pull with Portiforo might do you some good, so I hiked to the palace and did my little best to give you a boost. But," he added, with a show of vexation, "I can't understand why the president should have told you of my humble efforts. He promised that he wouldn't mention it."

"I'm glad that he did," the Camera Chap said impulsively. "It was a mighty decent thing for you to do, Gale, considering that the relations between us have been—er—somewhat strained. Without meaning any offense, I'd like to know why you did it?"

The *News* man shrugged his shoulders. "After all, blood is thicker than water," he responded sentimentally. "I couldn't stand by and see a countryman of mine made a target for Baracoan bullets, when it was in my power to save him, even though that countryman hadn't acted quite fairly to me in the past. Hang it all! I flatter myself I'm big enough to do a good turn even for an enemy."

"Well, we're not going to be enemies any longer," the good-natured snapshot expert declared, once more impulsively offering his hand to his supposed benefactor, who accepted it without a qualm.

Lieutenant Ridder, who had encountered Hawley outside the national palace, and accompanied him to the steamship office, had listened to this conversation with some surprise. "Who's your friend, Frank?" he inquired with a frown, after they had left Gale. "I can't say that I'm stuck on his looks. On first impression, I'd size him up as a mighty slippery proposition. And as for owing your liberty to him, I think you're mistaken about that. I know of somebody else who deserves most of the credit."

"Who is he?" the Camera Chap demanded eagerly.

The naval officer's eyes twinkled. "It isn't a he—it's a young woman. I wonder if you could guess her name."

"Miss Throgmorton?"

"Good guess," Ridder chuckled. "Yes; it was the United States minister's daughter that did the trick for you. She forced her father to use his influence with Portiforo."

"Forced him? How do you know?"

"She told me so herself. I suppose she'd be angry with me if she knew I was telling you a word about it, but I think it only right that you should hear of her efforts in your behalf. She went to her governor and told him that if you were guilty she was guilty also, as she had assisted you to take that mysterious snapshot—she didn't tell me what it was—and that unless you were set free she was going to give herself up to the authorities as accessory before the fact. There's some class to a girl who'll go that far to help a friend."

"Some class!" Hawley repeated, a tender look in his eyes. "Say! She's the pluckiest, whitest girl I ever met."

The navy man grinned. "Well, you and she could form a mutual admiration society," he confided to his companion. "You certainly stand high with her, old man. She——"

He stopped short at a sharp exclamation from his companion. To his surprise he observed that, although his remark ought to have been of great interest to the latter, he was paying no attention to it. They were walking along the Avenida Bolivar, and the camera man's gaze was directed toward a man on the opposite side of the wide street. This man wore the uniform of an officer of the Baracoan army, and he wore spectacles of dark-blue glass.

"That's mighty queer," Ridder heard his companion mutter.

"Are you referring to the glasses?" the sailor inquired. "It is rather odd to find a fellow in the service with such weak sight. In our own army they'd retire him for disability, but I suppose anything is good enough for Baracoa. Do you know who the fellow is? He seems to know you from the way he's staring over here."

Hawley nodded. "Yes, I know him; his name is Reyes—Captain Ernesto Reyes, of the engineers. But what puzzles me is why he should be wearing those goggles. He didn't wear any glasses at all a couple of days ago."

A little later the two men parted company, Ridder announcing that he had to go back to the ship. Much as he liked him, Hawley was not sorry to be rid of him just then. He was eager to make a call at the United States legation, and as the person he hoped to see there was not Minister Throgmorton, he preferred to go alone. When he arrived at the legation, a disappointment awaited him. The old colored servant informed him that Miss Virginia was not at home.

The visitor was surprised and chagrined to hear this, as a glimpse he had caught of a pretty face at one of the upper windows apprised him that this announcement was not to be taken literally. His face lighted up, however, at some supplementary information which the servant imparted to him. "Miss Virginia is not at home now, sir," the old darky repeated with a broad grin, "but," he added in a mysterious whisper, "she's gwine out horseback ridin' this afternoon. She done tol' me to be sure and tell you that."

That afternoon, Hawley hired a mount and met his fair ally at the old trysting place. The girl had dismounted and was standing in the middle of the road talking to her steed as though he were a human being, when the

Camera Chap galloped up. She ran eagerly to meet him, both her hands outstretched and her eyes shining joyously.

"This is almost too good to be true," she cried, as he jumped from his horse. "When I heard what they did to poor Doctor Bonsal this morning, I was half crazy with fear on your account. You certainly have had a narrow escape, Mr. Hawley."

"Yes; and I understand that I owe it largely to you that I am now free," he said, his voice trembling. "I can't begin to tell you how much I——"

"Nonsense," she interrupted, a rosy tinge making itself visible beneath her fair skin. "Who told you that? It is to the President of the United States that you owe your freedom."

"The president!" the Camera Chap cried.

Virginia smiled. "Didn't my father tell you that? Well, it's the truth. He didn't tell it to me, either; but he received a code message from the White House yesterday, and he was so careless as to leave it on his desk when he went out. I suppose I ought to be very much ashamed of myself, but my curiosity forced me to work out the translation with the aid of the code book. What a very important man you must be, Mr. Hawley, to have the president so concerned about you. But tell me what happened at the palace! What did that tyrant have to say to you?"

Her companion laughed. "I must say, in justice to him, that he didn't act much like a tyrant to-day. If it hadn't been for the things we know about him, I would almost have thought from the way he treated me that he really was the genial, benevolent old gentleman he looks to be when his face is in repose."

"Did he exact any promise from you in return for your release?" the girl inquired anxiously.

"Only one. I am to leave Baracoa on to-morrow's boat."

Virginia's face clouded. "Of course, I expected that," she said, with a sigh. "Still, it's a great pity that you have to go."

Her words brought a joyous expression to Hawley's face. "Do you really care?" he asked.

"Of course I care," she answered, her color deepening; "but not on my own account—at least," she added, with sweet candor, "not wholly on my own account. I was thinking of poor President Felix. You are going to leave him to his fate? Of course, I don't blame you for going," she explained quickly, observing the hurt expression which came to his face. "It would be suicide for you to stay after what has happened, and you have already made enough sacrifices in his behalf. Still, it does seem a great pity that we can't do anything for him—that all our efforts should have been for nothing."

"Yes, it does seem a great pity," the Camera Chap agreed. "Tell me, Miss Throgmorton," he said with apparent irrelevancy, "do you happen to know what is the matter with Captain Reyes' eyes? I saw him on the Avenida Bolivar to-day, and he was wearing spectacles with thick blue lenses."

Virginia frowned, as though she resented this evident attempt on his part to change the subject. "Yes, I have seen them," she replied coldly, "I met him this morning as he was returning from the oculist. He had been complaining of weak eyes for some time, and yesterday the specialist ordered those glasses. But what has that got to do with poor President Felix?"

"Nothing, of course," Hawley answered with a queer smile. "Nothing whatever. I was merely curious about those blue spectacles."

CHAPTER XXXV.
WIRELESS WARNING.

Just as the steamship *Eldorado*, bound for New York, was about to leave her dock at Puerto Cabero, a touring car with a closed top dashed up to the wharf, and two women alighted and went aboard the ship. One of this pair, whose slender form was clad in black, wore a heavy veil which concealed her features, but Hawley, who was standing near the gangway when they arrived, gave a start of surprise. Despite the veil, he recognized the women as Señora Felix and her maid. The Camera Chap had not heard that the wife of the ex-president was to be among his fellow passengers. Later on, he learned that her departure from her native land was not a voluntary act. Her husband's successor to the presidency had sent her a curt notice the day before that the government of Baracoa expected her to sail on the *Eldorado*, and that if she saw fit to disappoint the government's expectation in this respect, she might have to stand trial on the painful charge of being in league with the government's enemies.

Although Hawley did not know at the time that the unfortunate woman was an exile, he could see from the way in which her slender form trembled that she was under stress of great emotion, and his heart was filled with sympathy for her, but although she passed close to where he was standing, he did not attempt to address her or even to salute her. He was keenly alive to the fact that he was an object of close scrutiny from several keen-eyed swarthy men who stood on the pier, and he realized the great necessity of treating the señora as a total stranger while they were looking on. But later, as the boat was passing out of the bay, and the Camera Chap stood against the rail of the promenade deck, gazing with mixed sensations at the grim, gray walls of El Torro fortress, he became suddenly aware that somebody was standing close beside him, and, turning, discovered Señora Felix.

The woman leaned over the rail, and her eyes were fixed yearningly on the fortress. She had raised her veil, and the sympathetic young man beside her could see the tears running down her haggard face. A sound as though she were choking came from her throat.

They were all alone. The rest of the passengers were on the other side of the deck absorbed in watching and waving salutes to the American battleship, which was an object of greater interest to them than the fortress. Under cover of this privacy, the Camera Chap thought there would be no harm in whispering a word of comfort to his unhappy neighbor. But, to his amazement, at the first sound of his voice, she wheeled on him with the fury of a tigress. "You!" she cried, her eyes blazing, her voice quavering with rage. "How dare you presume to address me after what you have done? Are you so lacking in shame, sir, that you would intrude upon the grief of a woman whose nearest and dearest you and your selfish government have murdered?"

"My dear señora!" the president's photographic envoy protested gently.

"Yes, murdered!" the frantic woman repeated fiercely, paying no heed to his interruption. "Your intolerable interference amounts to that. Things were bad enough before you came to Baracoa, at least, there was some hope then. But now—now——" Her voice broke, and she covered her face with her hands.

"My dear señora," the Camera Chap repeated, taking advantage of this lull in the storm of denunciation, "I regret exceedingly that you should feel so bitter toward me, for I assure you—empty as the words may sound—that I would gladly give up my life to serve you and your husband."

If the poor woman had been in a saner mood, she would have realized that the man who uttered these words had already proved the sincerity of them by the great risk he had run for her cause, but she merely laughed bitterly.

"Your life, señor!" she cried. "Such a sacrifice as that was not required of you. All that you were asked to do was to give up your selfish ambition—to go back to your heartless president and tell him that the life of a noble man and a woman's broken heart were far more important in your eyes than a laurel for your own brow and a diplomatic triumph for your government. But you refused to listen to the pleadings of a devoted wife. You persisted in going ahead with your ruthless, blundering plans, not caring what might happen to your victim so long as you could boast to the world of your wonderful snapshot achievement."

Hawley saw that there was no use in trying to defend himself by pointing out to her that he had not made his unsuccessful attempt until he had been led to believe, from his conversation with the commander of the United States battleship, that the captive of El Torro would be protected after the snapshot had been taken, and that, moreover, it was the information which had come to him concerning the precarious condition of General Replife's health which had caused him to decide that desperate measures were absolutely necessary. In her present mood, he realized, such argument would have been useless. Besides, his thought was not to defend himself against her bitter accusations. Big-hearted chap that he was, his sole desire was to comfort her, if that were possible.

"Tell me, señora," he begged, after an anxious glance at the group of passengers crowded against the opposite rail, "do you know definitely that anything has happened to President Felix, or are you merely giving expression to your apprehensions?"

Again she laughed bitterly. "Is it not to be taken for granted that the consequence of your mad act of the other night would be the assassination of my husband? Do you suppose for a minute that those ruffians would let him live now that they are aware that their secret is known?"

"But you do not know of his death?" the Camera Chap persisted. "You have not actually heard that they have done what you fear?"

She shook her head. "No, I have not heard," she said wearily. "It is scarcely to be supposed that they would proclaim their crime to the whole world. Assassins are not in the habit of advertising their deeds, señor."

Her reply relieved him of a great fear which her previous utterances had created in his mind. "Let us hope that your anxiety is groundless," he said soothingly. "I suppose, señora, you have heard the good news from the hospital. It was announced to-day that the condition of the minister of war is much improved. He surprised the surgeons by rallying when they thought there was no hope, and now they say that he is practically out of danger. And Replife's life means President Felix's life. Now that Portiforo knows that Replife is going to live, he will not dare resort to assassination."

The woman refused to be comforted by these arguments. "Who can tell how far that tyrant will dare to go, now that you have opened his eyes to the fact that the conspiracy is known?" she asked despairingly. Then she went below, and Hawley did not see her again for the rest of the voyage, for she kept to her stateroom, even having her meals served there. But the next morning her maid handed him a note, the pathetic contents of which afforded him much satisfaction:

"Please forgive me for my unkindness of yesterday. The sight of that terrible building, so long the tomb of that poor, noble martyr, made me beside myself. In my calmer moments I realized that I might have done you an injustice. I believe that you are brave and generous, and that possibly what you did you may have thought was for the best. For the risks that you have run and the sacrifices that you have made I am not ungrateful; and if, as I cannot help fearing, terrible consequences to me and mine have been the result of your gallant if indiscreet attempt, you have my forgiveness, señor."

"Poor little woman," said the Camera Chap to himself, as he finished reading this message of forgiveness. "If only——" His thought was interrupted by a hand laid on his shoulder. Turning hastily, he looked into Gale's grinning countenance.

"A love letter?" the reporter inquired banteringly, pointing to the note.

"Not exactly," Hawley replied with a laugh, hastily thrusting the missive into his pocket.

"Seemed to me that it was a lady's handwriting," the *News* man remarked.

The Camera Chap frowned. "How do you know that?" he demanded indignantly. "Did you dare look——" Then he abruptly cut himself short, resolved not to quarrel with the man to whom, he believed, he partly owed his freedom, and possibly his life.

"I couldn't help noticing the handwriting as I accidentally glanced over your shoulder," Gale explained.

"You didn't read the letter, did you?" Hawley inquired. His tone was anxious, for he had not heard the reporter step up behind him, and, consequently, had no way of knowing how long he had been there.

"Certainly not," Gale replied in an aggrieved tone. "Don't you give me credit for having any breeding?"

Except for this slightly unpleasant incident, Gale and the Camera Chap got along well together until the *Eldorado* stopped at San Juan, Porto Rico. There the *News* man made a queer discovery. When the vessel weighed anchor and started out for her trip to New York, Hawley was not on board. He had gone ashore, explaining that he desired to make a purchase, and had mysteriously disappeared.

When the ship's officers and the other passengers learned of this disappearance, they were inclined to believe that the snapshot man's failure to show up was entirely accidental. But Gale, evidently, was not of that opinion, for, with a malicious smile on his face, he hurried to the wireless room and sent off a dispatch. The message was addressed: "Portiforo, National Palace, San Cristobal," and ran as follows:

"Hawley missing at San Juan. Have reason to believe he is on his way back to Baracoa. Look out for him.

"GALE."

After sending this warning to the sly fox at Baracoa he felt more cheerful. He had not a desire in the world to help the president of the little southern republic in any way; it was entirely his own satisfaction that was to be furthered by his actions.

CHAPTER XXXVI.
A WELCOME INTRUSION.

The day after Hawley's departure from Baracoa, Lieutenant Ridder called at the United States legation with a message from the commander of the *Kearsarge* to Minister Throgmorton. On his way out, he encountered Virginia, and eagerly availed himself of the opportunity to renew his acquaintance with that captivating young woman.

The naval officer was flattered by the cordiality which she displayed toward him, but was astonished and concerned to observe that when he mentioned the name of his friend Hawley a frown came to her face and she hurriedly changed the subject, as though it were distasteful to her. He went back to his ship wondering what could have happened to bring about this change in her sentiments toward the man for whom she had previously manifested such warm regard. If Virginia had been asked to explain why she was displeased with the Camera Chap, she probably would have found difficulty in stating her grievance against him. As she had told him, she could not with logic or justice blame him for going away, knowing what would happen to him if he ventured to remain on Baracoan soil. Yet she was disappointed in him, and his departure had aroused within her a feeling of resentment.

Possibly it was because he had appeared to accept the situation with such irritating cheerfulness, or it may have been that she had formed such an exalted opinion of his heroic qualities that she had half expected— unreasonable though she knew such expectation to be—that, at the last moment, he would defy Portiforo and his order of banishment and not leave Baracoa without making one more attempt to rescue the unfortunate prisoner of El Torro.

If Lieutenant Ridder had been a less loyal and unselfish friend, he might have sought to take advantage of Virginia's changed attitude toward the snapshot man and her evident liking for himself; for the daughter of the United States envoy had made such a great impression on him at their first meeting that he couldn't help feeling envious of Hawley's good luck. Not being at all the kind of fellow to seek to "butt in" on an absent friend's romance, however, he made it a point to steer clear of the embassy, and when, several days later, a tinted, perfumed note was handed to him by an orderly on the battleship, a frown came to his face as he read its contents. The note was from Miss Throgmorton, and it ran as follows:

"My Dear Mr. Ridder: I am wondering why I have not seen you lately. Are they keeping you a prisoner on the ship? If not, and it is possible for you to come ashore this afternoon, I should like very much to have a talk with you.

"I am going for a ride into the country, after luncheon. If you could find it convenient to meet me, then come to San Cristobal, and be at the northern gate of the Botanical Gardens, between one and two o'clock. You will find an old colored man waiting there. He will provide you with a mount and conduct you to a place where we can talk without danger of being spied upon. I hope you won't think me too unconventional in writing to you like this, but I positively must see you on a matter of life and death."

At first his almost quixotic sense of fairness caused him to decide that he would send some excuse for not keeping this appointment, for he suspected that the last paragraph of the note must be more or less of an exaggeration; but presently he reproached himself for his lack of gallantry. He felt sure that Miss Throgmorton was too nice a girl to have urged such an unconventional meeting unless the circumstances justified it.

Promptly at one o'clock that afternoon, he arrived at the northern gate of the Botanical Gardens, and was met by old Uncle Peter, who conducted him to a near-by stable where two horses, already saddled, were waiting for them. Half an hour later, as they galloped along a desolate stretch of dusty road, the navy man caught sight of a girl on a pony coming toward them, and his pulses quickened as he recognized the trim, graceful figure.

"I suppose you are just burning with curiosity as to why I have sent for you," Virginia said, with a smile, as they dismounted.

"Anxiety would be a better word," he answered. "The tone of your note was so alarming that it is a great relief to me to find that you can still smile."

The girl sighed. "I suppose I have no right to smile," she said sadly, "for I really am in great trouble."

"What is it?" he demanded eagerly. "If I can help, Miss Throgmorton, you know you can count on me."

"Yes, I know that I can," she answered softly. "That is why I have sent for you. I—but we had better not talk here. We will go to the top of this hill. We shall be more safe up there."

Leaving Uncle Peter in charge of their horses, they climbed the hillock, and Virginia invited her companion to seat himself beside her on a bowlder, under the feathery branches of a bamboo tree. "This is where—er—Mr. Hawley and I always met when we had secrets to discuss," she announced.

"It commands a view of the road in both directions, so there is no danger of anybody creeping up on us unseen."

With an excess of caution which made him smile, she gazed up into the branches of the solitary tree under which they were sitting. Then she continued, lowering her voice almost to a whisper: "I am going to begin, Mr. Ridder, by telling you what picture it was that Mr. Hawley and I were trying to take at the fortress the other night."

"Is it necessary that I should know?" he asked. He felt somewhat uncomfortable, for he could not help suspecting that it might be her evident pique against the Camera Chap which prompted her to give him the information, which, until now, neither she nor Hawley had seen fit to confide to him.

"If Mr. Hawley knew what I am doing," the girl said, as though reading his thoughts, "I feel sure that he would approve, for he couldn't be unreasonable enough to expect that just because he has given up the task of freeing poor President Felix, nothing else is to be done."

"Freeing President Felix?" the naval officer repeated, looking at her in bewilderment.

The girl nodded. "It was his picture that we were trying to get the other night. It was to rescue him that Mr. Hawley came to Baracoa. And now that he has gone, and Señora Felix has gone, and they have done away with poor Doctor Bonsal, there is nobody left but me to fight for the freedom of that unhappy man. But I can't do it alone," she added wistfully. "I am only a girl, and I realize my helplessness. I've got to have assistance, and that is why I have decided to take you into the secret. I know that you are brave, and generous, and trustworthy, Mr. Ridder."

The navy man bowed. "I am sure, at least, that you will find me trustworthy," he said simply. "If you really think it best for me to know, I shall be glad to hear the facts of the case, Miss Throgmorton, and to give you any help that I can."

Thereupon Virginia proceeded to tell him the tragic story of the missing president of Baracoa, and when she had finished, the lieutenant's face was very grim.

"It is the most amazing story I ever heard!" he declared. "It fairly makes my blood boil to think of that poor fellow being caged up there in the fortress with a battleship flying the Stars and Stripes less than half a mile away. But he's not going to be there much longer," he added, a determined expression coming to his strong face. "You're quite right, Miss Throgmorton, we've got to set him free. If you'll permit me, I'll speak to the captain about it as soon as I get back to the ship. I'll tell him the story, and———"

Virginia cut him short with a gesture of disapproval. "No, you mustn't do that. What I have told you is in the strictest confidence. If I thought that any good would come of it, I would have gone to Captain Cortrell myself, long before this. But I know that he would take no action in the matter. You know how he acted in the case of Mr. Hawley. And if he couldn't see his way to do anything for an American citizen, we can be sure he wouldn't interfere to help a man who has no claims on our government."

"I think you do him an injustice," her companion protested, resenting the somewhat bitter tone in which she spoke of his commanding officer. "There isn't a better-hearted or braver officer in the service than our old man. But, of course, he isn't always free to do what he'd like to do. The commanding officer of a battleship has got to think of pleasing Washington, D. C., before he can think of pleasing himself. How about your father, Miss Throgmorton? Surely the American minister wouldn't stand for such a conspiracy?"

Virginia sighed. "My father refuses to believe that there is any such conspiracy," she said. "Knowing how favorably disposed father was toward that tyrant Portiforo, I have always realized the futility of trying to enlist him in our cause. But yesterday," she added with a frown, "it occurred to me that, after all, it was worth trying. I was desperate, and saw no other way of helping poor President Felix. So I went to my father and told him my story. He laughed at me and told me that I was suffering from hallucinations, and when I insisted, he became very angry and forbade me ever to mention the subject to him or to anybody else again."

A puzzled expression came to the naval officer's face. "That's queer," he muttered under his breath.

"No, Mr. Ridder," Virginia continued, "we can't hope for any help from either Captain Cortrell or my father. We've got to handle this thing ourselves."

"But what can we do?"

Virginia looked at him reproachfully. "The other day, when your friend Mr. Hawley was locked up, you were ready to go to the jail and attempt a rescue by force," she reminded him. "Wouldn't you do as much for this unhappy man?"

The lieutenant hesitated. "If I were sure that such an attempt would be successful, I wouldn't mind tackling it," he said. "But if I were to fail, Miss

Throgmorton, you must realize what it would mean. There'd be the deuce to pay in Washington, and——"

"You didn't think of that when Mr. Hawley was in danger," Virginia protested indignantly. "You were quite ready to risk your career in the navy, and possibly your life, then."

"But Hawley was my friend, and I was under great obligations to him, besides."

"Does that make such a great difference?" the girl inquired somewhat coldly. "Are you willing to remain inactive while an innocent man is suffering a fate worse than death? Do you not feel an obligation to expose the villainy of these rascals? If so, I must say that I am disappointed in you, Mr. Ridder."

For a few seconds the lieutenant remained silent. Then suddenly his face lighted up. "You are right, Miss Throgmorton," he said, "I can't leave Baracoa without making an attempt to set Felix free. I don't know how we'll go about it, but we'll find a way—you and I together." He jumped to his feet, and, shading his eyes with his hand, looked toward the point in the road where Uncle Peter was waiting with the horses.

"Hello!" he exclaimed. "Who's that talking with your colored man? Looks like a tramp."

"More likely a spy," Virginia remarked, frowning. "I quite expected that I would be followed. Well, of all the audacity! Look! He's actually coming up to us."

Sure enough, the stranger, having exchanged a few words with the old darky, was climbing up the hill toward them, walking with the shambling gait of a native mendicant. He was a dark-haired, swarthy man, apparently past middle age. He was tall, but his figure was so bent that he appeared to be undersized. There was a five days' growth of hair on his chin, his clothing was in rags, and his feet were bare. Altogether, he was by no means a prepossessing person.

"A thousand pardons, señor, for this intrusion," he whined, addressing Ridder in Spanish, "but if you would earn the undying gratitude of a starving wretch, you can do so by separating yourself from a few cents. American money will do."

"Go away," the navy man growled. He spoke with unwonted roughness, which was due in part to Virginia's suspicion that the intruder was probably a spy, and partly to the fact that although the lieutenant's knowledge of Spanish was limited, he was sufficiently familiar with that language to realize the insolence with which the beggar spoke. *"Onda pronto!"* he exclaimed, with a threatening gesture.

He was startled by a cry from Virginia—a cry of mingled astonishment and joy. "Mr. Hawley!" the girl exclaimed with a half-hysterical laugh.

"Hawley!" Ridder exclaimed staring incredulously at the human scarecrow. "Well, I'll be hanged if it isn't!"

For a few seconds the ragged mendicant appeared bewildered. He stared blankly at the couple. Then suddenly a broad grin appeared on his swarthy countenance. "This is a bitter disappointment," he declared ruefully. "I had been hoping that this get-up of mine was good enough to deceive even your sharp eyes, Miss Throgmorton."

CHAPTER XXXVII.
A NEW PLAN.

"So you have come back!" said Virginia, her face radiant, a thrill of admiration in her voice.

"Of course," the Camera Chap said simply. "Did you think that I wouldn't? Surely you didn't think me capable of being such a wretched quitter?"

The girl's face showed her remorse. "Forgive me," she said. "Of course, I ought to have known that even so great a risk couldn't keep you away. But you really should not have done it," she protested, with a contrariness which amused Ridder. "You are taking your life in your hands. If any of Portiforo's spies should recognize you——"

"I am in hopes that the eyes of Portiforo's spies won't be as sharp as yours," said the president's photographic envoy, shrugging his shoulders. "It seems to me that this disguise is pretty good."

"It is splendid!" Virginia declared. "And your mannerisms, too. I had no idea that you were such an accomplished actor. I can't explain how I knew it was you—certainly there was nothing about you to give you away. I guess it must have been my instinct which told me," she added, with a blush.

"I must admit you had me completely fooled, old man," declared Ridder, with a grin. "It's a wonderful make-up." He looked his friend over from head to foot and laughed. "Ye gods, you certainly are some spectacle!"

Hawley's face reflected his grin. "Talking about spectacles," he said, "how's our friend, Captain Reyes? Can either of you tell me whether he's still wearing those blue goggles?"

"He was wearing them as late as this morning," Virginia informed him, with a gleam of comprehension of the Camera Chap's apparently irrelevant interest in the eyesight of the custodian of President Felix. "I met him to-day on the Avenida Juarez, and he told me that his eyes were giving him a lot of trouble, but are greatly improved since he has worn the glasses. The specialist has ordered him to wear them both night and day."

"Night and day!" the snapshot adventurer echoed joyously. "That's better than I dared hope for. Of course, I ought to be ashamed of myself for gloating over another man's misfortune, but I can't help regarding this as a gift from the gods. But tell me," he added, a shade of anxiety flitting across his face, "is Reyes still at the fortress, or have they put him on the sick list?"

"He is still on duty," Virginia announced. "I asked him, this morning, why he didn't lay off until his eyes were better, and he told me that his superiors had urged him to do so, but that he had insisted that he was capable of attending to his duties, and that they had let him have his way in the matter."

Hawley exhaled a deep breath of relief. "Now I know that we're going to win out," he chuckled. "Fortune wouldn't have put so many things our way if she weren't on our side."

"But what do you expect to gain by those blue spectacles?" Lieutenant Ridder demanded. "I can't see how they're going to help us free Felix."

The Camera Chap gave a start of surprise, and turned, with an inquiring glance, to Virginia.

"I—I felt that I had to tell him," the latter stammered contritely. "I thought—I didn't know that you were coming back, and it was necessary to have somebody to help me."

"That's all right, Miss Throgmorton," Hawley assured her. "I'm glad Ridder's been initiated into the order. If you hadn't told him, I should have done so myself. For in order to put through the little scheme I have in mind, old man," he announced, addressing the lieutenant, "I shall need your help."

"I shall be glad to do whatever I can," Ridder replied. "The story which Miss Throgmorton has told me about Felix has got me so agitated that I'm ready to go the limit in order to help free him."

"What I want you to do," said Hawley, "is to make arrangements for a dinner to be held on board the *Kearsarge*."

"A dinner?"

"A banquet to be given by the officers of the visiting battleship to the officers of the fortress," the snapshot adventurer explained. "I believe such affairs are not unusual?"

"Generally it is the other way around—the other fellows wine and dine us first, and then we return the compliment," the navy man said. "However, I guess I won't have any difficulty in persuading the captain to reverse the usual order of things in this case. But what's the idea? Is this dinner part of your scheme for rescuing Felix?"

"A very important part of it," the Camera Chap informed him. "If you can bring it about and manage to have our friend of the blue glasses among those present, I have every hope of success. I'll outline the idea to you. I am confident that you'll both be as enthusiastic over it as I am."

But, greatly to his surprise, when he told them what he had in mind, they failed to display the amount of enthusiasm which he had expected.

"It would be sheer madness for you to attempt such a desperate thing," was Virginia's verdict. "You would surely be caught. Anxious as I am to see President Felix set free, I must beg you to give up all thought of carrying out this plan, Mr. Hawley."

"It's a clever scheme," declared Ridder. "I take off my hat to you, old man, for your ingenuity in having thought of it, and your grit in being willing to put it through; but I agree with Miss Throgmorton that it is much too risky a proposition. You might stand a slim chance of getting the picture, but you'd stand a much greater chance of being backed up against an adobe wall with a firing squad using you for target practice. Besides, it isn't fair that you should do the whole thing all by yourself. Now that you've taken me into the secret, we ought to divide up the work and the danger."

The Camera Chap smiled. "There'll be work and danger enough for you, too," he promised. "If I'm caught and it comes out that you were mixed up in the plot—and I'm afraid that's bound to come out—I can see a peck of trouble coming your way. Portiforo will probably demand your surrender as accessory, and even if your skipper refuses to give you up, there'll probably be a court-martial in Washington in store for you, and possibly dismissal from the service. All this, of course, is to be dreaded only in the event of failure. But I'm not going to fail. I disagree with you both about my scheme not being practical. Of course, if we had to go up against a well-organized, highly disciplined garrison, I'd have to admit that our chances of success were scant. But Portiforo's army is a joke. Those soldiers at the fortress remind me of a lot of supes in a comic-opera chorus. With a crowd like that to deal with, it would be possible to get away with almost anything. If Felix is still in the same cell—if they haven't moved him—it's going to be mere child's play to get the snapshot and make my escape—much easier than our other attempt, Miss Throgmorton."

"But if they have moved him?" Virginia suggested fearfully. "And it is very likely that they have. It is only reasonable to suppose that after our last attempt, those scoundrels would have taken that precaution. If they have him locked up in another dungeon—one that cannot be reached from the outside—what are you going to do then?"

He shrugged his shoulders. "In that event," he replied carelessly, "my job is going to be a little more difficult, of course. I shall have to go inside the fortress and hunt around until I find him. But let's be optimistic."

Although they still demurred at the project, they failed to dampen his ardor or persuade him to give it up.

CHAPTER XXXVIII.
LIKE A BAD PENNY.

When Virginia returned to the embassy, an unpleasant surprise awaited her in the form of a good-looking, dapper young man who greeted her with a sardonic grin.

"Hardly expected to see me back again, I suppose?" he remarked quizzically.

"I certainly did not," the girl replied coldly. "I supposed that you were in New York by this time, Mr. Gale."

"I changed my mind just after the boat sailed out of San Juan harbor, and went ashore in the pilot boat," the reporter informed her. "There were certain reasons why I deemed it advisable to return to Baracoa, so I cabled the office that they'd have to struggle along without me for a little while longer, and caught the next boat back to Puerto Cabero." He chuckled. "I rather thought you'd be astonished to see me, Virginia. Almost as astonished, I'll wager, as you were to see our friend Hawley come back again."

The girl gave an involuntary start of surprise, and her face paled. "Then you——" she began, but caught herself quickly. "Mr. Hawley back again!" she exclaimed, with an air of incredulity which was well simulated. "Surely that can't be possible!"

Gale smiled triumphantly. The sentence which she had left uncompleted and her momentary agitation had not escaped his notice. "Yes, he's back," he said, with sarcasm. "Didn't you know that? I had an idea that you might have seen him."

"Surely you wouldn't expect him to show his face in San Cristobal, considering the circumstances under which he left," the girl returned, her blue eyes boldly meeting his searching gaze.

"Perhaps not," Gale rejoined, after a slight pause, during which he did some rapid thinking. "Perhaps I was wrong in assuming that he has returned to Baracoa at all. He disappeared from the ship at San Juan, and I had an idea that he might have come back here."

"Is that why you returned, too?" Virginia demanded scornfully. "Were you lured back by the hope of finding him in Portiforo's clutches again, and being able to gloat over his fate?"

"Certainly not," the reporter answered emphatically. "I'm not bothering about Hawley at all. I came back here on a matter of business."

Part of his statement was the truth. It was not merely malice which had caused the man to postpone his return to New York and hurry back to San Cristobal as soon as he had discovered that Hawley was missing from the steamer. He had a professional reason for taking this step. He decided that he might have acted somewhat rashly in notifying his office that there was nothing in the weird rumors concerning Felix's incarceration in El Torro fortress. A certain note which the wife of the missing president of Baracoa had written to the Camera Chap, part of which he had managed to read over the latter's shoulder, on the promenade deck of the steamship, had opened the reporter's eyes to the possibility that he might have made a big mistake. He concluded that he had better seek to rectify that mistake by returning to Baracoa and making another attempt to get at the facts concerning Felix.

"I am sorry to find that you took me seriously the other day when we had that talk concerning Hawley," he said to Virginia. "I don't really wish the fellow any harm. He and I are good friends, now—I suppose he's told you of the large part I had in getting him set free—and I should regret exceedingly seeing him in trouble again. I am glad to learn that he hasn't shown up in San Cristobal. I was afraid that he might have shipped from San Juan in a tramp steamer headed this way. But, as you say, it is scarcely likely that he would have done such a rash thing."

He spoke without the slightest tinge of irony in his tone. It had suddenly occurred to him that it would be a good idea to give his host's daughter the impression this his suspicions were lulled. More was to be gained, he decided, by watching her closely for the next few days than by endeavoring to bluff her into an admission that she knew of the Camera Chap's return to Baracoa and the reason thereof. That Hawley had returned to Baracoa he now felt quite sure. Virginia's demeanor had confirmed what, until then, had been merely a suspicion on his part. And that the snapshot adventurer's motive in coming back was to have another try at getting Felix's picture, Gale was equally certain. For the next three days he proceeded to carry out his plan of keeping a close watch on his host's daughter. He felt sure that sooner or later she would communicate in some way with the Camera Chap. Probably they were hatching out some scheme together for landing the precious snapshot. If so, by watching the fruition of that scheme, he hoped at least to gain some valuable information as to the whereabouts of Felix. Perhaps, even, if he played his cards right, he might be able to force Hawley to share the picture with him, in the event of the latter's success. A still more alluring prospect was the possibility of letting that expert snapshotter get the picture, and then, by working some clever trick, getting it away from him so that he could hand to his paper one of the greatest photographic scoops which had ever startled Park Row. Difficult as he realized this last feat would be, the *News* man did not consider it impossible of fulfillment.

He subjected Virginia to an espionage which would have done credit to one of Portiforo's professional spies, shrewdly suspecting that she was the keystone to the whole situation. But if the girl was in communication with the Camera Chap she was managing it with a skill and cautiousness which outclassed his keen powers of observation; for he was unable to detect even any indication that she had knowledge of Hawley's whereabouts. One discovery he did make, though: she seemed to have grown very friendly with a certain good-looking, husky young officer of the battleship *Kearsarge*. Gale learned that this man's name was Ridder. He and Virginia met frequently and with a secretiveness which made the reporter wonder whether the daughter of his host hadn't already forgotten all about Hawley and was going through the early stages of a new romance. Strange to say, it did not occur to Gale that the naval officer might be acting as an intermediary between Virginia and the exiled snapshotter. He began to feel less positive that the latter had returned to Baracoa. At all events, he was pretty sure that the Camera Chap hadn't ventured to show his face in the capital or its environs, for he had reason to believe that Portiforo's spies were keeping a sharp lookout for that unwelcome visitor, and if he had been there it was scarcely likely that those human ferrets wouldn't have unearthed him by this time.

Having come to this conclusion, the reporter gradually ceased his close watch of Virginia's movements, and spent most of his time in Puerto Cabero, cultivating the acquaintance of the soldiers of the fortress, particularly that of Captain Ernesto Reyes. He managed to persuade the latter to take him on another tour of inspection through the prison of El Torro, but was unable to find any trace of Felix there.

One day, as he sat drinking with Reyes in a café much frequented by officers of the army, the captain asked him whether he had received an invitation to the banquet on the warship.

"What banquet is that?" Gale inquired curiously.

Captain Reyes produced a card on which was engraved a formal invitation requesting his presence at a dinner to be tendered by the officers of the *Kearsarge* to the officers of El Torro garrison.

"I supposed that surely you would receive an invitation, Señor Gale," the army officer remarked. "The American minister and Miss Throgmorton are going to be there, so it is queer that you should have been overlooked."

"Maybe mine will arrive later," the reporter said. "Are you going to attend?"

The other announced that he expected to be among those present. "I was going to send my regrets at first, on account of my eyesight," he declared. "I was afraid that with these glasses I should not be exactly an ornament at the festive board, and in such a well-lighted room I would not dare to leave them off. But Miss Throgmorton insisted upon my accepting the invitation."

"Miss Throgmorton?" There was an inflection of surprise in Gale's tone.

The gallant captain smiled complacently. "She told me that it would spoil the whole evening for her if I were not present. So what could I do, my friend? Of course, as a gentleman and a soldier, I could not disappoint a lady—especially one so charming as the daughter of the American minister."

Gale looked thoughtfully at his wine. "I wonder why she should be so anxious to have you there," he muttered. "It strikes me as being deucedly queer."

His companion's manner showed that he resented the remark. "I see nothing so very queer about it," he said indignantly. "I do not wish to appear boastful. Otherwise, perhaps, it would not be difficult for me to explain why Miss Throgmorton finds such evident pleasure in my society."

CHAPTER XXXIX.
CAUSE FOR ANXIETY.

When Gale returned to the embassy he found an invitation to the dinner awaiting him. Minister Throgmorton had mentioned to Captain Cortrell that he had a guest stopping at his home, and the commander of the warship had been prompt to take the hint. The reporter accepted the invitation with alacrity. As a rule, he was not fond of formal dinners. In the course of his reportorial experience he had attended many of them in an official capacity, and he had come to regard such functions as decidedly boresome. The solid and liquid refreshments were, in his opinion, but poor compensation for the ordeal of having to listen to the long-winded, dry speeches which always came afterward. But he expected to find much to interest him at this dinner on the battleship. What his friend Captain Reyes had told him made him so eager to attend that even if he had not received an invitation he had fully decided that he was going to find some way of being present.

Virginia's behavior increased his suspicion that there was a peculiar significance attached to the affair. The girl appeared strangely anxious and ill at ease. If she had been a débutante looking forward to her first formal party, she could scarcely have evinced more nervousness and considering that, because of her father's position, such festivities were common occurrences in her life, her state of mind struck the observant newspaper man as being somewhat remarkable.

A conversation which he overheard between the girl and Lieutenant Ridder a day before the event enlightened him to some extent as to the cause of Virginia's anxiety. The naval officer had called at the legation, and, on his way out through the garden, he stopped to exchange a few words with her.

"Everything is coming along fine," he informed her, unaware, of course, that the *News* man, concealed behind some shrubbery, was listening with intense eagerness. "The more I think about the scheme, the more I begin to believe that it is going to work out all right."

"But suppose Reyes should, at the last minute, change his mind and fail to show up?" Virginia suggested timorously. "That would spoil everything."

"Yes; that would spoil everything—for the time being," Ridder agreed. "We should have to postpone the attempt. But why should we suppose anything so gloomy, my dear Miss Throgmorton? He has accepted the invitation, and he has assured you that he will be there." A smile lighted up his face.

"If you want to make absolutely sure that he won't disappoint us, why don't you ask him to call for you and escort you to the dinner? If he has any blood in his veins, he would jump at such an opportunity, and once he's made the engagement he couldn't be so unchivalrous as to back out."

Virginia received this suggestion with an ejaculation of delight. "If he escorted me to the dinner, it would be his duty, of course, to see me home, also," she murmured, talking more to herself than to her companion. "That is a splendid idea of yours, Mr. Ridder—probably even a better one than you supposed. It has given me a big inspiration. I see a way, now, to change our original plans so as to reduce the danger of accidents to a minimum."

"What is it?" the naval officer demanded eagerly.

To the eavesdropper's keen disappointment, the pair walked away from that spot before the girl answered, so he was unable to learn the nature of the inspiration which had come to her. However, incomplete and puzzling though it was, he felt that he had good cause to congratulate himself on the information he had already gleaned.

The next morning, Virginia sent a charmingly worded note to Captain Reyes, and, as Ridder had expected, the Baracoan was much flattered by this fresh proof of Miss Throgmorton's favor, and eagerly grabbed at the opportunity which her note offered him to be her companion on the trip from the capital to the warship.

Moreover, he triumphantly exhibited the note to his friend Gale, later that day, as a proof of his intimacy with the fair daughter of the United States envoy.

The reporter smiled sardonically as he read the dainty missive. "Doesn't it strike you as the least bit odd, my dear Ernesto, that Miss Throgmorton should put you to the trouble of coming all the way from the fortress to the embassy to call for her when she has both her father and myself to escort her?" he suggested.

Reyes laughed quizzically. "Ah, my unfortunate friend, I cannot blame you for being jealous!" he exclaimed.

Gale shrugged his shoulders, but let the taunt pass without verbal comment. He had suddenly changed his mind as to the advisability of striving to make the army officer see the matter from his viewpoint. The thought had come to him that, after all, it would be better not to interfere with Virginia's mysterious plans at the present stage of the game. It would be time enough to open Reyes' eyes when the situation had taken more definite shape.

Resplendent in gold lace and gilt buttons, the Baracoan called at the embassy that evening, so late that he found Virginia on the verge of tears. Her father and Gale had left for the battleship nearly an hour earlier, and ever since then she had been almost frantic with impatience and fear that her escort was not going to show up at all. She received his apologies graciously, however, as they motored swiftly down the steep roads which led to Puerto Cabero. Not for all the world would he have been guilty of such a sad breach of decorum, her penitent companion assured her, if it had not been absolutely unavoidable. His duties at the fortress had made it impossible for him to get away earlier.

"In fact, my dear señorita," he announced, "if I had not made this engagement with you—which, of course, could not be broken under any circumstances—I fear I should have had to disappoint our hosts this evening and remain on duty at the fortress. On account of our latest advices regarding the enemy, our commanding officer did not deem it advisable that so many of his staff should absent themselves from the fortress at one time. Half of us were asked at the last minute to send our regrets to the *Kearsarge* and remain on duty, and, at first, I was among those selected to stay behind; but when I had explained to the general about my appointment with you, he agreed with me that I must go."

"Then I am very glad that I asked you to be my escort," Virginia declared with a fervor which went to his head like a strong wine. "But what do you mean by advices regarding the enemy? To what enemy do you refer?" she inquired nervously.

He looked at her in astonishment. "To the revolutionists, of course, señorita. That traitor Rodriguez and his band of ruffians have proven somewhat stronger than we had imagined. To-day they overcame a detachment of Federal troops at Santa Barbara and seized the railroad. It is believed that, emboldened by their success, the beggars are now contemplating a forced march on the capital."

"But surely you do not fear an attack upon the fortress to-night?" Virginia inquired, her voice tense with anxiety.

Her companion laughed contemptuously. "Certainly not. There is no occasion for alarm, señorita. Those fellows will never get within a hundred miles of the capital. When they get up against Villaria's brigade they will be annihilated. Still, it would be bad generalship not to be prepared. I believe you have a saying in your language about eternal vigilance being the guarantee of safety. That is why our garrison has been placed on a strictly war basis and half of our staff has found it impossible to be the guests of the American officers this evening."

What he had said caused Virginia to feel uneasy, but she made a valiant attempt to conceal her state of mind from him. "I am glad to hear that the fortress is in no danger—from the insurrectos," she said, and her escort was astonished at the emphasis with which she spoke.

He favored her with a searching glance from behind his blue spectacles. From her past actions, he had good reason to believe that she was in sympathy with the enemies of the Portiforo administration. He did not feel any great bitterness toward her on that account. The fact that she was a woman, and a very pretty one, made him inclined to view her past offenses with indulgence. But it chafed him to hear her now expressing views, which, he was compelled to believe, could not be sincere.

"You do not desire the revolutionary cause to triumph, señorita?" he inquired, a strain of irony in his tone.

Virginia shrugged her shoulders. "To be quite frank with you, I don't care whether they triumph or not. It is all the same to me which side wins," she replied carelessly.

"Then why are you so glad that the fortress is in no danger of attack?"

"Because," she answered serenely, "if the insurrectos were to be so inconsiderate as to attack El Torro to-night, I fear it would interfere with our dinner."

Reyes laughed heartily. "Oh, is that the reason? Well, have no fear, my dear Señorita Throgmorton. I assure you that there is not the slightest danger of our appetites being spoiled by any such interruption."

A little later they arrived at the seaport, and, alighting from the car, entered one of the battleship's launches which was waiting at the landing for them. As they stepped to the deck of the *Kearsarge*, Lieutenant Ridder greeted them. That young officer's face, which, a minute before, had worn a strained, worried expression, was now illuminated by a broad smile. "I'm glad to see you," he said to the girl. "I was beginning to be afraid that you weren't coming."

She smiled in a manner which showed that she appreciated the fact that, while to others his words might have sounded like a compliment, they were intended to be congratulatory. But a second later the smile disappeared from her lips. She glanced furtively at Reyes, and saw that he was occupied at the moment, chatting with one of the ship's officers, and she eagerly availed herself of this opportunity for a few confidential words with Ridder.

"There is danger," she whispered. "I am afraid we must give up the idea. I have just learned that they are very much on their guard at the fortress. They are awaiting a possible attack of the revolutionists, and the whole garrison is unusually wide awake. Under the circumstances it would be madness to go ahead to-night. Tell Mr. Hawley——"

The naval officer interrupted her with a deprecatory gesture. "It is no use," he whispered. "I have already told him. I knew about the danger. Half our guests have sent their regrets, and some of those who are here have told us the reason. I have been trying my hardest to persuade Hawley that, under the circumstances, he couldn't possibly get away with his scheme to-night, but the plucky old chap won't listen. He says that we've made our plans, and it's too late to change them now. He insists upon going through with it."

CHAPTER XL.
AN INTERRUPTED DINNER.

The guests of the *Kearsarge* had no cause to complain of the measure of Uncle Sam's hospitality. If the scene of the banquet had been a first-class hotel, the preparations could scarcely have been more elaborate. The big battleship presented a spectacle of dazzling splendor. From bow to stern, masthead to lower deck, her grim lines had been beautified by a blaze of electric lights, flags, Japanese lanterns, bunting, and flowers. The wardroom being too small to accommodate the big dinner party, the spacious upper deck had been converted into an open-air dining room. At tables set together so as to form a huge horseshoe, covered with fine linen and laden with massive silver, the guests were served with a feast of rare daintiness.

There were several women present at the banquet, for the officers of the garrison had been invited to bring their wives, sweethearts, sisters, and daughters. Gale had discovered that the girl next to him was the niece of the commandant of the fortress, and he exerted himself to be agreeable to her, not only because she was a young woman of fascinating personality, but because, always having an eye for the main chance, he foresaw that her relationship to the man in charge of El Torro garrison might come in useful to him later on.

Although he kept up a sprightly conversation with her and appeared to give her his entire attention, he was all the time keeping a close watch on Virginia and Captain Reyes. That interesting pair, as luck would have it, sat almost directly opposite to him, and he was able to observe every move they made.

Just as the last course of the dinner had been served and the speeches were about to begin, Gale saw the daughter of the American minister lean back in the chair and half close her eyes, while a look of distress came to her pretty face.

This action was not lost upon Captain Reyes. He bent toward her solicitously. "What is the matter, señorita?" he inquired. "Are you ill?"

"Maybe it will pass away soon," the girl answered, apparently making a brave effort to pull herself together. But she seemed to grow worse instead of better, for presently she whispered, in response to an anxious inquiry from the captain: "If my father were not down on the program for a speech I think I should ask him to take me home."

"There is no need to bother your father, señorita," Reyes said promptly. "If you wish to go home, I am at your service."

"You are very kind," Virginia said faintly, flashing him a grateful smile; "but, of course, I could not dream of taking you away. I must try to wait until my father has finished his speech. I wish he was first on the list, but I am afraid——"

"I shan't mind it at all," her escort cut in eagerly. "In fact, I shall be delighted to accompany you." And his eagerness was not feigned, for he was glad to exchange the terrors of the postprandial oratory for the pleasure of a boat ride and automobile jaunt with this pretty girl.

"Well, if you insist," said the latter, "let us try to leave as unobtrusively as possible. I think the trip home will do me good."

They left the table so quietly that few noticed their departure; but a few minutes later, as they were stepping toward the port gangway, Reyes became aware of a hand placed on his shoulder, and, turning, learned that Gale had followed them out.

"A word with you," the reporter whispered. "It is of the utmost importance."

The frown which came to the other's face showed that he resented this intrusion, but something in Gale's manner caused him to draw back and allow Virginia to go on alone.

"What is it?" he demanded sharply. "I must say, señor, that I am beginning to grow very weary of this confounded interference——"

"Where are you going?" the *News* man cut him short. "Tell me quickly: Has she fooled you into going away with her?"

"Fooled me!" The Baracoan's frown deepened into a scowl. "I do not understand," he said haughtily. "Miss Throgmorton is feeling indisposed and I am taking her home."

To his astonishment and indignation, Gale received this with an ironical laugh. "I guess it is about time to open your eyes," he said. "I am wise now to the whole game." He whispered a few words in the army officer's ear. What he said caused the latter to give a start of surprise.

"This is astounding!" Reyes muttered. "Are you sure?"

"Of course I am not sure," the reporter replied. "But you'll see that I am right."

Virginia, noting her escort's absence from her side, turned at the head of the gangway, and a worried look came to her face as she saw with whom he was talking.

"The launch is waiting for us, Captain Reyes," she called out impatiently. "Are you ready?"

The Baracoan hesitated a moment. Then, with sudden decision, he whispered a few words to Gale, stepped to the girl's side, and assisted her down the ladder. As they got into the boat, Gale followed them. "Guess I'm going ashore, too," the reporter said, with a grin. "I have some business which needs my immediate attention."

Virginia glanced at her escort's face. She observed with concern that he did not seem to resent this intrusion.

CHAPTER XLI.
A BOLD ATTEMPT.

About fifteen minutes after the gray steam launch containing Virginia, Reyes, and Gale had left the battleship, another of the *Kearsarge's* hooded fifty-footers darted away from the starboard gangway apparently, from the course she took, bound for the landing at Puerto Cabero. But after this little craft had gone far enough away to be out of sight of the battleship, it suddenly changed its course, and, making a wide detour, sped toward the fortress of El Torro.

Presently the lone sentry, pacing the narrow strip of land in front of that ugly gray building, brought his rifle smartly down from his shoulder as the boat reached the beach and a tall figure stepped ashore.

"Halt! Who goes there?" the picket demanded. But without waiting for an answer he abandoned his menacing attitude and respectfully presented arms. For, although it was dark, he was able to discern that the man who had stepped ashore from the battleship's launch wore the uniform of a captain of the army of Baracoa, and that his eyes were screened by a pair of familiar blue spectacles. The newcomer stiffly acknowledged the salute, then turned to shake hands with the natty young American naval officer in charge of the launch's crew. "Well, good-by, Captain Reyes," the sentry heard the naval officer say, addressing the bespectacled man in Spanish. "Sorry that you are obliged to leave us before the fun is all over. I trust we shall meet again soon."

The launch started back toward the battleship, whose gayly illuminated outline the sentry had been gazing at wistfully all night, wishing that he wore epaulets so that he, too, might be wining and dining instead of doing wearisome picket duty; but after the little boat had gone a short way it stopped, as though something might be the matter with its machinery.

The sentry might have paid more attention to this maneuver if the bespectacled man in the captain's uniform had not at that moment addressed him.

"You can go," the latter announced. "You are relieved. I will take your place."

The words, which were in Spanish, were spoken with a thickness which, in the picket's opinion, seemed to account for the unusualness of the incident. He observed, too, that the other swayed as he spoke. By which token he deduced that the supply of champagne aboard the battleship had been plentiful.

As the sentry hesitated, the man with the epaulets turned upon him fiercely. "What are you waiting for?" he demanded. "Do you not understand? You are relieved." His utterance had grown even thicker than before, and his voice did not sound much like that of Captain Reyes, but, considering his condition, the soldier saw nothing strange about that. Promptly the latter once more presented arms. Tipsy or sober, the man in the blue spectacles was his superior officer, and it was not for a common soldier to question his orders.

Watching this scene from the launch, Lieutenant Ridder exhaled a deep breath of relief as he saw the sentry walk away and disappear within the fortress. "He got away with it, all right," he muttered joyously. "But," he added grimly, "the worst is yet to come."

The next five minutes were the most anxious ones that Ridder had ever passed through in all his life. As he sat, with his hands gripping the wheel of the launch, straining his eyes in an effort to see what was going on ashore, his teeth were clenched and his heart was pounding against his ribs.

The man in the blue spectacles had disappeared behind a row of tall bushes in front of the fortress. Presently—it seemed like ages to the anxious naval officer—there came from behind this foliage a flash of light and a dull boom like an explosion of wet powder.

Ridder gave vent to an ejaculation of joy. "By Jove, he's done it!" he muttered. "Good old Hawley!" As he saw a slim figure dart out from behind the bushes and approach the water's edge, he gave the wheel in his hand a swift turn and sent the launch dashing toward the beach.

But short as was the distance the boat had to cover to reach his comrade, he was too late. Led by a stout man in civilian garb, a swarm of soldiers had rushed out of the fortress and seized the Camera Chap just as the latter, perceiving that the launch would not get to him in time, was about to throw himself into the water.

"What have we here?" exclaimed the corpulent person in civilian garb, savagely tearing the blue spectacles from the prisoner's face. Then, as he recognized Hawley, he uttered an exclamation of mingled astonishment and joy.

"Ah, I perceive it is our brave and ingenious Yankee snapshotter!" he sneered. "So you have come back to Baracoa, señor! Permit me to compliment you upon the brilliancy of your latest exploit, and to condole with you that such a brave and clever attempt should have met with such poor success. We——"

He did not finish the sentence, for at that moment Lieutenant Ridder with the three sailors of the launch at his heels, rushed up to the group.

"Let this man go!" the naval officer bellowed, brandishing a revolver. "He's an American citizen, and you daren't touch him."

The fat man laughed ironically. "You appear to have an extremely vague idea of international law, my impetuous friend," he remarked; "surprisingly vague, in view of the uniform you wear. I should advise you, señor, to go back to your ship, and to congratulate yourself that you, too, are not placed under arrest. Unless you depart immediately, the consequences are liable to be serious for both yourself and your country."

"For my country!" Ridder began derisively. "Why, you chump——"

"Hold on, there, old man!" Hawley broke in, smiling at his friend's recklessness. "You'd better do as he says, and go back to the ship. You can't do any good, and, if you attempt to interfere, you may indeed cause international complications. Especially," he added, with a chuckle, "if you are guilty of such a grave breach of decorum as to call his excellency, the President of Baracoa, a chump."

Ridder gave a start of surprise. Until that moment, the identity of the stout man in civilian attire had not been known to him. With the instinctive respect which his training as a naval officer caused him to feel for the head of a sister republic, no matter what he might think of the man personally, for a moment he was abashed at what he had done. But a second later he was guilty of a still greater breach of decorum.

Stepping up to Portiforo, before anybody could realize what he was about to do, he pressed the muzzle of his revolver against that startled dignitary's "corporation." "So this is the president!" he cried, with a triumphant laugh. "Well, so much the better! We may be outnumbered, but I guess we hold the trump card. Get into the boat, Frank, old man, and beat it back to the ship. These fellows can't stop you."

"You wouldn't dare!" the president gasped, his bloated face turning pale. "Do you realize, señor, that this is the greatest outrage in all history?"

Lieutenant Ridder, of the United States navy, did realize that. He was aware that his mad act was likely to "raise the deuce at Washington," cause a howl of protest to go up from every nation on the globe, and possibly bring on an international trouble. He had every reason to believe, too, that even if he managed to escape Portiforo's vengeance—which contingency was extremely doubtful—he was going to be put out of the service for acting in a manner unbecoming an officer and a gentleman. But, just the same, he kept the muzzle of his revolver pressed against the stomach of the chief gentleman of Baracoa. For he was not Lieutenant Ridder, of the United States navy at that moment. He was plain John Ridder, of New York City, who had once had the life almost kicked out of him by a gang of toughs in New York's Chinatown, and who, ever since then, had been yearning for an opportunity to pay his debt to the plucky young man who had saved him from that fate. Possibly his actions were influenced also by the consideration that while the person whom he was threatening was the ruler of a friendly nation, he was also a tyrant and a usurper, and that his rascality might be revealed to the world if only Hawley could get away with the photographic proof of the dastardly conspiracy.

"I assure you, Mr. Portiforo, that I do mean exactly what I say," he said quietly. "You had better instruct your soldiers to let go of my friend and permit him to enter the launch, for as sure as there are bullets in this gun— and I hope, for your sake, you have no doubts on that score—if they attempt to stop him there's going to be an immediate change of administration in Baracoa."

Desperate as was his act, it might have succeeded, for the soldiers who held the Camera Chap captive, appreciating the peril of their president, looked to the latter irresolutely for instructions, and Portiforo, realizing that, temporarily, at least, this rash young man with the bulldog jaw held, as he had boasted, the trump card, was about to give orders to his soldiers to do as Ridder demanded. But just at that moment, the naval officer's arms were pinned to his sides, and his right wrist was grasped so tightly that the revolver fell to the ground.

A second launch from the battleship had landed quietly at the fortress, and two men, disembarking therefrom, had run along the beach toward the group. It was one of these men who, taking in the situation, had crept up stealthily behind Ridder and taken him by surprise.

As the lieutenant struggled in the grasp of his assailant and a half dozen of the soldiers who went to the latter's assistance, Portiforo's face resumed its normal hue, and he expressed his relief by a hearty chuckle.

"Well done, Captain Reyes!" he cried approvingly. "Splendid work, my brave Ernesto!"

CHAPTER XLII.
GALE TURNS A TRICK.

Virginia Throgmorton, congratulating herself upon the success of the ruse by which she hoped to get Captain Reyes safely out of the way while the Camera Chap was carrying out his daring plan, had received an unpleasant surprise when the launch containing the Baracoan army officer, Gale, and herself reached the landing at Puerto Cabero.

Instead of disembarking there, Reyes had turned apologetically to the girl. "I am filled with a thousand regrets, señorita, to be compelled to transfer the privilege of escorting you to your home to our friend Señor Gale," he said. "Not for a great deal would I forego the opportunity, but a soldier must place duty before pleasure, and I find I have an important duty to perform which demands my immediate attention."

"A duty!" Virginia exclaimed apprehensively. "Where? Are you going back to the battleship?"

The Baracoan's reply had filled her with dismay. "No, señorita; I am going to the fortress," he announced.

The significant smile which accompanied these words increased the girl's apprehensions. "But I do not wish Mr. Gale to escort me home," she objected, refusing to recognize defeat. "In fact, there are reasons why I cannot consent to that arrangement. I must insist that you go with me, Captain Reyes. I shall be terribly disappointed if you don't."

"I am sorry, señorita," he answered firmly, "but I am compelled to deny myself the pleasure."

"Then I will go back to the battleship," Virginia announced, with sudden decision. "I have changed my mind about going home."

The captain bowed. "Very well, señorita. But I must ask you to be good enough to go a little out of your way. I presume you won't object to putting me down at the fortress first."

The girl frowned. Her one idea, now, was to return to the *Kearsarge* in the hope that she might be able to intercept Hawley before he set out on his hazardous expedition, and warn him that their plan had gone awry. "I hate to be disobliging," she said to Reyes, "but you will have to wait." She turned to the sailor at the wheel. "Back to the battleship—as quickly as you can," she requested quietly.

"I beg your pardon," said the Baracoan. "But I must insist. My business is urgent. We will first go to the fortress."

Virginia gave him an indignant glance. "I think you are horrid to-night, Captain Reyes! I did not think that you could be so rude to a woman. However," she continued, suddenly changing her mind as a new idea came to her, "it shall be as you say. We will take you to your fortress first. After all, it will mean only a few minutes' delay."

Reyes and Gale exchanged a smile of triumph. Possibly they would not have felt so jubilant, however, if they had guessed what Virginia had in mind. It had occurred to her that it might be too late to intercept Hawley, that he might already have started out for the fortress, in which case she believed she saw a way of rendering him valuable assistance by assenting to Reyes' request.

As they drew near to El Torro, which loomed up blue-black in the moonlight, they caught sight of another navy launch heading for the fortress, and the girl's pretty face became grim. She knew who was in that boat.

Reyes and Gale appeared to have the same knowledge. They jumped to their feet excitedly. "Hurry!" the Baracoan cried tensely to the man at the wheel. "If you get us there before that other boat lands I will make it well worth your while."

But the jack-tar paid no attention to what he said. He was listening at that moment to Virginia, who had leaned forward and was whispering something in his ear.

In response to her request, the man grinned, and, giving the wheel a sharp turn, changed the craft's course, at the same time slackening her speed.

"What are you doing!" Reyes cried angrily, aghast at this maneuver. "I am Captain Reyes, of the army of Baracoa. If you don't obey my orders, my man, you will get into trouble."

"You'd better do as he says!" exclaimed Gale, addressing the sailor threateningly. "He is a guest of your ship, and an intimate friend of Captain Cortrell."

"And I am Miss Throgmorton, the daughter of the United States minister," Virginia said, observing that the man at the wheel seemed to hesitate. "If you do as I tell you, I will answer for it that everything will be all right. Pay no attention to these men."

The jack-tar grinned, and the launch kept to her new course—away from El Torro. Virginia laughed happily as she viewed the discomfiture of the pair.

"You will not be so merry, to-morrow, señorita," the Baracoan said to her savagely. "You will get into great trouble for this service you have rendered to the enemies of our government—and, this time, neither your sex nor your father's influence will save you."

The girl shrugged her shoulders. "To-morrow is a long way off," she informed him serenely. "Lots of things can happen before then."

A little later an exclamation of dismay came from Gale. His eyes were turned anxiously toward the fortress. It was a clear moonlight night, and, although they were some distance off, he could discern what was taking place on the beach. The other launch had landed, and a tall figure had gone ashore. "He's getting away with it!" the *News* man growled, as he saw the flash of light go up from behind the clump of bushes, and, immediately afterward, caught sight of the dim outline of a man running toward the water's edge.

A laugh, half hysterical, came from Virginia, but it changed suddenly to an involuntary cry of despair. A shadowy group had rushed out from the fortress and seized the fugitive.

In striking contrast to her distress was the delight of Reyes and Gale. "Hurrah! They've got him!" the reporter cried. "Congratulations, Ernesto, old sport! We may have missed the first part of the performance, but at all events we shall be in time for the finale."

Reyes turned with a mocking smile to Virginia. "Now that your charming little conspiracy has failed, perhaps you won't mind permitting us to go ashore, señorita," he suggested. "You must realize that it can no longer do you any good to hold us here."

The girl sighed. "Yes; you might as well let them land now," she instructed the sailor at the wheel. "As he says, nothing is to be gained by detaining them any longer."

The launch landed some distance away from the point where the Camera Chap was struggling in the grasp of the captives. As Reyes and the reporter ran eagerly along the beach toward the group, they saw Lieutenant Ridder suddenly project himself into the tableau and threaten Portiforo with a revolver.

They did not know, then, that the man thus threatened was Portiforo. They had no expectation of finding the president there, for his visit to the fortress had been in the nature of a little surprise party to the garrison. But, as they drew nearer, Gale recognized the corpulent form of the chief executive of Baracoa, and announced his discovery to his companion, who promptly proceeded to distinguish himself by stealing up behind Ridder and throwing his arms around that reckless young man.

"Excellently done, my brave Ernesto!" Portiforo chuckled as the soldiers went to Reyes' assistance and took charge of the discomfited American naval officer. "Possibly, señor," he sneered, addressing Ridder, "you will regret, now, that you did not take advantage of my good nature and go back to your ship while you had the chance. Of course, after the outrage you have committed, you must realize that your uniform cannot save you from the consequences of your mad act."

Ridder shrugged his shoulders. "I'm ready to take my medicine," he said quietly. "I trust, however, Mr. President," he added anxiously, pointing to the three sailors who had followed him ashore, "you will not find it necessary to hold these men. They have done nothing."

Portiforo held a brief debate with himself, and decided to permit the sailors to return to the *Kearsarge*. They appeared to be loath to leave their young officer, who was very popular with all the men, but he smilingly ordered them to go, and they put back to the ship in the launch.

"Take these rascals and lock them both up!" the president commanded fiercely, pointing to the Camera Chap and the navy man. "Until further orders, nobody is to be permitted to communicate with either of them. But wait a minute! There is one little detail which almost escaped my attention. Before we lock him up, we will first relieve Señor Hawley of the camera with which he took that audacious flash-light picture."

"Here it is, Señor Presidente," announced Gale, bending down and picking up a small pocket kodak which was lying on the ground near the Camera Chap's feet and handing it to Portiforo. "Guess he was trying to get rid of the evidence," he added, with a grin.

"Thank you, Señor Gale," said the president, regarding the camera with great satisfaction. "This is a dainty little thing. We will have the film developed as soon as possible," he continued, with a sardonic smile. "I have heard much of Señor Hawley's great skill as a photographer, and I am most anxious to see for myself what kind of work he can do."

"Will you let me have a copy of the picture, Señor Presidente?" the *News* reporter requested, seemingly with great eagerness.

A scowl darkened Portiforo's face for an instant. Then he smiled and shook his head. "It is painful to me to have to refuse you anything, my friend," he said, "but I fear that would be impossible."

Gale appeared to be keenly disappointed, but his demeanor was only a pose; for he had every reason to believe that when the film was developed, the result would be a blank, inasmuch as he knew that the camera which he had handed Portiforo had never been used.

The *News* man, himself, had bought that camera, a few days previously, in San Cristobal, and had carried it in his pocket when he went to the *Kearsarge* dinner, anticipating that it might come in handy. Being rather clever at sleight-of-hand work, it had been a simple matter for him to drop his own kodak, unseen, at the Camera Chap's feet.

With equal dexterity, he had pocketed the small camera which Hawley had used to take the flash-light picture of President Felix, and which, a few minutes earlier, he, alone, had observed the Camera Chap attempt to conceal by thrusting it into some bushes near which he was standing.

CHAPTER XLIII.
A LITTLE KEEPSAKE.

Later that night, Gale returned to San Cristobal very well satisfied with himself and his evening's work. He had every reason to believe that he carried in his pocket the photographic proof of President Felix's incarceration in El Torro fortress; for he deemed it exceedingly unlikely that Hawley would have ventured to take the flash light unless he had found Felix; and, as for the picture turning out successfully, knowing the Camera Chap's skill as a snapshotter and his ability to get results, even under the most unfavorable technical conditions, the *News* man felt sanguine on that score.

He thrilled with anticipatory joy as he pictured to himself the glory which would be his when his paper should startle the world by launching his big photographic scoop. But keen though he was to have the film developed, he felt constrained to postpone that detail for a few days. He did not possess the necessary knowledge or materials with which to do the work himself, and, although there were a couple of studios in San Cristobal which made a specialty of doing developing and printing for amateur photographers, he was afraid to trust the precious film to them, particularly as they were run by natives who might recognize the subject of his picture. So he decided to wait until he got to New York and have the negative developed by the experts in the *Daily News* office.

There was a boat leaving Puerto Cabero for New York the following morning, and he resolved to book passage on her. His work being done, there was nothing now to keep him in Baracoa, except possibly his desire to wait to see what was going to happen to the Camera Chap. It would have filled his mean, malicious soul with joy to be able to go back to Park Row and boast to "the boys" that he had been a personal eyewitness of the snapshot adventurer's fate, but he put the temptation aside, resolved to subordinate pleasure to duty. He realized the necessity of getting the picture of Felix to his paper as speedily as possible.

Before he sailed, however, he at least had the satisfaction of learning definitely what his rival's fate was to be. Justice in Baracoa, under the Portiforo administration, was swift—on occasions. The country being under martial law on account of the revolution, the case of the Camera Chap and Lieutenant Ridder, of the United States navy, was tried before a military court. The court convened that morning, and, after less than an hour's deliberation, arrived at a verdict that the interests of the government of Baracoa demanded that capital punishment should be the fate of both prisoners, and that the sentence of the court should be carried out within twenty-four hours.

When Minister Throgmorton heard of these verdicts he hurried to the palace and held a long conference with the president. After his visit, it was officially announced that the government of Baracoa had decided to pardon one of the two American prisoners. The man who was to receive clemency, it was stated, was Lieutenant Ridder. Although his offense was grievous, President Portiforo was disposed to be magnanimous, and if the state department at Washington would give its assurance that the young man would be dishonorably dismissed from the United States navy, he would be allowed to go free within a few days.

In the case of Señor Hawley, however, the government of Baracoa announced there could be no deviation from the sentence of the court. This was the second time he had offended, and President Portiforo felt that he must be made an example of, "as a lesson to all those who espoused the revolutionary cause."

Virginia was in despair when she heard the tidings from her father. "I have done my best," the latter assured her. "I have argued and pleaded with President Portiforo on behalf of Hawley, but find it impossible to persuade him to mitigate the sentence of that unfortunate young man."

"Couldn't you have got him to postpone the carrying out of the sentence for a few days?" the girl said bitterly. "That would have given us time to do something."

The diplomat shook his head. "I did my best," he repeated. "Portiforo positively refused to grant even a stay of execution in Hawley's case. I had great difficulty in persuading him to extend clemency to Ridder, and that was the most that I was able to accomplish. He was absolutely obdurate as regards the other prisoner. He informed me that he wouldn't grant any mercy to Hawley, even if the President of the United States were to ask it of him as a personal favor."

He viewed his daughter's distress with solicitude. "I am extremely sorry, my dear," he said gently; "although I am not favorably impressed with Mr. Hawley, and still less so with the odious yellow journal he represents. I should have liked to get him out of his scrape, for your sake—now that you have confided to me the depth of your feeling toward him."

Preceding Minister Throgmorton's visit to the palace, Virginia, in her desire to save the Camera Chap, had laid bare to her father the innermost secret of her heart. He had been amazed by the revelation. He had known all along, of course, of the friendship that existed between her and Hawley, but inasmuch as they had known each other only a few weeks, he had not suspected the full extent of her regard for the photographic adventurer. His daughter's happiness being more to him than any other consideration, he had put aside his own prejudices and really had done his utmost to persuade his friend Portiforo to spare Hawley's life.

"There is just one concession that I was able to wring from the president," the minister now announced. "It isn't much, my poor girl, but it may give you a little comfort: He has consented to permit you to see the prisoner. Personally, my dear, I would advise against your availing yourself of this privilege. Such a meeting, I fear, would only add to your distress. However, I will permit you to follow your own wishes in the matter. If you desire to go to the prison, here is a pass which the president made out for you."

Virginia took the paper from him with pathetic eagerness, and less than five minutes later she was speeding on her way to the fortress.

The meeting between her and the president's photographic envoy took place under somewhat disadvantageous circumstances. Two of the prison officials insisted on being present during the interview, and Virginia was not allowed to enter the cell; she had to converse with the condemned man through the bars.

She found the Camera Chap apparently resigned to his fate. His face was pale and haggard, but he bore himself with a cheerfulness that amazed her, great as was her estimate of his courage.

"Brace up, little girl," he said gently, putting out his hand to her through the bars. "You mustn't take it like that, you know. Things haven't turned out exactly as pleasant as we had hoped," he continued, with a whimsical smile, "but I assure you that I am not a bit sorry I came to Baracoa. If I hadn't, I should never have had the privilege of knowing you, and I assure you that blessed privilege is ample compensation for—whatever is coming my way later on."

Presently he inquired of the two prison officials whether he would be permitted to dispose of some of his personal effects as keepsakes, and they told him that there would be no objection to this proceeding, which was a privilege always granted to condemned prisoners.

Eagerly he drew from his finger a seal ring, and handed it to Virginia. "I ask you to be good enough to wear this as a souvenir of our friendship," he said. He smiled ruefully. "I had hoped to present it to you under more favorable circumstances. And there is one other favor I would beg of you to grant: I have a friend in New York who, I feel sure, would be glad to receive a keepsake from me. Tom Paxton, managing editor of the New York *Sentinel*, has always admired this tobacco pouch of mine." He took from his pocket a leather pouch of unique design. "I would like him to have it. It isn't much, but I know he will appreciate the circumstances under which it is given. Yes," he repeated, with peculiar emphasis, "I am quite sure he will appreciate the circumstances. Would you mind seeing that he gets it, Miss Throgmorton?"

As the girl took the pouch which he held to her, she noted an expression on Hawley's face which puzzled her.

It was not until she had arrived at the boat landing at Puerto Cabero that a suspicion of the truth dawned upon her mind. With a sudden thrill of hope, she opened the leather wallet with frantic eagerness, and an exclamation of delight escaped from her lips. Underneath a thin covering of granulated tobacco, the pouch contained a small cylindrical article, the nature of which Virginia immediately recognized. It was a light-proof roll of film from a small pocket camera.

CHAPTER XLIV.
THE DEVELOPED FILM.

For a few seconds Virginia stood staring as though fascinated at the little significant package in her hand, but was brought to herself by a sudden consciousness that somebody was standing close by her watching her intently. She raised her eyes and encountered those of the soft-footed Señor Lopez. There was an expression on the spy's face which caused the girl to thrust the film roll and the pouch hurriedly into the hand bag she was carrying, and to step hastily into the automobile waiting for her at the wharf.

"Home, señorita?" the native chauffeur inquired.

She was about to give an affirmative response, but suddenly changed her mind as an idea came to her. "No," she answered. "Take me to the residence of Sir Godfrey Montague, the British minister, as quickly as you can."

As the car started, she glanced back, and saw that Lopez was just entering another automobile. She guessed that the man was about to attempt to follow her, and a grim expression came to her face as she opened her hand bag and tentatively examined a dainty, pearl-handled, little revolver which was among its contents. Her fears, however, so far as Lopez were concerned, proved groundless, for when her car arrived in San Cristobal and drew up in front of the British embassy, the spy was not in sight.

Virginia sent in her card to Beatrice Montague, the diplomat's daughter. She knew that the latter was an enthusiastic amateur photographer and did her own developing and printing—which was the reason she had decided to call upon her now.

"I want you to do me a favor, Beatrice," she said, as soon as the English girl came into the reception room to greet her. "I have a film here which I want developed and a print made from it as quickly as possible."

"Surely," the other responded, wondering greatly at her visitor's flushed face and agitated manner. "Come up to the dark room, dear. I didn't know that you, too, had become a camera fiend."

She led the way upstairs to the chamber which she had fitted up as her laboratory. Here, under the rays of a ruby lamp, the girls opened the roll of film and submerged it in the necessary chemical solutions. A little later, as her friend held the wet gelatin against the lamp, Virginia gave vent to a joyous cry. "He did it!" she exclaimed, with a hysterical laugh. "He has succeeded, after all."

"Who did what?" Miss Montague asked curiously. "What is this negative, Virginia? It looks to me like an old man gazing out of a barred window."

"That's what it is," her visitor answered happily. "An old man gazing out of a barred window. How soon can you let me have a print of this, Beatrice? Please hurry. Every minute counts."

In a little while the picture was ready. As the British minister's daughter took it out of the printing frame, she stared in astonishment at the finished product. In its negative form, of course, she had not been able to identify the subject; but now it occurred to her that there was something hauntingly familiar about the haggard, wistful face that peered at her from the barred window.

"I've seen this man before somewhere," she announced; "but I can't recall where———" She stopped short, and an expression of astonishment came to her face. "How extraordinary!" she exclaimed. "Do you know, my dear, if it weren't so very absurd, I should say that this was a snapshot of former President Felix. To be sure, it looks much older than he did at the time of his disappearance, but the features are very much like his, as I recall them. It is truly a remarkable resemblance."

Virginia smiled. "Isn't it, though? Please hurry up and finish this print so that it won't fade. I'll tell you all about it later on, but I haven't time now." Without waiting for the print to dry, she placed it in her hand bag and hurried out to the waiting automobile. "Back to Puerto Cabero—as fast as we can go," she said to her chauffeur.

As she spoke, she glanced up the street and caught sight of another automobile standing at the corner. In that car sat Señor Lopez. She saw him bend forward in his seat and give an order to his driver, and she was not surprised, when her car started, to observe that the other followed. The discovery prompted her to take the precaution of transferring the precious snapshot from her bag to her blouse, but evidently the spy was content with merely watching her movements and had no intention of trying to wrest the picture from her, for he trailed behind her car all the way to the seaport, and once when their motor broke down on a lonely stretch of road and they had to stop ten minutes for repairs, Lopez's chariot also came to a halt a short distance behind.

A launch from the *Kearsarge* was waiting at the wharf as the girl stepped from the automobile and went down to the water's edge. She inquired of one of the crew whether the captain was on board the warship, and, receiving an affirmative response, requested to be taken out to him immediately.

Captain Cortrell received her with a grim smile. "I can guess the object of your visit, Miss Throgmorton," he said sadly. "But I regret to say that I am powerless to do anything in behalf of—— Why, what is this?" He stared in astonishment at the picture the girl had handed him.

"Who sent this photograph?" he demanded, an eager expression on his weather-beaten face.

"Mr. Hawley," she answered. "He couldn't bring it himself," she explained with a smile, "so I undertook to be his messenger. I was in hopes that it might alter the situation so far as he is concerned."

Without an apology, the battleship's commander turned from her and disappeared inside his cabin, leaving Virginia standing outside. He opened a drawer of his desk, and took therefrom the bulky envelope that contained his sealed orders.

When he returned to Virginia, a few minutes later, his face was wreathed in smiles. "You were right, Miss Throgmorton," he said, "in assuming that the picture you have brought me from Mr. Hawley would alter the situation. It has changed matters considerably."

CHAPTER XLV.
TWO LACONIC ORDERS.

While the American minister's daughter was visiting the *Kearsarge's* commander, Señor Lopez was dashing back to the capital, working the motor of his car to its utmost capacity in his desire to get there as soon as possible. He had watched the girl go aboard the warship, and then he had proceeded to the fortress. What he learned there had caused him to realize the necessity of reaching the palace without delay.

President Portiforo was in consultation with his cabinet when the spy reached the palace. They were discussing a dispatch which had recently arrived, and that the missive contained news of a startling character was evident from the worried, scared expression on the countenance of the chief executive of Baracoa.

"The report seems incredible," Portiforo declared, his voice quavering. "If it is true—and I suppose there can be no doubt of that—I must admit that thing looks bad—exceedingly bad. Villa's defeat is a blow we can scarcely hope to survive. There is now practically nothing to keep Rodriguez from reaching the capital. By forced marches he ought to be here within another twenty-four hours." A sickly smile creased his face. "By this time to-morrow the crowds on the street will shout: 'Viva el Presidente Rodriguez!' It looks to me, gentlemen, as if the time had come for us to take a little trip abroad for the benefit of our health."

The members of his cabinet received this suggestion with gloomy nods of assent.

Portiforo leaned forward in his chair. "But before we go," he went on, lowering his voice, "there is one little matter we must not overlook. To-morrow, no doubt, the enemy will be in possession of El Torro." He turned to a tall, bearded man with a very pale face who sat at his right hand. "Surely you will agree with me, my dear Replife, that before that happens we must do—what would have been done long ere this if it had not been for your sentimental objections."

Minister of War Replife, just out of the hospital, sighed, and a shadow flitted across his pallid countenance. "I don't like it," he said hoarsely. "I can't bear the thought of it. It is impossible for me to forget that he was once my friend. We have done him enough wrong, as it is, without——"

"We've got to think of ourselves now," Portiforo broke in impatiently. "This is no time for maudlin sentiment, my friend. Unless we—er—take

- 183 -

steps to remove the evidence, by to-morrow night the whole world will know our secret, and there will be no refuge for us, wherever we may flee. As political refugees, we should be received with honor and sympathy abroad, but as fugitive criminals we could not expect nearly so pleasant a reception."

All the members of the cabinet except Replife received this argument with approval. While they were discussing it, a secretary entered the room and announced that the spy, Lopez, was outside insisting that he must see the president immediately on a matter of the greatest importance.

Lopez was admitted at once. The tidings he brought caused Portiforo and his cabinet to exchange glances of alarm.

"You are positive that it was a roll of film Miss Throgmorton had in her hand?" the president inquired.

"I am absolutely sure of that, Señor Presidente. And I am equally sure that she took it to the British minister's residence to have the film developed, and that the picture is now in the hands of the commander of the Yankee warship."

A scowl darkened the president's bloated face. "Then why didn't you get it away from her?" he growled. "Surely you must have had plenty of opportunity."

Lopez bared his large, exceedingly white teeth in a deprecatory smile. "If I had known then what I know now, of course I should have taken that step, Señor Presidente—although I am not a man of violence. But I must admit that Señorita Throgmorton's actions puzzled me—until after I had been to the fortress. I was content to watch her, to find out what it all meant. But when I learned at the fortress that the prisoner Hawley had handed her a tobacco pouch to send as a keepsake to his editor, the significance of that incident dawned upon me. I happen to know that the daughter of the British minister is an amateur photographer, so it was easy to guess why Señorita Throgmorton visited her—and why she then hurried to the Yankee warship."

The scowl on Portiforo's face deepened. "But I can't understand how that confounded photographer could have managed to retain possession of the snapshot!" he muttered. "I took his camera away from him that night, and it was loaded with film."

Lopez shrugged his shoulders. "Señor Hawley is an exceedingly ingenious and resourceful young man," he remarked. "After the several exhibitions of his cleverness which he has given us, I think we can assume that he had the sagacity and foresight to change the film roll of his camera immediately after taking the picture."

The president nodded gloomily. "Yes; he might have done it that way. We ought to have been more careful in searching him afterward," he said. "I suppose, my dear Replife," he continued, turning with a grim smile to the secretary of war, "you now fully agree with the rest of us as to the necessity of carrying out immediately the step we were discussing. The startling news that Lopez has brought us emphasizes the danger of delaying the matter."

General Replife shook his head. "On the contrary, I think the news which Lopez has brought is a strong argument why you should spare the life of the unhappy Felix," he urged. "What good would it do you to put him out of the way now? Such a step would only make things worse for ourselves. The photographic evidence of our guilt is now in the hands of the United States government. Whether he is found in El Torro or not, the world will know from that snapshot that he *was* locked up there. And if he is done away with it will, of course, add to the price which we will have to pay later on."

Some of Portiforo's advisers were impressed by this argument. They looked at their chief anxiously. The latter leaned back in his chair, a look of uncertainty on his face. It was evident from his demeanor that he appreciated the force of this plea for their victim's life.

Then suddenly his beady eyes snapped, and his cruel lips parted in a snarl. "We will take our chances on the price we may have to pay—if we are caught," he said. "There is a possibility that we shall be able to convince the world that the snapshot is a daring fraud. Photographic evidence has been manufactured before now; and"—he smiled sardonically—"the man who took the picture will not, then, be here to refute our claims."

He reached for pen and paper on the big mahogany table before him, and began to write rapidly. When he had finished, he turned to Lopez. "Go back to the fortress and deliver these immediately," he said to him. "One of them is for the commandant; the other for Captain Reyes. Wait there until both orders are carried out, and then come back and report."

Lopez bowed, and put the two papers in his pocket. Then he hurried back to Puerto Cabero. During the journey, he read the two papers, and their contents caused him to bare his teeth in a malicious smile.

The missive addressed to Captain Reyes was somewhat ambiguous. It said merely, "The time has come."

Portiforo knew Reyes would have no difficulty in grasping the purport of that laconic sentence. The other order, addressed to the commandant of the fortress, was less vaguely worded. It commanded that official to proceed immediately with the execution of the American prisoner, Hawley.

Before two hours had elapsed, Lopez returned to the palace. The cabinet members had departed. Portiforo was in his private suite, nervously pacing the floor.

"Well?" he said hoarsely, as his envoy entered. "Has it been done?"

The spy shook his head. His face was white, his manner agitated. His breath came in great gasps, as though he had been running hard.

"I was too late, Señor Presidente," he answered.

"Too late?"

"When I arrived there, I found El Torro in possession of marines from the *Kearsarge*. I can't understand how they managed it—I didn't wait to gather particulars—but they took the garrison by surprise, and captured the fortress with scarcely a struggle."

Portiforo sank weakly into a chair. "Incredible!" he gasped. "And the prisoners?"

Lopez made a despairing gesture. "I regret to say that our birds have flown, Señor Presidente. Felix, Hawley, and Ridder are now safely aboard the Yankee warship."

CHAPTER XLVI.
BESIDE THE GREAT GUN.

In the captain's cabin of the *Kearsarge* a white-haired, emaciated man, with tears streaming down his pallid cheeks, was vociferously assuring the commander of the warship of his undying gratitude.

"My dear sir, you don't owe any thanks to me," the latter protested gruffly. "The man to whom you owe your freedom is Mr. Hawley. Anxious though I was to serve you, I could have done nothing if it hadn't been for him."

President Felix raised his faded eyes to the beamed ceiling of the cabin. "And to think that I misjudged the motives of that heroic young man!" he said remorsefully. "It seemed to me preposterous that he could save me with his camera. I did him the injustice of supposing that he was merely a professional photographer trying to get a sensational picture and not caring what happened to me afterward as a result of his exploit."

"And yet you assisted him by standing at the bars of your dungeon and posing for his camera?" Captain Cortrell exclaimed, in a surprised tone.

A glow came to the liberated martyr's eyes. "That was because I saw the possibility of being vindicated in the eyes of the world," he replied. "That was all that I dared hope for, señor—vindication, not freedom. I believed that Mr. Hawley's daring exploit would cause my enemies to resort to desperate measures, but I was in hopes that afterward—after my death—the picture might be published in the United States and my reputation cleared. Even if Mr. Hawley had done me only that service, it would have been enough," he added fervently.

"Well, thank goodness, he was able to accomplish more than that," said the naval officer heartily.

"How shall I ever be able to repay him?" said Felix brokenly.

While this conversation was taking place in the captain's cabin, the Camera Chap was standing under the shadow of one of the warship's great guns, looking into the blue eyes of Virginia Throgmorton, and earnestly assuring her that to her alone was due the successful outcome of his adventure.

"I was sure, when I handed you that pouch, that you would grasp the idea," he said, a note of profound admiration in his voice. "Any other girl might have failed to understand."

Virginia laughed and blushed at the same time. "I am so glad that I did understand," she said earnestly. "It wasn't cleverness, of course—it was just instinct. But suppose I had taken you literally and sent on that keepsake to your friend, Mr. Paxton, without examining it!" She shuddered at the thought.

Hawley smiled grimly. "In that event, I guess the *Sentinel* would have had a big picture scoop. Tom Paxton would have realized what that film meant, of course, as soon as he saw it, and would have played up the snapshot for all it was worth." Suddenly he smiled as a thought came to him. "What has become of our friend Gale?"

Virginia informed him that the *News* man had gone back to New York.

"I supposed as much," Hawley chuckled. "I guess he was in a hurry to go back to his office and hand them his big picture scoop. In spite of the seriousness of the situation, I could scarcely keep from laughing, that night, when I saw him fool Portiforo by pocketing my camera and handing him another, not suspecting that while he was working that cunning little trick he was being hoaxed himself." He chuckled again. "I would give a whole lot to see his face when he arrives at the *News* office and develops that perfectly blank film."

Virginia frowned. "Serves him right," she said. "I don't like to be vindictive, but I hope his editor discharges him." She sighed. "I can't understand why my father should have taken such a fancy to that contemptible fellow. But then," she added, with a rueful smile, "poor dad has shown himself to be a very poor judge of men."

Hawley nodded.

"I am sorry for your father, Virginia. I presume it will be a great blow to him—the way things have turned out."

"I am afraid it will," the girl said wistfully. "He had such great faith in that tyrant Portiforo. And I suppose he will be asked to resign his post. It isn't to be expected that Washington will continue him here under the circumstances. Personally I shall not be sorry to return to the United States, but I fear that dad will feel keenly the disgrace of being recalled."

The Camera Chap made no comment on this, but there was a thought in his mind which did not find expression until a few days later when he arrived at Washington and presented himself at the White House.

The President of the United States received his photographic envoy with marked cordiality, and gazed appreciatively at the snapshot which the latter handed him with the simple announcement: "Here is the picture, Mr. President, which you instructed me to take."

The chief executive smiled quizzically. "I must compliment you on the manner in which you have carried out my instructions, sir," he said formally. "Thank you for the picture. I fear that you must have had considerable trouble in getting it." Then suddenly the quizzical smile left his face, and his hand went out and grasped that of Hawley in a strenuous grip. "Well done, sir," he exclaimed, in a tone that was by no means formal. "I shan't forget your splendid, plucky work, my boy."

It was a little late when the subject of reward was brought up, and the president was offering the Camera Chap a lucrative position in the United States secret service, that the latter spoke the thought which was in his mind when he had that conversation with Virginia on board the *Kearsarge*.

"I don't want anything for myself, sir," Hawley said. "But—if you won't think me too presumptuous—I would like to ask a favor on behalf of somebody else. I understand that there is talk of Minister Throgmorton being recalled as a result of the latest developments in Baracoa. If you could see your way to permit him to retain his post it would be giving me a greater reward than I deserve."

The president shook his head. "I regret to say that is out of the question," he replied. "I am convinced that Mr. Throgmorton acted with perfect sincerity in upholding Portiforo and refusing to believe the rumor about the conspiracy against Felix, but a man capable of such bad judgment is scarcely fit to represent this government abroad. Besides, Mr. Throgmorton has no desire to continue in his post. He has sent me his resignation to take effect immediately. He feels naturally that it would be embarrassing to him to remain in Baracoa under the Felix administration. He and his daughter have sailed for the United States."

And the president wondered why this announcement brought such a joyous expression to the Camera Chap's face.

THE END.